COLD MALICE

QUENTIN BATES

ISIS
LARGE
PRINT

First published in Great Britain 2020
by
Constable
An imprint of Little, Brown Book Group

First Isis Edition
published 2020
by arrangement with
Little, Brown Book Group
An Hachette UK Company

A catalogue record for this book is available
from the British Library.

ISBN 978–1–78541–914–0

Published by
Ulverscroft Limited
Anstey, Leicestershire

Set by Words & Graphics Ltd.
Anstey, Leicestershire
Printed and bound in Great Britain by
TJ Books Limited, Padstow, Cornwall

This book is printed on acid-free paper

Til Sólu

PROLOGUE

December 2004

He didn't see the carnage for himself. Afterwards he thought back to it whenever the past kept sleep at bay, convincing himself that he had experienced the fear as the savage blue sea crashed onto the beachfront houses and hotels, sweeping cars, people, shacks and stalls before it and then sucking them back in its grasp as it retreated. He was sure he could hear the screams, the frantic calls, the wailing as people's homes and loved ones vanished in the churning water.

He *had* seen it all, but from the comfort of a bar, watching it on the tinny TV set fixed high on the wall, wondering if it was a hoax and then recognising on the screen the hotel where he had left his family: wife, three children and the mother-in-law he had always disliked from a not always polite distance.

She was the real reason he hadn't been sober for three days and was in the bar a dozen miles from the beach. Katla had made it plain that a holiday was needed for them to bond as a family, the unmistakable subtext to the demand being that if there were no holiday then Ingvar might as well start looking for love elsewhere, as she certainly would. So he arranged the three-week break, and then found that Katla's mother had also booked the same three weeks at the same hotel. They had even been on the same flight, for crying out loud.

It was more than a man could stand. Every day he spent less time with the family, leaving the children to romp in the pool or laze in front of the TV and his wife and her mother to shop and bask in the sun, while he snatched a holiday of his own, drinking with a couple of German guys who had found themselves in much the same situation.

He ordered another beer, having to call to the barman, who, like the rest of the handful of people in the place, stood mesmerised by the grainy footage being replayed over and over and the manic non-stop commentary.

As the scale of the disaster unfolded in snatches of news bulletins, he felt a warm surge of anticipation; the chance he had already been planning for.

He raised a silent glass to himself.

Happy New Year to me.

It was time to start walking.

December 2010

Erik Petter Tallaksen didn't struggle as the strong hand covered his nose and mouth for far longer than was needed to end his life, but the man in the white coat wanted to be absolutely certain. He reflected that the

2

unfortunate man had probably only had at most a week or two to live, and he was doing him a favour by cutting short the painful process.

It didn't do any harm that there was a handsome bonus coming his way for helping this wreck of a man out of this world so his name could live on without him.

The hostel was silent. At three o'clock on a rain-battered winter Tuesday night few people were about, and the grey van was parked out of sight at the back of the hostel where the CCTV couldn't quite make out the number.

"That's everything?" asked the pale-faced man with the accent and the sharp eyes, scanning both Jens and the back door of the hostel.

"Belongings, such as they are. Birth certificate. Danish passport. Social security paperwork . . . his identification number's there," Jens said, a finger pointing to the ten-digit code. "That's all there is."

"No family? No visitors?"

Jens shook his head.

"He's been in here on and off for the last eight months. No pals other than a few other junkies. He's never had a visitor and nobody has ever asked about him."

"Criminal record?"

"Sorry. Can't help you there. At any rate, the police haven't been to see him so I guess he's as clean as any lifelong smackhead's ever likely to be."

"He's only in his thirties?" the man said in surprise, riffling the pages of the dog-eared passport.

3

"Yeah. He looks twice that. But that's what twenty years of smack and speed do to you. I'm amazed he lasted as long as he did."

The pale man shivered in his thick coat and nodded to his broad-shouldered friend, who effortlessly swung the zipped grey bag containing Erik Petter Tallaksen's earthly remains into the back of the van. Now it was Jens's turn to shiver at the scant respect shown to the dead man, but the bulging envelope that he stuffed into his trouser pocket overcame any qualms.

"You need any more?" he asked hopefully.

"Yeah," the pale man said after a moment's pause. "Not right away. Give me a call when there's a suitable candidate, someone who's not going to be missed."

Jens wondered if he should put out a hand to be shaken at the conclusion of a business deal they were both satisfied with, but decided against it.

The van disappeared into the rain and he made his way back to the warden's office to pour himself a celebratory mug of coffee and wait for his shift to be over.

"Anything exciting?" Evabritt asked when she turned up at six to take over.

"Not much," Jens yawned. "Oh, Erik Petter left."

"He left?" She frowned. "He's in no condition to be out on his own."

"I tried to convince him he was better off here, at least until daylight," Jens said sadly. "But he wouldn't have it. He was adamant he was getting the train over to Copenhagen for Christmas."

"Home to Denmark?"

4

"I guess so."

"He didn't have any money. How was he going to get home if he didn't even have the train fare?"

"I don't know," Jens said, injecting as much regret as he could into his voice. "Maybe he'll be back if he gets chucked out of the station."

"You didn't lend him the train fare, did you?" Evabritt asked, head cocked on one side.

Jens made himself look guilty.

"You shouldn't, you know." She tousled his hair fondly and sighed. "You know what these people are like. Well, I'll get his room cleaned today and I don't suppose it'll be long before there'll be some other lost soul needing it."

"Let's hope not," Jens said.

The sea and the dawn sky melded into an enfolding grey blanket as the boat shoved its way through the chop of the waves. The skipper sat in the wheelhouse chair and gnawed his fingernails, eyes on the screens in front of him. It wasn't likely, but considering the nature of the bundle nestling under the gunwale where it couldn't be easily seen, a chance visit right now from the Coast Guard or those busybodies from the fisheries patrol would at best be hard to explain and at worst disastrous. He had no business being here, far outside his usual fishing grounds, and that in itself was suspicious. In fact, he was away from anyone's fishing grounds, in a patch of the Baltic where the mustard gas and explosives dumped after a couple of wars had ensured that any kind of fishing was out of the question.

He brooded that if he hadn't had debts, he'd have told them to go and fuck themselves sideways.

Eventually he eased back the throttle and the engine's rumble died away to a throaty mutter beneath his feet, the boat rocking in the unpredictable Baltic swell. He unzipped the bag, tried not to look at the emaciated face that gazed back at him, its eyes half closed, and hurriedly dropped a couple of yards of chain inside, adding some worn shackles for good measure. He zipped the bag shut and punched holes in it, surprised at how its tough fabric resisted his knife. It was also a surprise how little the bag and its contents weighed as he rolled it over the gunwale and watched it disappear from sight to join the rusting shells and canisters of poison far below.

He shuddered to himself, put the boat back into gear and felt a surge of relief as he pushed the throttle lever forward as far as it would go. That was a debt paid, one of many, but he wondered how long it would be before another favour he could hardly refuse would be requested.

CHAPTER
ONE

*Stiff south-westerly wind, veering north-westerly
later in the day. Mainly fair with some light
cloud cover, moderate precipitation by evening.
Snow showers or sleet overnight on high ground.
Temperatures around 0°C.*

Winter 2020

"It was the neighbour who cut him down and called
the ambulance," the young police officer with ginger
stubble sprouting from his chin said apologetically, as if
he should have been there to stop it happening.

The breeze hardly rippled the surface of the lake, a
translucent shade alternating between grey and pale
blue as the cloud cover broke to let in shafts of the late
afternoon sunlight before reforming to blot them out.
Gunna shut the car door and didn't bother to lock it.

"Not to worry. Suicide, right?"

"Looks like it. He was hanging from a rope slung
over a beam in the barn and there was a chair that had
been kicked away. Classic stuff, isn't it?"

Gunna shivered. Violent crimes were invariably
deeply unpleasant to deal with, but there was a depth of
sadness about someone taking their own life, as if the
misery that could drive a person to such an extreme

permeated the walls and the ground where it had happened. This tranquil spot would never be a happy one as long as that rootless ghost was around.

The place felt mournful on this icy day with the chill stealing down from the hills. The wooden house was set back from the track that ran along the shoreline, half hidden behind spindly trees, and the young officer ushered Gunna past it to a barn tucked away behind, the curved metal sheets of its walls faded and rusted to the same shade as the scrub grass that surrounded it.

The corpse lay where it had been taken down, a blanket draped over it. A second young officer, his face pale, tried to look as if he knew what he was doing.

It was the contents of the barn that took her by surprise. One long bench was scattered with brushes, palette knives and screwed-up tubes of paint among other debris, and canvases were stacked carelessly against one wall. Gunna made out landscapes and upside-down human figures among them before she turned her attention to the blanket.

"It's not very nice," the young officer told her needlessly.

"They never are," she said, drawing back the cover to see lank dark hair, thin at the crown, and a face that looked deeply weary. She had no desire to see the man's neck, the makeshift noose still around it.

"What's the neighbour's name?"

"I don't know. I haven't asked."

"Always get the names," Gunna told him gently as the other officer nodded morbid agreement from the doorway. "Always."

8

"He's in the house," the young officer said. "With the doctor."

Gunna carefully replaced the blanket. "We have an identity for this poor guy, do we?"

"His name's Áskell Hafberg," the young man said. "The artist."

"I'd never have guessed. Now, the doctor and the neighbour. Lead me to them."

A squat man in a matching camouflage hat and waistcoat over a traditional patterned sweater sat in an armchair with a glass of something amber cradled in his hands while the doctor scribbled on a pad.

"G'day, Ingólfur." Gunna greeted the doctor and held out a hand to the shocked neighbour, who put down his whisky and jumped to his feet. "I'm Gunnhildur Gísladóttir from CID. You're the gentleman who raised the alarm?"

"Good morning," he said, teeth chattering. "That's me. Jónatan Bjarnason. I live next door during the summer."

Gunna drew up a hard kitchen chair and they both sat down. "You found Áskell?"

Jónatan shuddered. "I was only going to ask him if I could borrow a can of petrol for my outboard. I wanted to catch a few fish for dinner. Normally he'd lend me a few litres of fuel and I'd pay him in fish. He wasn't in the house, and I figured he wasn't home. I knew he wouldn't mind, so I went out to the barn to get the can, and there he was."

He shuddered again and sipped his whisky.

"So you cut him down?"

9

"I did. I had no idea how long he'd been there, all night or just a few seconds. When he was on the ground I realised he was stone cold, so he must have been there a long time. Christ, what a sight," he said, shoulders shaking at the recollection.

"You knew him well?"

"As well as anyone round here. Áskell knew damn all about insurance — that was my business before I retired, by the way — and I know nothing about art. So we talked mostly about fishing and books and occasionally we'd play a game of chess. He didn't much like people with an opinion on art, so I suppose that's why we got on so well."

"He fished as well, I suppose?"

"He used to. Until his wife died."

"When was that?" Gunna asked, and the doctor looked up enquiringly.

"About five years ago. She drowned, just out there by the end of the jetty. He'd never fish in the lake again after that. He was happy to swim in it sometimes, said it brought them closer together. But he wouldn't put a hook in there again."

"But he didn't mind you doing it?"

"That was different, he said."

Gunna nodded and looked through the window to the stubby jetty with its rickety planks.

"When did you last see him?"

"The day before yesterday."

"And how was he?"

"Miserable. Drunk and miserable. He still missed Birna terribly. He'd miss her more than usual, have a drink, miss her some more and that would go on for a week every now and again. I always thought he should have gone to the doctor, but he wouldn't have it."

"Birna was his wife?" Gunna asked, the sound of the name chiming with a memory somewhere deep inside as Jónatan nodded. "Had he been drinking steadily these last few days, do you know?"

"He had." Jónatan coughed as the last of the whisky hit the back of his throat. "He wasn't a happy man."

Gunna flipped through her notebook and extracted a card.

"That's me and where to find me if there's anything you want to talk about or anything you might remember. I need your name and a contact number and I'll have to get a full statement from you later. You're going to be out here all week, are you?"

Jónatan shrugged and stood up. His shoulders sagged and he shook his head doubtfully. "I was going to be, but I'm not so sure now. At any rate, I don't live far from the police station, so if I'm not here, you can find me in town."

Gunna followed him to the door and watched as he stumped down the track, shoulders hunched and hands deep in the pockets of his waistcoat, without looking back.

"What do you reckon, Ingólfur?"

The doctor looked up from his notes. "Time of death around midnight, I'd guess. I'm sure the post-mortem will tell us he had been drinking."

"Cause of death? Not that I need to ask."

"Broken neck. Very quick and efficient. So many people manage to screw this up and end up strangling themselves, but this fellow did a good job of it."

Helgi felt hot and even more uncomfortable as he waited at the bar, his patience wearing thin, until the barman finally approached, his expression asking wordlessly what sir would like to drink. Helgi opened his mouth to speak, but the voice was someone else's.

"A brandy. Double."

The gruff voice at his side ordered with the authority of someone used to being listened to, and Helgi turned, ready to argue that he had been waiting for what felt like the best part of the day for the last beer of the exhausting holiday that had left him longing to get back to the familiarity of work.

"Hey, pal . . ." he began, as the barman took a glass from the rack overhead and poured.

"What? Were you waiting?" said a bronzed man with a face that looked as if it had been chipped from rock, glancing down at Helgi, who felt suddenly inadequate in his baggy shirt and with the skin peeling from the top of his sunburned head.

"I was waiting," Helgi said. "Until you jumped in."

"Sorry, bud," the man said, dropping a twenty-euro note on the bar and placing a finger on it. He nodded his head sideways in Helgi's direction. "Get this gentleman a drink as well, would you?"

Disarmed, Helgi's frustration evaporated.

"Thanks. I'll have a brandy as well."

"Make it a double," the stranger ordered, lifting his glass in salutation. "Your health," he said in a grave voice. He sipped, rolled the spirit across his tongue for a moment, savouring it, then threw the rest down his throat in one smooth motion. He replaced the glass on the bar, nodded, and walked away without waiting for his change.

The name nagged at her all the way back to town from Áskell Hafberg's house overlooking the lake at Hafravatn. It was still nagging at her as she parked in the yard behind the police station at Hverfisgata, and by the time she was halfway up the stairs, she was cursing her own inability to remember why it rang a bell.

"Busy, Gunnhildur?" Ívar Laxdal asked, striding towards her, trench coat belted over his barrel frame.

"A suicide up by Hafravatn. Helgi's still on holiday and Eiríkur's busy, so I thought I'd have a little drive in the country," she said, and watched his eyebrows close up into a single dark bar of a frown. "Not a pretty sight," she added. "I drew the short straw on this one."

Ívar Laxdal nodded sagely. "One has to do that sometimes and let the youngsters have the exciting stuff."

Gunna wondered how Helgi, still stricken with panic at the onset of deep middle age, could be described as a youngster, but let it pass.

"Anyone we know?"

"Áskell Hafberg. He was an artist, apparently, although I've never heard of him. Hanged himself from a beam in his workshop."

"Hafberg?" Ívar Laxdal asked, gaping for a moment then quickly recovering his composure. "I didn't even know he still lived in Iceland."

"You seem to know more about him than I do. Would you like to fill in the gaps in my knowledge?" Gunna invited, getting over the shock of having seen Ívar Laxdal lost for words, albeit fleetingly, for the first time.

He pursed his lips and looked into the distance through windows that could have done with a wash, or at least a decent shower of rain.

"Áskell Hafberg. Well I never," he said quietly, half to himself, before returning to reality. "A truly fine artist, deeply talented in my view and scandalously overlooked. At an artistic level he never fitted in with the establishment, if that's what you can call it, and he rubbed them badly up the wrong way because he simply didn't care. His paintings had a unique passion and a depth to them, and they sold, which is why I suppose the cultural mafia never liked him, however much they pretended to." He paused. "I have two pieces of Áskell Hafberg's work at home," he added with a touch of shyness, and this time Gunna was astonished to hear the inscrutable Ívar Laxdal talk with such knowledge and feeling about art.

"You collect art?" she asked finally.

"I do," Ívar Laxdal replied seriously. "When I can afford it. I have two of Hafberg's early works. One of them I bought from the artist something like thirty-five years ago. I always knew it would be worth something."

"And the price has probably gone up now, or it will when news gets out that he's dead."

"And suicide, Gunnhildur? No sign of anything suspicious?"

Gunna shook her head. "Nothing that I could see. He'd been drinking for a few days, apparently."

"The curse of the artistic temperament. Look after it, will you? I'd appreciate it if you'd do it sensitively," he added in a bleak tone. "One of Iceland's finer artists, and maybe his death is what's needed to get him greater recognition." He carried on towards the top of the stairs, waving a gloved hand in farewell.

Gunna had her hand on the office door when she realised what she should have done and hurried for the lift, emerging at the ground floor and making for the car park. She waved as Ívar Laxdal's black Volvo rolled towards her and came to a halt.

"Sorry," she panted as the window hissed down. "I should have asked you upstairs. Since you know about his art, do you know anything about Áskell Hafberg's private life?"

"He was something of a hell-raiser by all accounts, at least as a young man," Ívar Laxdal said slowly. "An *enfant terrible*, as the French would say. Children, I believe; several wives, including other men's. He lived abroad for a long time and I thought he still did."

"And Birna? Does that name mean anything to you?"

Ívar Laxdal shook his head and frowned.

"I can tell you about his work, but not much about the man, I'm afraid, other than that his wife died in tragic circumstances a few years ago."

★　★　★

They had the aisle between them, Halla with the boys securely strapped in and their iPads in their hands in one row of seats, and Helgi sitting opposite, watching as Halla tried to make herself comfortable, folding her hands across her swelling belly. Pregnancy suited her, Helgi thought, feeling pleasantly fuzzy courtesy of the windfall double brandy in the departure lounge. The aircraft was ready to go and the plane bumped across the tarmac. Helgi felt Halla's hand on his arm and for a moment they clasped hands across the aisle until the acceleration pressed them back into their seats and she turned away to make sure that Nonni and Svavar were still engrossed in their games.

It hadn't been a wonderful holiday, Helgi thought. If Halla's parents had just let them use the villa in Portugal, it would have been great, but the interfering old busybodies had insisted on being there as well, which would have been fine for a day or two but was far from all right for a whole two weeks. The villa was large and comfortable, close to the golf course that was so dear to the old man's heart, but the walls were paper-thin and Helgi reflected that while he could live with a chaste goodnight kiss on the cheek, every night for two weeks was too much for a grown man.

He felt the brandy's effects and wondered if he dared order another one once the drinks trolley appeared, or if that would prompt tutting and a frown from across the aisle.

He closed his eyes as the aircraft lifted off, and his thoughts drifted back to the brandy, and the bar, and

16

the slab-shouldered man who had walked away without picking up the handful of coins that were his change.

There was something there that irritated him, a resemblance to someone he had once known, and being unable to call the name to mind infuriated him. The line of the man's jaw and the slight cleft in his chin, the abrupt tone and the eyes narrowing as he realised he had been challenged for jumping the queue were somehow familiar. He tried to recall the few words the man had spoken, in easy, clipped English. There was an accent there behind the gravel in his voice that tugged at Helgi's memory, and he settled into a troubled doze.

The brandy had worn off by the time they landed and found there was a delay and a couple of hours to wait for their evening connecting flight to Iceland. Halla settled herself and the two sleepy boys in a snack bar in a quiet corner of the departure lounge. Helgi reflected that it would be a late arrival, and Halla's sister would be less than cheerful when she came to collect them from the airport. He shrugged mentally. That could be Halla's problem. Standing in yet another queue, this time for coffee and fizzy drinks for the boys, he wondered idly if he had picked the right girl. He had slept with Stella a couple of times in his restless single years, but somehow had ended up with the warm, maternal Halla instead of her career-minded and resolutely childless sister, who would probably have suited him better.

He sighed as he carried a tray back to the table. Halla had become pregnant almost immediately, mirroring his first marriage, and Nonni and Svavar had

17

arrived in quick succession, adding to the three sons they collectively already had between them: Halla's boy and Helgi's two from his first marriage. It nagged at him that this latest pregnancy hadn't been discussed, it had just happened; as if it was meant to be, as Halla had happily told him.

Halla slept placidly through the second flight. This time Helgi sat with the boys, trying to read a paperback as they chattered at his side. He realised as the aircraft came in to land at Keflavík airport that for at least half an hour he had been turning the pages without taking in a single thing that had happened in the book. He sighed to himself, glanced out of the window and shivered as he saw below the long floodlit strip of Reykjanesbraut, the highway leading through the lava fields from the airport at Keflavík to Reykjavík. He told himself that he'd need to brace himself for the coming cold shock waiting for them outside the terminal building.

While Halla had been restored by three hours of slumber on the flight, Helgi took a deep breath at the carousel, telling himself that the third airport of the day was the last one and in less than an hour he could climb into his own bed. He hauled the cases from the carousel, cursed at the weight as he stacked them on a trolley and steered them towards the Nothing to Declare sign, just as a broad-shouldered figure strode past him, a leather bag hung on one shoulder and a modest case on wheels at his heels.

Helgi stopped dead for a second, and then pushed the trolley as hard as he could, the boys scampering behind him as he tried to catch a glimpse of the man again, ransacking his memory to recall the name that ought to go with the face that had suddenly appeared first at a busy Portuguese airport, and then striding confidently into the Icelandic night.

He dropped Erik Petter Tallaksen's passport on the table and wondered why he was there.

He had brooded all the way from Vigo to the airport across the border in Porto and during the stopover at Schiphol. He knew it was dangerous, that this was the worst place in the world for him to be. This was precisely where some long-lost schoolmate or relative could run into him in the street with a smile, innocently asking where he had been all these years. Then they'd remember the rest of the story and any chance of staying under the radar would be gone if he wasn't able to bluff it out by sticking to English.

But it had to be done. It had been too long. Fifteen years was a big chunk of any lifetime, during which his parents had died, his siblings had become grandparents and his wife had married someone new. With the whole world online these days, it hadn't been hard to keep track of people and events back home. Now he would have to do his best to not attract any attention to himself.

Once he had walked out of the airport into the chill outside and taken his place on the bus with the tourists, he had felt vulnerable. He longed to turn around, walk back into the terminal building and buy himself a one-way ticket right back to the sunshine and the place he now thought of as home.

He hadn't set foot in his native country in fifteen years, had hardly spoken a word of his own language for just as long. Occasionally he had heard snatches of conversation, especially when he had been in Denmark or Norway, and had grinned to himself as these Icelanders abroad blithely assumed that they could drink and argue at the tops of their voices without fear of being understood.

Sitting in this bare and ruinously expensive hotel room with its view of a lot more city lights than he remembered from the old days, he felt the walls closing in on him, the doubts tugging at his conscience. It had been a mad decision, made on the spur of the moment. But there were things he had to attend to, people he needed to see — even if he dared not let them see him.

It was past midnight when Halla finally put the key in the lock and pushed the door open. Helgi followed with Svavar in his arms. Still on his feet but practically asleep, Nonni shuffled in a daze towards the room he shared with his brother.

"Shoes off, Nonni," Helgi said quietly.

He took the sleeping Svavar straight to the boys' bedroom and laid him in the bunk bed. He gently pulled off his shoes and tucked the duvet around him, while Nonni shambled in, yawning, and crawled gratefully into his own bunk.

20

"Good lad," Helgi said, kissing the top of his head. "My turn in five minutes," he muttered to himself as he switched off the light.

Halla leaned against the counter, one hand on her belly and the other cradling a steaming mug.

"There's hot water if you want some tea," she said as Helgi dropped into one of the kitchen chairs. "You're going to work tomorrow, aren't you?"

"Anxious to get rid of me, are you?"

"Idiot," she said fondly, sitting opposite him and taking his hand. "Was that a terrible holiday?"

"Much as I'm fond of your parents, you can have too much of a good thing." Helgi yawned. "The only moment we had to ourselves was when they took the kids to the market and left us behind."

"Yeah. That was a fun couple of hours."

"They weren't out of the drive before we had our clothes off," Helgi said. "We could try a rerun?"

"In your dreams, old man. Five months gone and we've been travelling all day. Do you really imagine I have the energy for that kind of stuff?"

"A man can live in hope," he said seriously. "And yes. I have to go back to work tomorrow. Twelve till eight."

"I'm quite proud of you, Helgi. You know that?"

Helgi sent her a suspicious look.

"Why?"

"Because we spent almost two weeks with my parents in the same house and you didn't complain. Well, not all that much. But on top of that, you didn't call Gunna once to find out how she was doing."

"Gunna's a big girl. She can look after herself."

Halla sipped her tea and sighed. "It was a lovely break, and I suppose it'll be the last one for a while."

"It'll be the last one we can afford, especially if we're going to try and move to somewhere bigger next year."

"I know. I haven't even wanted to think about house prices while we've been away. I'll bet they've gone up another five per cent while we were in Portugal."

"Let's hope the underworld has been busy and there's some overtime to be had. We could do with it."

Halla gave him a tired smile.

"You're back at work already, Helgi. I can tell. What was all that at the airport?"

"What d'you mean?"

"You went right into cop mode at the airport in Porto. Don't think I can't tell. What was that all about?"

"Oh, nothing," Helgi said, stretching his arms over his head and then reaching out to place one hand on the bulge that touched the kitchen table. "Just a face in the crowd. Someone I thought I recognised, but I can't put a name to the face. It's frustrating."

"It comes with age, old man."

"Maturity, you mean, young lady."

"Whatever." Halla yawned. "Come on. Old people like you need their sleep."

Halla slept on her side, a hand by her face and a curl of her hair wrapped around one finger. Helgi drifted between sleep and half wakefulness as the trials of the day seeped out of his bones and faces flashed through his mind.

22

He sat up in bed with a start.

"Ingvar," he said, his voice urgent. "It was Ingvar Sturlaugsson."

"What's the matter?" Halla asked sleepily as Helgi lay back on the pillow.

"Nothing, love. Just a face from the past," he said absently, patting the bulge, his mind elsewhere. "Go back to sleep."

CHAPTER
TWO

Moderate southerly wind veering south-westerly,
later gaining strength and backing easterly
overnight. Clear skies, cloud cover by evening
with possible rain or snow showers.
Temperatures 0°–5°C.

Áskell Hafberg's neighbour sat on the bench by his back door looking morosely out over the lake.

"It's a beautiful place on a summer's day," he said in a mournful voice. A fresher wind had left the dull grey water scarred with sharp-edged wavelets and the trees swung their leafless heads in sympathy. The hills were hidden behind banks of grey cloud that seemed to hover hardly clear of the rooftop of Jónatan's one-room summer house.

"Next of kin? Any ideas?" Gunna asked.

"If you go in the house, there's a number on a scrap of paper pinned to the wall by the phone," Jónatan said. "I think it's Ursula's number. That's Birna's daughter, lives in Sweden."

"She's the only one? She's not Áskell's daughter?"

"To be honest, I never asked. I don't think so. I know Áskell has, or had, a son. But he hasn't been seen for years."

"How long had Áskell lived here?"

"Longer than I have, at any rate, and I inherited this place almost thirty years ago. It was a wreck then. My uncle used it for a week now and then when he went shooting ptarmigan, but he never looked after it. When he died, it came to us. My brothers and sisters weren't interested in it, so they sold me their shares and I fixed the place up. Since I retired, I've spent more time out here than at home."

"And Áskell was already here?"

Jónatan sipped coffee from a thick earthenware mug and Gunna cradled a similar one in her hands.

"Yeah. Áskell lived here. Not all the time, but back then he was here a few months a year. He'd be abroad for weeks and months at a time, but these last few years he was here more and more, and after Birna died he hardly left the place. I used to go shopping for him so he didn't have to go into town more than he had to. Dear God, but she was lovely."

"Remind me again, what exactly happened to her?" Gunna asked. She had already looked it up, but wanted to hear Jónatan's opinion.

"Who knows? I certainly don't. Like I told you, she drowned. Just down there," he said, pointing. He looked away to hide the fact that he needed to brush away a tear. "Under the jetty."

"And how did Áskell cope?"

"He didn't cope," Jónatan said. "The pair of them argued and fought, but I've never seen two people who were as much in each other's pockets as they were. Birna was always sweet to me, never a cross word, always polite and friendly."

"Was she like that with everyone?"

"Everyone except Áskell. They needled each other. It stoked him up, got him going. He always said he did his best work when they'd had a shouting match about who had hung the front door key on the wrong hook. They'd have a row about whose turn it was to cut the grass, and then he'd sneak off to the barn, fire up the stove and work for thirty hours straight."

"And after she died? Was he still able to paint?"

"In fits and starts. Sometimes I'd see him sitting on the end of the jetty down there with his feet in the water. That meant he was psyching himself up and he'd be in the barn for days on end. I normally knew when he was working because I'd smell the woodsmoke from that old stove in there."

"When did you see him last?"

"Three days ago," Jónatan said. "I got a whiff of woodsmoke in the morning so I decided I'd leave him to it. He never made a fuss if he was disturbed, and I'm not sure it worried him. If his head was full of ideas, he'd just ignore you." He coughed and sipped. "Well. Not ignore. That's not quite right. He'd get so absorbed in what he was doing that I'm sure he just didn't notice when somebody went in there."

"And yesterday, no smoke?"

"Exactly. I reckoned he'd worked himself to a standstill and would take it easy for a day or two." Jónatan shifted on the seat and folded his arms around himself, his empty mug tucked in his embrace. "So tell me, what do you make of it all?"

Gunna shrugged. "I don't know yet. I'll have to conclude my investigation. But I have to say it seems clear enough that he took his own life."

"He wasn't a happy man. But I hope you do a better job than that fuckwit who was here a few years ago."

"What do you mean?"

"The idiot who investigated Birna's death," Jónatan said, unable to hide the bitterness in his voice. "I don't know the name of the guy who was in charge; to be honest, I only saw him the once. Let's just say that he didn't tire himself out asking too many questions."

"Why do you say that?" Gunna asked, her curiosity aroused. "Was there any question about Birna's death?"

"I don't want to say too much." Jónatan sighed. "And I probably already have. But what the hell, they're both dead now."

"Go on."

He pulled off his hat and scratched his head nervously. "It's like this," he said. "Áskell was always certain that she didn't drown. Birna knew the lake well and people used to think she was crazy because she swam regularly, a couple of times a week at least. She wouldn't just drown, and especially not in water that's knee-deep. You get my meaning? It was something that only ever came up when he'd had more to drink than usual. But there was never any doubt in his mind, and now he's gone as well."

There was no need for them, but Gunna pulled on a pair of latex gloves from force of habit. She watched her breath turn to clouds in the cold air of Áskell Hafberg's workshop. It was one of the old military sheds of the kind the British army had erected everywhere they had been stationed eighty years ago, sheets of heavy corrugated iron that curved in a half-moon to form the body of the building, the ends finished with sheets of plywood nailed to a timber frame. This one had presumably been used as a garage at some point, as it had heavy double doors that looked out over the lake beyond.

She searched through drawers, finding nothing but artist's materials, empty cigarette packets, a few carpentry tools in a deep bottom drawer under the bench, pencils sharpened to needle-like points and slotted into a case, and empty bottles everywhere. She went slowly through the canvases stacked against the back wall, admiring them. Many of the landscapes, in pale shades and clean lines, showed the lake outside in its many moods, from emerald summer to grey, angry winter. Those at the front of the stacks were darker, with sharper, more jagged lines. Winter seemed to be more in evidence as the artist had slashed at the canvas with his brushes, in contrast to the detail and care that appeared to have gone into the earlier canvases. Sometimes they were pure lake-scapes, the hillsides on the far side setting a distant backdrop, while in others there would be an indistinct figure or even two in the picture.

At the back of the workshop a pile of roughly framed canvases leaned against the wall and Gunna lifted them one by one, turning them around as she did so, arranging them so that a series of paintings of a snub-nosed dark-haired woman appeared. There were head-and-shoulders portraits, hurried sketches in charcoal, several formal portraits of the woman seated in a chair and one of her cross-legged on lush grass with the slope-shouldered hills across the lake in the background. Gunna lifted this one up and held it to let the light fall on it better, examining the woman's laughing face with the curtain of dark hair around it, rendered in shades of black and grey that up close looked contrived but that fell into place as she put the painting down and stepped back.

She shook her head, perplexed, as she stared at the picture, troubled by something that felt familiar but which she could not identify.

Looking at one picture, a portrait in a formal pose, she had the unsettling feeling of being watched, until she realised that a pair of half-concealed eyes and an indistinct face were hidden in the waves of the sitter's cascade of dark hair that filled more than half of the canvas.

She put it down, facing the wall, and picked up another, this one a charcoal drawing different from the others, not in quick, dashing strokes, but in painstaking detail, so precise that from arm's length it looked as lifelike as a photograph. The woman looked back at her out of the frame, head tilted knowingly, as if the artist had caught her with a snapshot just as she was looking around to respond to a joke that had taken her pleasantly by surprise. In one corner was a signature, Á. Hafb., Birna, and a date so recent that it had to have been painted only a few weeks before.

Opening the barn's door as far as it would go to let in light, Gunna propped the portrait against a bench and took a photograph of it with her phone. She replaced it with another, and put the phone back in her pocket with half a dozen images of the mysterious woman with the enigmatic smile.

Erik Petter Tallaksen's shiny passport, a driving licence that had seen better days and a gold credit card were enough to secure him a rental car. He was almost tempted to take the offered upgrade, but decided that flashy wasn't going to be his style for the next few days.

He started with a few old haunts, through the centre of the city and the western end where he had lived as a young man, first as a hard-up student making his way to navigation college every day and later as a working seaman with pockets full of cash during the occasional trip off. The narrow streets seemed more cramped now, even though the city had been smartened up. The sight of the harbour was a shock, with only a handful of boats to be seen, and most of those looked to have been rocking at their moorings for a long time. So much had gone, and there was so much more that was new. What had once been bare ground had been built over as shopping centres, and warehouses had sprung up, but he was relieved to see that a couple of cafés he remembered were still there and promised himself lunch at one or the other before reminding himself that wasn't going to be a smart idea for someone who wanted to stay off the radar.

The city's Shadow District was what took him by surprise. He'd known the place had changed, but the reality of it was a shock. Practically the whole of Lindargata had gone, the rambling timber houses clad in their distinctive corrugated iron sheets swept away and replaced by high-rises dwarfing the old Ministry building on Skúlagata that had for so many years been the area's largest landmark. The ramshackle old houses containing odd-shaped apartments and bedsits carved from once grand residences had disappeared. All the places where there had always been moonshine, dope or girls to be found had gone, and he guessed that the fun had moved away from the city centre to a suburb somewhere.

He managed to lose himself in the new one-way streets that had replaced the old narrow alleys, and found his way eventually to Hlemmur to discover that the bus station where the drunks used to hang out had become a smart food hall populated by chattering youngsters sharing plates of pasta. He wondered where the dubious characters who had previously huddled on benches a stone's throw from the central police station had gone.

He shook off his regret for the vanished city and cruised through as if he were just another tourist, following the satnav to cope with the network of new roads and housing estates that had risen from the rocks since he had last been there.

Without meaning to, he found himself in the suburb where he and Katla had lived, and where his former wife now lived with her new guy and, as far as he was aware, the two younger children. He took the turns almost unconsciously along what had been his habitual route, until he stopped fifty metres from the house he had built. Back then it had been on the edge of the city, backed by lava fields. Now the rocks and the wilderness had given way to another estate, leaving what had once been the silent periphery firmly in central suburbia.

He wondered if anyone might be at home, not that he had any intention of knocking on what he still thought of as his own front door.

He had easily been able to follow the family's progress from a distance, thanks to the social media that chronicled every aspect of life in Iceland. He had known when his parents had died, when his brothers and sisters had become parents and finally grandparents, when his own children had started a new school or been on holiday, when his eldest son had graduated from college and then when the boy had been sent to prison, first for a moment's foolishness and then a second time for something worse. He had watched with an interest that he found disturbing as Katla had eventually moved his replacement into the house that his disappearance had paid off.

He wondered what her reaction would be if he were to walk in through the door, shrug his jacket off onto the back of the kitchen chair as he had always done all those years ago, pour himself a mug of coffee to sip as he leafed through the paper with his feet up on a stool. That had always driven her to distraction back then. If he were to do it now, she'd be reaching for the sharpest knife in the kitchen drawer.

The house echoed and the floorboards creaked as Gunna made her way inside. It was an old place, built in the fifties, she guessed, probably as a summer cottage back when Hafravatn would have been far outside the city's limits. It had been panelled in wood that had darkened with age and nicotine, and there were pools of darkness in the corners that were hardly banished when she clicked on the two working lights of the dim hall.

A dialling tone buzzed in her ear as she listened to the distant phone ring in Sweden, wondering if the number on the slip of paper tacked to the wall by a mirror gradually losing its silver backing meant anything, or even if it was still Ursula's number.

"Hallo," sang a voice, deep but female, when the phone was finally picked up.

"Hallo, am I speaking to Ursula?" Gunna asked in English, and there was a sudden silence, the sound of something being swallowed hurriedly.

"This is Ursula." The voice was cool and suspicious.

"My name's Gunnhildur Gísladóttir and I'm a police officer with the Reykjavík CID. Do you speak Icelandic or is English better?"

"Let's just stick to English, shall we?" Ursula decided. "What's the problem? What are you looking for?"

"Can you tell me what your relationship is with Áskell Hafberg?"

"He's my sort-of stepfather, I guess. Why? What's he done now?"

"In that case, my condolences. He passed away yesterday."

This time the silence was a longer one.

"Hello?" Gunna asked finally. "Still there?"

"Er . . . yeah. I'm still here."

"I understand it must be a shock for you. Were you close?"

Ursula sighed. "What happened? Finally drank himself to death?"

"No. I'm afraid not. There's no easy way to break this, but he committed suicide."

"Shit. Look, OK, thanks for letting me know. But why are you calling me?"

"This is the only number I have for anyone who may have been related to him. You said he was your stepfather. He was married to your mother, I take it?"

"Yeah. She died a few years ago."

"That was Birna?"

"That's her. I don't know if they ever did get married, but they lived together for years . . . Don't do that!" Ursula called. "Listen, I'm sorry. This really is a bad time and the kids will rip the place apart if I take my eyes off them for five minutes. Can we speak later?"

Gunna heard the first note of concern in her voice, a half-stifled sob.

"No problem. I'm at the house now and I'm going back to the station. I'll give you a call when I get there."

"Fine. In an hour?"

The place had been practically in the countryside when he had bought the land, an oblong plot that had seemed vast back then. That was when he had been a single man and the patch of building land had been a spur-of-the-moment investment. He didn't have to build on it right away, but he had been doing well for himself as the only Icelander in the crew of a trawler from Greenland that had called in at Reykjavík with an injured crewman. A replacement had been needed, and that single trip had turned into years as he had worked up to occasional relief skipper on one of the same company's older trawlers.

The concrete base of the house had been laid one spring. Even then he still hadn't intended to continue with it, convinced that sooner or later he'd sell it as it was to some young couple looking to build their own home.

Then he had met Katla and everything changed. They hadn't been able to keep their hands off each other, and within a few months they were living together in the cheapest rented flat they could find while every trip off and every spare penny he could earn or land a loan for had been swallowed up as the house rapidly took shape. Within a year they'd moved into one end of it while the other end remained a shell with plastic sheeting nailed across the windows as he earned to pay the plasterer to polish the walls to a shine and the electrician to finish wiring the place. Meanwhile Katla produced three children in the space of a few years during which it seemed they only saw each other for long enough for her to get pregnant yet again.

He parked the car at the end of the street. He hadn't meant to come here at all. In fact, he had been determined to keep well away, but he had been unerringly drawn to the place, trying to get his bearings now that the suburbs had sprawled beyond their old limits instead of being bordered by an undulating expanse of moss-grown rock and tussocks of grass.

His Greenland job had come to an end when he had moved in with Katla and the first child was on the way. Eight-week absences weren't acceptable for a man with a young family, so he had regretfully left and taken a berth closer to home, and before long was sailing as the chief mate on a local boat.

It had been a refit that had changed everything. The old man had left it to Ingvar to steam the ship across to Gdynia where a planned five weeks of repairs and maintenance had turned into eighteen by the time he gave up in desperation and jumped at the offer of a berth on a trawler working off West Africa. The money was erratic but generous when it came through; the downside was the longer absences. The surprise was that he enjoyed everything about it: the heat and the strange spicy food, the oddball people he had to work with, the Russians, the Norwegians, the Spanish and the Moroccans who respected him as the muscular skipper who could effortlessly splice a warp and who always found fish, but who could also turn on the charm when he needed to. After that, when he had stepped into the fleet manager's role, he had revelled in the intrigue, the cat-and-mouse of bribing the right person just enough over a lavish dinner and a visit to an expensive brothel to get the licences that would keep the ships working, or just the bustle and buzz of making sure the boats got to sea, that everything came together and nobody who needed a quiet backhander went unpaid, that the fuel guy was slipped enough to not dilute the diesel with too much water.

One of the breaks between seasons took him home with a stack of cash that had been easily enough to pay for the last of the work on the house and get the plot around it landscaped, but by then a tired coldness had crept between him and Katla.

He fought the impulse to duck down, recognising one of his former neighbours driving past, taken aback to see how grey Sigvaldi had grown in the intervening years. Thinking about it, he was just surprised that Sigvaldi hadn't moved in those years, and he wondered how many of the other neighbours were still there. Then there was that flash bastard Valgeir, with whom Katla had conducted an on-off affair, and who had then moved in permanently after she had been so tragically widowed.

He sighed. He could hardly blame her, an attractive and demanding woman with three lively children, no shortage of cash and a husband who had been making increasingly infrequent appearances. It wasn't as if he'd been blameless either. The lure of raucous bars and young women in not many tight clothes had been more than he had been able to resist. He told himself that he had made an effort, but once he was aware of what had been going on with Valgeir in the next street, he hadn't let it bother his conscience too much.

The house looked good, neat and freshly painted. The garden was tidy behind the hedge he had planted as a row of thin sticks, now a bushy barrier to prying eyes. He wondered if Katla had been keeping it maintained, or if her new guy had seen to all that.

The real money had come with the joint venture between himself and a Spanish group who had seen his success in securing licences to fish where nobody else could. The venture had been their idea, running old but well-maintained trawlers that landed catches every few days to a new factory in a dust-blown port that appeared to have grown out of the dunes. There had even been enough to buy an apartment in Cangas, across the water from Vigo, where his new employers had their surprisingly modest office, although he had never bothered to tell Katla about the place.

He had seen more than he needed to, and started the engine. The street was depressingly similar to the last time he had been here all those years ago. The trees and bushes in people's gardens were bigger, there were a few more cars parked outside houses that looked precisely the same as they had back then. He didn't dare go much closer to his own house, and wondered if it really was his own house any more. It had to be Katla's, and before that it would have belonged briefly to an insurance company until they paid out and handed it over to the widow he guessed hadn't grieved too much for him.

He grinned to himself at the thought that he was legally dead, and as such it wasn't as if he could own property any more.

He clicked on the radio, put the car into gear and, against his own better judgement, drove along the street, resisting the temptation to slow down outside what had once been his house. It wasn't as if there was anything to be seen. The hedge hid it from view. A brief glimpse up the path showed him the same front door, the one he had painted bright red one summer morning, now firmly closed, but there was nobody to be seen. That was fine, he told himself. He had no desire to encounter Katla, and even less inclination to bump into her new husband, but he wondered which of his children still lived in the house their father had built.

Back at her desk at the Hverfisgata police station, it took Gunna a few minutes to find the files, and she forgot the time as she started to read, coming back to reality with a jerk as she remembered and hastily dialled Ursula's number.

"Hallo?" the voice on the other end sang.

"Hi, Ursula, Gunnhildur Gísladóttir here again. Sorry, I got tied up and couldn't get to the phone earlier," she lied.

"That's all right. I've been wondering. What happened to Áskell? Can you tell me?"

"I'm sorry to have to tell you that he hanged himself some time the night before last," Gunna said. "I'm very sorry."

"And that's something the police investigate?"

"It is for the moment, until we're sure there were no external factors."

"You think there might have been?"

"We don't know yet. I'll have to wait for all kinds of lab results and I'm trying to track down his next of kin, which is why I called you."

"Áskell had no brothers or sisters, and I don't recall him or my mother mentioning any close relatives."

"He didn't have children of his own?"

"There's a son called Úlfur, but we lost touch years ago."

"But he's not your brother? Apologies, I need to get a handle on who is who. You're not Áskell's daughter?"

"No, I'm not, but I grew up with him around. Áskell had Úlfur when he was still a teenager, so he'd be in his forties now, if he's alive. Áskell and my mother hooked up after he had split with Ulli's mum, so Úlfur was like a stepbrother to me."

"And he has no children?"

Ursula was silent and Gunna could hear the faint pops and crashes of a cartoon in the background.

"That's a question, isn't it? Who knows? There might well be a bunch of little Úlfurs running around somewhere that nobody knows about. He was pretty popular until he started to hit the bottle hard and gave up washing."

"Gave up washing?"

"Well, not consciously, I suppose. He just had other stuff to think about. Like where the next drink or hit was coming from."

Gunna scrolled the screen in front of her as they spoke, looking at odd words in the report on Ursula's mother's death. "Your mother," she said. "Losing her hit Áskell hard?"

"It hit all of us hard. I really don't want to talk about that, especially as . . ." Ursula's voice tailed off.

"Especially as?" Gunna asked, intrigued, and she heard Ursula take a deep breath.

"Look, I said I didn't want to discuss it. There were things about my mother's death that didn't add up, and nobody asked too many questions. All right? So maybe you can understand why the police aren't top of my list of favourite people."

There was a harshness to her tone that had been hidden and which now appeared clearly.

"I'm sorry if you feel that way. Look, I've just dug out the report on your mother's death and I'll read through it now," Gunna said, scrolling to the top. Her heart sank to see that Örlygur Sveinsson had been the investigating officer. "In the meantime, there's Áskell's house and studio that will need to be dealt with, so a next of kin will have to be found, otherwise I suppose everything will go to the state. There are a lot of paintings there, and as far as I can see, most of them are of your mother."

"Are there many?" Ursula asked after a pause.

"Several dozen, I'd say. One of my colleagues will be cataloguing everything in the next day or so."

"I don't know . . ." Ursula said, half to herself. "Listen, I'll see if I can get my guy's family to look after the kids for a few days and I might be able to get a flight over. Give me your number and I'll call you back."

★ ★ ★

41

He felt the breath sucked out of him. His heart hammered and he fought the urge to duck out of sight.

Three teenagers dressed from top to toe in black stalked along the street, and he watched them in the mirror as they approached the rental car where he had parked at the side of the road to spend a few minutes scrolling through his emails.

The one in the middle looked to be the alpha male of the group, half a head taller than the others and with a hawk-like face under a ragged black fringe. He was flanked by two wingmen, smaller versions of himself in much the same black uniform hung with silver trinkets. The one on the far side, furthest from the car, was the one who had snatched Ingvar's breath as he instantly recognised his own father's features in the boy's face: heavy brows and the square jaw with the dimpled chin.

He wondered for a moment what to do, whether to quickly put the car in gear and drive away before they could have a chance of seeing him, or to sit tight and wait for them to walk past, hoping that the lad on the end would not be curious enough to glance into the car.

He longed to speak to the boy, look him in the eye, ask how he was, even apologise for having disappeared from his life. But this wasn't the moment, not with his two friends at his side. He had no idea how any kind of meeting would turn out. How would the boy react to being introduced to the father he believed had died when he was a toddler? Anger? Frustration? Joy?

The three youths strode past the car without a glance to either side, and he realised that he had been gripping the steering wheel so hard that his fingers had turned white.

Helgi admitted to himself as he drove to work that he liked his job. He relished the constant challenge, the fact that one day was rarely anything like the one before, and he genuinely liked his colleagues. He and Gunna had clicked from the start. Fair enough, he mused as his Skoda nosed through the downtown traffic, she could be brusque to the point of rudeness. He chuckled at the thought that rudeness was an understatement. Gunna had no problem in being downright offensive if she felt it was called for, and it was a brave man who picked an argument with her. But Helgi had never once fallen foul of her. Once or twice he'd been told in no uncertain terms of the error of his ways, but that was an indicator that she was under pressure, and he never took it badly.

Young Eiríkur was different, he reflected, listening to the Skoda cough and splutter as he pulled up at the lights on Sæbraut. Helgi and Gunna were both from out of town and were much the same age, while city kid Eiríkur was a dozen years younger and Helgi had the feeling that he was marking time as a police officer, that sooner or later his real calling would snatch at him and take him elsewhere.

He parked in the yard behind the Hverfisgata police headquarters and shivered as he got out of the car. Relaxing under the Portuguese sun had left him poorly prepared for this bleak winter weather, with a snowstorm forecast to tighten its grip on Reykjavík.

"The traveller returns," Gunna announced as Helgi elbowed the door open. "Take a seat, young man, and tell us simple island folk of your adventures in the big wild world. Good holiday, was it?"

Eiríkur grinned and waved from behind his computer in the corner, but said nothing.

"And good day to you, ladies and gentlemen. I'm delighted to see you're alive and well," Helgi said, dropping into his chair. He glanced under the desk, checking that nobody had interfered with his personal library. "Let's say it was good in parts. Portugal is a delight. The food was wonderful, the wine was nectar, my wife is gorgeous and blooming, but thirteen days with her parents under the same roof was . . ." He searched for the right expression. "Let's just say it was challenging."

"So you've come back to us refreshed and suntanned, ready for the fray?"

"I wouldn't say that, but you'd better tell me what's new."

"Uniform. That's what's new."

"For detectives? You are joking. Please tell me you're joking."

Gunna shook her head, and jerked a thumb towards Eiríkur.

"Not a bit of it. Take our youthful colleague here, properly dressed at last."

Helgi looked aghast as he saw that Eiríkur was dressed in uniform trousers and a police-issue T-shirt.

"Directive from upstairs," Gunna explained. "We're expected to be in uniform from now on, except when on specific jobs when uniform would be a disadvantage. So you've until the end of the week to get yourself properly kitted out."

Helgi frowned and surveyed Gunna's checked shirt and jeans.

"I see you're following the rules to the letter," he observed.

"I'm fighting a rearguard action. But I'll have to give in sooner or later. Not without a fight, though."

"I'd expect no less of you, chief. Is there coffee in there?"

Gunna nodded and ushered him towards the cubbyhole that housed the coffee machine, a round table and walls festooned with scurrilous cartoons. She filled two mugs and handed him one.

"So was it a decent break?"

"It was," Helgi admitted. "Much needed. Now I just have to pay for it."

"How's Halla?"

"Big."

"Four months to go?"

"Yep. Another little millstone."

Helgi sat down and Gunna recognised the signs immediately as he knitted his fingers.

"What's up?"

"What would you do if you saw a ghost standing next to you?"

"Ghost stories, Helgi?" Gunna took a seat and leaned on the table as Helgi fussed with adding just the right

45

amount of milk to his coffee. "You're not going psychic, are you? Elves and stuff?"

"Careful what you say about them," Helgi muttered.

"Elves?"

"The Hidden People, I mean."

"You don't believe all that stuff, do you?"

Helgi took a deep breath and closed his eyes for a moment.

"I don't know," he said at last. "I've seen some strange things over the years, especially when I was growing up in the north, and I don't like to dismiss what my parents and grandparents firmly believed without being sure of my ground. And you?"

"I'm with you on the Hidden People," Gunna agreed. "It doesn't pay to upset them, but don't say so to Eiríkur. He doesn't approve. So what's this ghost stuff?"

"Ingvar Sturlaugsson stood next to me at a bar, and then he was gone."

"Helgi, are you sure you should be back at work?" Gunna leaned back in her chair and shook her head. "You're not making sense. Be so kind as to explain."

"Come on, Gunna," Helgi snapped in uncharacteristic irritation. "Ingvar Sturlaugsson. He disappeared in the tsunami, Boxing Day 2004. He and his family were on holiday in Thailand. He was the only Icelandic citizen who lost his life in that disaster. It was all over the papers and the TV at the time, interviews with his wife and all sorts."

Gunna's eyes widened and she put her elbows back on the table, fingers forming a steeple before her face.

"And you've seen this guy?"

"He bought me a drink, in broad daylight. I'm certain it was him."

"Go on."

"We were at the airport in Porto. I'd left Halla with the boys and went to get myself a quick one at the bar, and this guy barged in next to me and ordered a brandy, in English. Then he noticed me standing there, apologised for jumping the queue and told the barman to get me one as well. He knocked his back in one, dropped the barman a twenty-euro note and didn't even hang around for his change."

"And you're certain it was this Ingvar Sturlaugsson? How can you be sure? Did you know him?"

"Not really. But . . ." Helgi tapped the table, lips pursed. "Listen. I knew his brother Tryggvi's kids. And their sister Magga. And I knew the old couple as well, Sturlaugur and Fjóla. I suppose Ingvar must be a few years older than me, probably mid-fifties by now. He'd already left home when I was at school with Tryggvi's son. I remember seeing him now and again, but they were all alike, that family, each one of the kids the spitting image of old Sturlaugur." His words were coming out in a rush. "I saw this guy at the airport in Porto, like I said, and I was sure I knew him from somewhere. It wasn't until later that I realised. It was the likeness to old man Sturlaugur that was bugging me. I knew I'd seen that face before."

"It wasn't the brother's kid? The one you were at school with?"

"Karl? Hell, no. He would never have walked away without another word."

Gunna shrugged.

"So what do you want to do? You're absolutely sure it was him?"

"I wasn't right away, but I'm a lot more certain now."

"Go on."

"I saw him at Keflavík as well. He must have had the same connecting flight via Amsterdam. He's right here in Iceland. I saw him leave the terminal."

Gunna scratched her head.

"Convince me. What do you think happened back in 2004?"

"That's what's bugging me. I know he was involved in some fishing business overseas. I also know things had been pretty stormy between him and his wife, according to what I remember Karl telling me after Ingvar vanished. Remember, this was before I moved south; I was still in uniform up in Blönduós," Helgi said, wagging a finger. "Ingvar's body was never found after the tsunami, along with the thousands of others who disappeared. His relationship was disintegrating. His business was all overseas and the taxman was after him here. Plus, he was always a ruthless bastard."

"Complete confidence?"

"Of course. That's what you're paying for."

Bára had no doubt that the man's name wasn't Tallaksen, but his money was as good as anyone else's.

She had arranged to meet him at a coffee house in Hafnarfjörður, preferring to be on neutral territory. The

48

place had a meeting room upstairs that could be hired for as long as anyone wanted it, and she saw the look of bemusement on his face as he glanced around. One side of the room was almost an office, with a bare table and severe chairs, while the other side boasted a sofa with deep upholstery.

"How long do we have?" he asked.

"I have the room for forty-five minutes. We won't be disturbed."

"It took a while to find someone in this country who does this kind of work," he said.

Bára shrugged.

"There aren't all that many of us who do it, and we don't tend to advertise."

"Maybe you should. You might get a lot more work from people like me in other countries."

"Maybe," she said, and clicked on the light above the desk. "Shall we?"

His eyes flickered around the room, scanning the fittings and the single narrow window. The woman wasn't what he had expected, not that he had known exactly what to expect. It had taken weeks to track down someone to do the work he had wanted, and even longer to be sure that it would remain confidential. He liked the look of this young woman with her businesslike manner and her trim figure in a dark suit that was smart enough to appear before a judge while being neutral enough not to attract attention anywhere else.

He noticed the smart black boots rather than heels, and a white shirt buttoned high at the throat. No rings, no pendant, no earrings, and blonde hair thick on top and cropped to a pale stubble that glittered at the sides of her head.

Although he would have preferred the comfort of the sofa, she gestured towards the desk, opened a briefcase and took out a slim folder.

The man was interesting, and under other circumstances she would have been intrigued to know more. It felt strange to be speaking English to someone with whom she felt sure she shared a native language, but if the guy wanted to pretend to be a foreigner, that was his business and she didn't doubt that he had his reasons.

"I have compiled as complete a profile of these people as I'm able to without breaking privacy laws. Would you like me to go through the main points, or would you prefer to read this yourself?"

He sat opposite her, amused at her formal English.

"Give me a run-down and then I'll read through the details later."

Bára nodded and opened the folder.

"The family you asked for information about is four persons, all resident at the same address at Asparsel 90: a woman with three children. The woman is Thorkatla Einarsdóttir, born in 1976. In addition, there's a Valgeir Samúelsson also registered there. Thorkatla's children are Sturlaugur Ingvarsson, born in 1997, Tekla Ingvarsdóttir, born 1999, and Einar Ingvarsson, born 2001. As far as I'm able to establish, Sturlaugur has two narcotics-related convictions. He's currently serving a long sentence for murder. The girl is a student at the

50

Hamrahlíð college of Further Education and I gather she's an excellent student, a promising basketball player, part of the judo team and a gifted musician."

"And the youngest?"

"Still at school. But there are some problems. It seems there's a level of autism there; I can't say how serious it is. That's not information that's readily available."

"And Thorkatla?"

"No debts I was able to find other than a Toyota Rav that's being paid for in instalments, all up to date. The house is owned outright. Her husband disappeared some years ago, and was declared deceased much more quickly than is normally the case when there's no body, as he was thought to have lost his life in the Boxing Day tsunami in Thailand in 2004. He had a generous life insurance and that paid off the house and a bit more. It was a little before my time and I don't remember it myself, but I've been able to look up a lot of newspaper coverage of it, interviews and so on."

"What does she do now?"

"Runs a shop in the Kringlan shopping centre."

"Runs or owns?"

"She's one of the owners of the business. The other owner is Margrét Ásdís Hallgrímsdóttir, who now lives overseas. At any rate, her legal residence is registered abroad."

"Do you know where?"

"She lives in Denmark, as far as I'm able to establish."

Ingvar nodded to himself, as if caught up in a moment's deep reflection.

"The lad," he said suddenly. "Tell me about him, what went on there. How did he wind up in prison?"

"He was involved in a fight that turned nasty. According to the court documents, a person was stabbed during the altercation and later died. Sturlaugur was identified as the killer on the basis of forensic evidence: his fingerprints were on the weapon. He got fourteen years," Bára said, and looked up to see the big man's lips pursed in a brief flash of suppressed anger.

"We don't have time for chasing ghosts. You know how snowed under we are," Gunna said, glancing at the window. "Literally, if the forecast is to be believed."

"I know," Helgi agreed sadly. "But you know when you get that feeling in your guts . . ."

"That sinking feeling when you know something's going to turn to shit but you don't know exactly how or when?"

"That's it."

Gunna sipped her coffee and brooded while Helgi stared into space.

"All right," she said. "You tell me what you want to do about all this."

"I don't really know. I'd like to figure out whether or not this man *is* Ingvar Sturlaugsson."

"Has a crime been committed here?" Gunna asked. "If it has, is it well past the statute of limitations? After all, this guy disappeared almost fifteen years ago. You

52

know what I mean. Is there something here to investigate?"

"If it is him, then he has to be here under a false identity," Helgi pointed out. "That's a criminal offence in itself."

"I suppose there's a possibility he may have legally taken citizenship somewhere else in the last fifteen years. Obviously, he can hardly have renewed his Icelandic passport in the meantime. So I'm asking again, what do you want to do?"

"Tell you what. Just bring me up to speed on the caseload, and if you don't mind, I'll ask a few discreet questions about Ingvar when I have a minute."

Aware of what could happen when Helgi became determined to get to the bottom of something, Gunna narrowed her eyes.

"You're sure you're not going to be heading off into the wild blue yonder searching for this ghost?"

"Of course not," he said, failing to convince either her or himself. "What are we working on at the moment?"

Gunna drained the last drops of coffee from her mug and placed it by the sink.

"Eiríkur is chasing a series of assaults, a couple of cracked knees and broken arms. It looks like a little turf war being played out. None of the victims wants to say a word."

"Of course. They know the other knee won't last long if they do that."

"Exactly. It's that clique at the top end of Breiðholt at work."

"Erling Larsen and his little empire?"

"That's the one. But it'll be their pals rather than them. Erling and his brother Gunnar both moved out of town."

"Really?" Helgi asked in surprise. "Breiðholt boys through and through. Where did they go?"

"Gunnar went to Hafnir. He bought a couple of houses out there not long after the crash, back when they were dirt cheap. The theory is he's out there because there's peace and quiet. Hardly any neighbours, and it's the best part of an hour's drive from town. Nobody's banging on his door, and he delegates all the heavy lifting to his city goons. Erling bought a place somewhere near Hveragerði not long ago, mercifully outside our patch."

"Fair enough. I'll go though the case notes and Eiríkur can fill me in on the details. What are you up to?"

"Me? Just kicking back and eating chocolate while you boys do the hard work."

"I expected no less," Helgi grinned, getting to his feet.

"I have a messy suicide on my hands, I'm afraid."

"Ah. Rather you than me."

"Yeah, it's not pretty. But it'll be sorted out soon. Just dealing with the details," Gunna said, and Helgi saw a moment's uncertainty in her eyes.

"What?" he asked.

"Well . . ." she began. I just thought you ought to know that Anna Björg is here."

Helgi couldn't stop his face breaking into a grin.

"That's great. So she's finally moved south?"

"Gave up waiting for a promotion up north. She's in traffic, and lucky to have a job, considering the state of things," Gunna said. "Look, I know there's history there. It's none of my business, but I'm thinking of Halla . . ."

"Don't worry, that's all in the past," Helgi assured her. "Well, mostly."

Helgi waded through the hundreds of emails that had piled into his inbox during his absence, using a strategy that Gunna had passed on to him of deleting anything that looked official on the basis that if it were important it would be sent again. If nobody noticed, then he could safely assume that whatever it was didn't matter.

He made a point of dealing with all the paperwork that needed to be checked, signed and filed before starting on the case files that Gunna had pointed him towards. He frowned as he read through the statements and reports about the injuries that had been handed out to twenty-seven-year-old Freyr Ágústsson, whose left arm had been badly broken. Unsurprisingly, he hadn't been able to recognise any of his attackers, while his girlfriend, who had also been present, hadn't even been able to identify how many of them there were. The number varied from two to four at various points in her statement, and while Helgi could appreciate that it had been a fraught few minutes while the men had cornered the pair on a quiet street, it was also obvious that neither of them wanted to point a finger at whoever had smashed Freyr's elbow. He would undoubtedly be undergoing treatment and physiotherapy for months to come, and even then it looked unlikely that he would ever regain full use of that arm.

Reading between the lines, it was blindingly clear that the couple knew exactly who the attackers were and had no wish to bring further misfortune on themselves by identifying them. Helgi sympathised. There was every chance that whoever had done the job while the others held Freyr down would eventually get a year or two in prison before being patted on the back and asked not to do it again, while whoever had commissioned the job would regard informing the police of anything as an affront that could never be allowed to go unpunished. Another visit would probably leave Freyr a cripple for the rest of his life, and Helgi understood perfectly his reluctance to say anything.

The weapon had been discarded at the scene of the crime: a wooden club around a metre long, with one end formed into a rounded handle and the business end left unshaped with four flat faces.

"Gunna?" Helgi called as he looked at the photos on his screen.

"Yes?"

"The Freyr Ágústsson case? Has anyone checked on this club?"

She came over to his desk and looked over his shoulder.

"It's an ice club. The trawlers carry them for beating ice from rails and steelwork," she said. "Normally these guys use a baseball bat for their dirty work, so this is a new development."

"And they left it behind?"

Gunna shrugged.

"An ice club isn't expensive."

"But it's not the kind of thing just anyone would have lying around, is it? And I don't suppose there are many places that sell them."

"True," Gunna agreed. "It's on my very long list of things to chase up, but as you mentioned it, you can call round all the chandlery companies and see if any of them have sold an ice club to someone who doesn't look like a shipping magnate."

"You want the rumours?" Bára asked cautiously.

"I want to know what really happened there. I want to know who did what, not who got the blame for what."

Bára took a sheet of paper from her folder and placed it on the table between them.

"I had the feeling that you might want to know more, so I asked a few discreet questions, and this is a combination of hearsay and putting two and two together. There's nothing here that would stand up in court, I mean."

"Fine. Fire away."

"This young man has a bit of petty crime behind him, plus he was part of a dope ring that was growing cannabis on an industrial scale. From what I've been able to find out, they were caught by a routine sweep that checks electricity consumption, things like that. The group were busted and left owing their supplier, who wasn't happy that his investment had gone down the tube."

"This was whoever financed the whole thing?"

"Yes. These people don't do their own dirty work. They supply the materials and make a profit while someone else takes the risk. Sturlaugur Ingvarsson did a few months in prison. Aron Stefánsson received a suspended sentence. What it comes down to is that these lads are in hock to a gentleman called Erling Larsen, until such time as he decides that the debt is paid off, which is effectively never."

"All right. So how come the boy is in prison for murder?"

"As well as selling dope, stolen goods, women and a few other things, Erling Larsen is an occasional loan shark and collects debts for other people. He's well known to the police, but since business has been good for him, he's very much the figure in the background. It's pretty simple. Sturlaugur and Aron were told to collect money from someone, and if there was no money to be had, they were to do some damage, or so I'm told."

Bára poured water into a glass from the bottle on the desk and sipped before continuing, while Ingvar listened intently.

"Instead of breaking a couple of ribs or a finger, which could have been passed off as an accident, one of them slashed the guy's face and neck. These clowns also managed to do this downtown in a fairly public place instead of somewhere quiet, meaning the police were there almost right away and they were banged up.

Somehow Erling Larsen decided that Sturlaugur should be the one to do the time for it, and his lawyer packaged the whole thing up. I have no idea what the score is; it could be that the boy's debt will be written off if he does the time for someone Erling Larsen wants to protect, which I understand is Aron Stefánsson."

"So Sturlaugur could be doing this willingly?"

"I doubt if that's the case. But he may have accepted that this is the way it's going to be, whether he likes it or not. So Aron is a free man and I presume Sturlaugur imagines that once he's out of prison in six or seven years, that debt will be clear."

"Fuck," Ingvar said. "How do you know this? I mean, how can I be sure this information is reliable?"

Bára shrugged.

"I used to be a police officer myself. I have friends on the force. That's why I told you the other day that I have to stay within the law, although occasionally I can bend things a little. Anyway, this is what one of the officers who was involved with that case told me, and I've no reason to disbelieve him."

"Where do I find this Aron?" Ingvar said. "And how about Erling Larsen?"

"Gunna?"

"Speak, young man," she said without looking up.

"There's something here I need to follow up. But it's out of town."

"It's not up north, is it?"

Helgi grinned.

"No such luck. It's in Vogar. It's to do with those ice clubs. None of the companies in Reykjavík or Hafnarfjörður dealing in maritime stuff have sold any ice clubs for months. Nobody's needed to buy any."

"But?"

"But there's a guy in Vogar with a small workshop that makes these things, and he said he sold half a dozen just after New Year."

Gunna glanced at her watch.

"It's almost four now."

"And he said he'll be there until six."

"So you want to run down there quickly? Do you want to check there's a spare car in the pool?"

"Well," Helgi said, "I could take my own car, see this guy in Vogar and then go home from there. I'll be back bright and early in the morning."

There was something about the tone of his voice that made Gunna immediately suspicious.

"And?"

"There's something I want to check on at the airport as well. Two birds with one stone, so to speak."

"This concerns your ghostly sighting yesterday?"

"Could be," Helgi admitted.

"Go on. Just keep it discreet, and if there's any fallout later, then it's your problem."

"Thanks, chief." Helgi grinned and the door banged shut behind him.

Gunna was left alone at her desk. Helgi had returned from his holiday tanned and slimmer, but he seemed no less tired than when he had shut down his computer before going on holiday. Maybe his tan accentuated the lines around his eyes, but Gunna had the feeling that he had become noticeably older. No doubt Halla's latest pregnancy, which had come as an uncomfortable surprise to him, was taking its toll. Their apartment in Garðabær was already full to bursting with Halla's son by a previous relationship and the two boys they had already agreed were enough for any family — not to mention the frequent presence of Helgi's practically grown-up sons from his first marriage — and now there was another strain on the space available.

She knew for a fact that given the opportunity, Helgi would jump at the chance to transplant the family somewhere cheaper and quieter, preferably somewhere on the north coast, but she also knew that Reykjavík-born-and-bred Halla would hate the kind of one-horse town where he would feel at home.

She shut down her computer and shrugged on her jacket. It was time for her to head for her own rural backwater an hour away from the city, and she found herself increasingly questioning the wisdom of commuting back and forth. All the same, she told herself, she had tried city life before and it had been noisy and stressful even back then. Nowadays Reykjavík had grown and the volume of traffic and noise seemed to have been magnified, so there never failed to be a feeling of relief as she left the last roundabout outside Hafnarfjörður behind her on the way home every evening.

"What do you mean?" Bára asked in a sharp voice.

He shrugged and spread his hands wide.

"I mean how much does it cost for you to go beyond what's legal?"

"No. That's not an option." Bára shook her head. "I have to work within the law. I can push boundaries on occasions, but if I start crossing the line, then I won't work again. As well as that, I have to be quite . . ." She paused, searching for the word in her vocabulary of formal English. "I have to be quite scrupulous. If I come across something illegal and it turns out later that I didn't pass the information on to the police, then I could become an accessory along with everything that entails. So it's not worth the risk."

"That's a shame."

"Sorry. I have to stay within the law, Mr Tallaksen." She paused. "Just as I have to be strictly confidential."

It was on the tip of her tongue to switch to Icelandic, but she kept her thoughts to herself. She hadn't been able to avoid doing some digging into Thorkatla Einarsdóttir's missing husband, going through old news reports and interviews. Now that she was presented with the mysterious Erik Petter Tallaksen who had contacted her several weeks ago from an email address that couldn't be traced to any particular part of the world, she was certain that this burly, self-assured man with his cropped hair, beard and deep tan had to be the missing man.

"What is it you're after?" she asked, curious. "If you tell me what you're looking for, then I can tell you if it's something that can be done."

She watched as Erik Petter Tallaksen frowned. Now it was his turn to shake his head.

62

"It's all right. I'll think things over," he muttered eventually.

Bára placed a business card in the folder and slid it across the table to him.

"Thanks," he replied slowly, peering at it. "You'll send me your bill?"

Without a word, she clicked open her briefcase and extracted a single sheet of paper.

"Fine," he said, nodding. "Euros?"

"Yes please. The account number's there if you could transfer the balance," she said, standing up.

"I'll do it tonight. No problem."

"If that's everything, then I hope what I've been able to do has been of use to you. If you need me for anything else, my number's on the card."

A mischievous smile appeared at the corner of his mouth.

"Are you married, Ms Ingunnardóttir?" he asked lazily.

"As it happens, Mr Tallaksen, I'm not. Is that relevant?"

"Maybe." He shrugged. "A drink later? Or dinner?"

Bára allowed herself a smile.

"It's tempting," she said. "But you're a client and I like to keep things professional."

"I thought you were on holiday," Andri said as Helgi lowered himself into a chair in front of the bank of monitors and helped himself to a hard biscuit from the packet on the desk.

"I was until this morning," he said, his mouth full. "Dedicated, me. Got home last night, back on the treadmill this morning."

He dipped the other half of his biscuit in the mug of coffee that he had also helped himself to without waiting to be asked, and lifted it clear a fraction of a second before it was about to disintegrate.

Andri yawned and jerked his head at the screens.

"I don't suppose you're out here just for the fun of the drive to Keflavík. So what are you after?"

"Had to ask a potential witness out this way a few questions, so I thought I'd drop by and say hello."

"Yeah. Come on. What do you want me to look up?"

"Last night," Helgi said. "There was a man on the same flight as me. Can you find him on the recording from the jetway?"

"So it is business after all?" Andri said. "Anything that Customs ought to know about?"

His fingers flickered across the keyboard and with a couple of clicks of the mouse he retrieved the recording.

"Not sure. But if there is, you'll be the first to know. Let's say it's a hunch I want to follow up."

"So we're not in official territory here?"

Helgi shook his head.

"Let's call it a preliminary enquiry. Just trying to figure out if there's a case to look into or not."

On the screen, tired passengers trooped out of the jetway from the aircraft and into the terminal, every one of them passing under a camera that provided a crystal-clear image of them. Some marched ahead, some shuffled; all of them looked exhausted.

"Any idea how far along this guy is?"

"We were sat in the middle of the plane and I didn't see him when I went to the toilet at the front. So he must have been near the back. He got off after us, I reckon."

Andri fast-forwarded through the footage until Helgi saw himself appear, one drowsy child in his arms and the other holding his hand, while Halla followed behind them, her belly jutting forward like the prow of a ship.

"Fuck me, Helgi. Another one on the way?"

"Yeah," Helgi growled. "Now we've figured out what's causing them, we won't be doing that any more."

Andri slowed the playback and Helgi leaned forward to stare at the screen, watching passengers pass by in ones and twos.

"There," he said at last. "That's the one."

Andri paused the tape and Helgi studied the man's face. He was brawny and tanned, and stood straight-backed with both handles of a holdall hooked over one shoulder.

"Can you get a couple of stills?"

"Yeah, no problem."

Andri clicked. Helgi handed him a memory stick and Andri copied the images to it.

"Now the fun part of it is, can I put a name to the face?"

Andri sucked his teeth.

"Where did you fly from?"

"Porto."

"Schengen all the way?"

"Yep. Via Amsterdam," Helgi said.

"In that case, I can ask Portugal to help me out as he'll have had to look at the camera while he scanned his boarding pass. Flight number?"

Helgi fished in his coat pocket and took out the boarding pass from the night before. Andri noted down the flight number and time, typed an email, attached one of the images and sent it while Helgi was still wondering what he was doing.

"So what's this about? Dope?" Andri asked, leaning back in his chair.

"No idea at the moment," Helgi replied. "Like I said, just a hunch. Sometimes things don't feel right, y'know? I've a suspicion this guy isn't who he says he is. That's all I can say for the moment."

"All right. Give me the whole story later," Andri said. "You owe me a drink for that, so you can tell me over a couple of beers. That's if Halla still lets you off the leash."

"Occasionally." Helgi grinned. "If there's a story to tell, you'll get to hear it. If there's nothing, then no harm done. But I'll still owe you a beer."

Gunna eased her shoes off and propped her feet on the chair as she sank into the sofa. For once nobody was home, and she wondered how long the peace and quiet might last, clicking on the lamp behind her head and shuffling the sheaf of printouts she had brought with her and which she had not seriously expected to get a chance to look through.

The report was short, prepared and signed off by Örlygur Sveinsson, who had nominally been her superior officer in charge of the serious crime unit but in reality had already been off with a long-standing back problem by the time Gunna had been transferred to work with his team. He had never returned to work, and when he retired, his role hadn't been filled, as Ívar Laxdal had taken over anything that had been Örlygur's responsibility.

She decided from the dates that this must have been one of his last cases before he had been signed off, before her arrival at the Hverfisgata police station as a new detective following her years in uniform. She pursed her lips as she read, flipping through the half-dozen pages before starting again from the beginning.

Birna Bergthórsdóttir had been found in the water under the jetty below the house. As soon as Gunna saw the full name, she began to make connections and frowned as she read on. A post-mortem had concluded that she had been drinking, but not heavily. Injuries to her arms and hands were reckoned to have been sustained as she tried to climb out of the water onto the jetty. Gunna scowled to herself, putting the report down as she conjured up a mental image of the lake and the jetty.

She was deep in the report and failed to hear the outside door open and shut.

"Hæ, Gunna. You all right?"

Startled, she looked up to see Drífa's bulk in the doorway. "Hæ, yeah. Sorry. You took me by surprise. I was miles away."

She got to her feet and clicked on the main light. Drífa looked down and came forward a few steps, one hand on her protruding belly and the other below it as if taking the weight of the child within. Little Kjartan Gíslason peered shyly from behind a fold of his mother's coat.

"How are you?" Gunna asked. "Kicking, is he? Or she?"

"It's a boy," Drífa sighed. "I'm certain of it."

"You'd better sit yourself down," Gunna said, noticing the mascara that had run down one of Drífa's cheeks. "Are you all right, sweetheart? What's the matter?"

"Oh, I don't know. Nothing and everything," Drífa sniffed. "Everything's such a mess."

She perched uncomfortably on a stool and took a deep breath, visibly holding back tears. Gunna squatted down and felt a warm glow as Kjartan smiled at her. She helped him off with his coat and boots and swung him into the air.

"Who's Granny's big little boy, then?" she demanded as he giggled at her.

Drífa lay back on the sofa with her mountainous belly in the air.

"Parent problems again, Drífa?"

"Sort of. Mum wants me to move back to the west."

"She's applying the pressure, is she?"

Drífa nodded.

"Why's she so determined to have you next door? I can understand she'd like to have her grandchildren close to her, but things are a little more settled now, surely?"

"She's still not happy," Drífa said, and Gunna bit back a retort that that was no surprise. "You know, the last thing I want is to go back home, but I feel I'm under your feet all the time." Drífa spoke through sobs that she stifled in her bunched-up sleeve. "And Gísli . . ."

"When's he back?"

"They're landing this week and he'll be ashore until . . . well . . . a while, I hope."

"Listen, Drífa. You stay here as long as you need to. It's not a problem."

"But it is a problem. I can see that."

"It's not." Gunna sat on the other stool and patted Drífa's hand. "Don't imagine that I don't know how you're feeling. It wasn't exactly easy when I had Gísli, and it's not easy when you don't have family around."

"But you were at home with your parents, weren't you?"

"Yeah. That was the problem," Gunna said grimly. "If I could have got away, I would have done just that. Mind you, I was a few years younger than you are now and it just wasn't possible. You know what Gísli's grandmother's like, don't you?"

"I suppose so," Drífa sniffed, looking up with a wan smile. "I can imagine," she added, and Gunna shuddered briefly at the recollection.

"Go on," she said as Drífa got off the stool. "If you want a shower, you'd best have one now, before the others come back. I'll look after Kjartan and there'll be something to eat by the time you're finished in there."

"You're going to cook?" Drífa asked in ill-concealed astonishment.

"I can cook, you know. It's not on the curriculum at the police college, but I can look after myself. It's not as if Steini's always been here to feed us."

Drífa nodded and put her hands on her hips, stretching her back as she pushed her belly out alarmingly.

"How long have you been together, you and Steini?"

"Five or six years, I suppose."

"Really? I thought you'd been together for years."

Gunna looked over her shoulder as she opened the fridge. "No," she sighed. "Before that, it was just me, Laufey and Gísli for a lot of years. Go on, go and have a shower before the others get in," she said, pulling out packets of chops. "Food in half an hour for us and whoever else is here by then."

CHAPTER
THREE

Strong south-easterly wind, backing easterly by midday and rising to near gale. Rain followed by snow showers. Temperatures 0°–5°C, dropping to — 5–0°C overnight.

The hour's drive was more of a challenge than usual, courtesy of patches of ice on Reykjanesbraut, the road that snaked along the north coast of the Reykjanes peninsula and into Reykjavík. Gunna reflected that at one time, commuting more than a few minutes to work had been virtually unheard of, but the property boom had pushed people out of the city to the cheaper housing of the surrounding towns.

"This is symbolic of the diktats that are simply handed down to us from some bureaucrat and which we have no choice but to go along with. I'm asking you if you believe that can be right?"

The rasping voice coming through the radio had a truculence to it that grated, and Gunna glanced down to see which station it was tuned to.

"It's the same with immigration," the voice continued. "We have to allow free movement, even though nobody wants it."

"This is part of a wider economic package that you'll surely agree is beneficial to the economy as a whole?" a second voice suggested gently.

"Of course not. We could have one without the other, economic prosperity without the burden of these people piggybacking on our welfare state," the rasping voice snapped.

"You mean by doing all the grunt work that nobody else is prepared to do?" the second voice said. "Vilberg, don't you think you ought to do some homework once in a while? These people form a vital part of the workforce, not a burden on the state."

"Figures! Give us some concrete figures and not just this endless hearsay —"

Instead of switching channels, Gunna punched the off button on the radio with more force than was needed, irritated by the hectoring tone of the latest political figure to press every populist button. Once again she told herself that she would have to follow Laufey's advice and figure out how to link the car's radio to her phone so she could listen to audiobooks on the way to work instead of the radio news, which was invariably profoundly depressing.

For the first time since returning to the city force after the years stationed at the coastal village of Hvalvík, where she still lived, Gunna found herself idly contemplating moving closer to Reykjavík but immediately dismissed the idea. The peace of the village was worth far more than being closer to work, she decided, knowing that Steini would never even think of moving into the city after having escaped it.

It was the report on Birna Bergthórsdóttir's death that was bothering her. There were worrying holes in Örlygur Sveinsson's investigation and she wondered whether or not to take the problem to Ívar Laxdal. She decided that she would. After all, she reasoned, that was what he was there for.

She brooded as she drove through Reykjavík, the streets crisp with frost under the Pajero's wheels, reflecting that a visit to Örlygur Sveinsson in his comfortable retirement might also be required.

Ívar Laxdal's black Volvo was already parked behind the Hverfisgata police station when she arrived, exasperated after the stop-start city traffic. Deciding to seek him out, she discovered that he was nowhere to be found. His office, as usual, was practically empty, and Gunna wondered how such a senior figure could manage to be virtually free of the forms and paperwork that governed everyone else's life. Normally Ívar Laxdal had a habit of turning up whenever his presence was bound to be awkward, so she decided it was typical of the man to disappear just as she wanted to speak to him.

"Good morning," she greeted Eiríkur, already hunched over his desk. "Tough night?"

"The usual," he yawned back. "Up at one thirty, up at four and again at five."

"Seen the Laxdal?"

Eiríkur shook his head. "His car's outside." He looked up. "Problem?"

"Why do you ask?"

"Nothing. Just wondering," he said, returning to his computer screen.

"Morning. Any luck yesterday?" Gunna asked as soon as Helgi appeared, dropping his keys on the desk with a clatter.

"Good morning to you," he replied, yawned and sat down. "The ice club guy was worth going to see."

"Did you get anything useful out of him?"

"Yep. He's supplied clubs direct to a couple of ships, but we're not too worried about them as they're bona fide customers. Apart from those, he's sold only eight ice clubs this year. All to the same person in a single purchase."

"Could he give you a description?"

"Better than that. He gave me the car registration of the guy who bought them. Better still, this chap paid with his debit card and there's a copy of the receipt. Name, date and everything."

Gunna wrinkled her nose.

"That would indicate to me that he's a legitimate purchaser. If he was buying clubs to smash people's kneecaps, he'd have paid cash, surely."

"Maybe," Helgi agreed. "Or it was a stolen card. Or maybe he's just not that smart."

Gunna nodded.

"True. It wouldn't be the first time one of these idiots has tripped up making a rookie error. Is it anyone we know?"

Helgi watched as his computer came to life.

74

"I'm about to find out," he said, glasses on the end of his nose as he tapped at the keyboard.

"And?" Gunna asked, getting up and coming over to stand behind him as he punched the information in.

"Aron Stefánsson," Helgi muttered. "Age thirty, a couple of traffic offences, three months for repeated minor stuff, theft and a bit of grass. Looks promising to me."

"And the car?" Gunna prompted.

Helgi tapped at the keyboard again.

"Registered to Gréta Valdemarsdóttir, same address. Laugarnesvegur 96. She's fifty-four, so somehow I doubt she's his girlfriend," he observed. "I'll bet you anything she's his mother."

"You'd better go and find out, hadn't you?"

It was a short conversation. Ingvar punched the number into a cheap phone loaded with the unregistered pay-as-you-go SIM card he had bought on the flight, and listened to the ringtone.

"Yeah?"

The voice on the other end sounded both uninterested and irritated at the disturbance.

"It's me," Ingvar said, and listened to the silence. "Hey. You there?"

"Yep. You're taking a fucking risk, aren't you? And so am I."

"Sometimes you have to. You know that."

"I told you before, there's nothing I can do."

"Maybe. But if you can't, I can."

"You're crazy."

Ingvar grinned to himself at the consternation his call was stirring up.

"The car park opposite Kolaport. In an hour."

"I can't just walk out without a reason."

"Then find a reason."

"I'll do my best."

"Just be there."

He dropped the phone on the bedside table, where it spun in a circle before coming to rest. He reached for the other phone, the shiny one with the screen that lit up as he swiped a finger over it, and tapped an icon. A moment later, a slim face framed with tumbling hair so fair it was almost white in the sunlight appeared, with a laugh that showed flawless teeth.

"Hey, Lizzie honey. How goes it?"

He watched as she propped her phone against something on the table and rested her chin in her hands to look down at him.

"Missing you, of course."

"And I'm missing you as well, sweetheart. It's not as if we aren't used to being apart now and again."

"Yeah, I know," she said, her laughter tinkling. "But normally it's me that's away and you're always here when I get back."

"Nice to know you're looking forward to seeing me again."

"Who says I am? I have the bed all to myself," she giggled. "But give it a day or two and I might start to miss you."

Ingvar took in the perfect skin and the fair hair that she swept back from her face to tuck behind her ears.

"So how's Norway?"

"It's Iceland. It's OK, pretty quiet. It's chilly, and a cup of coffee and a bun here costs as much as a three-course lunch does for us."

"Crazy country, right?"

"Yeah. Crazy place. I'm not staying long."

He felt a sudden surge of desire as she sat back and he saw the thick dressing gown she was wrapped in.

"Aren't you up and dressed yet?"

"I've been in the pool. Twenty lengths. Keeping fit."

He felt his mouth go dry.

"Is there anything under that robe?" he asked, his voice husky.

"Now wouldn't you like to know?" Lizzie laughed, leaning closer to the phone screen, pale hair falling around her face.

"There's nothing I would like to know more . . . So put an old man out of his misery."

Lizzie shook her head and placed a finger to her lips. She slid her chair back and he saw with a pang the bright morning sunlight that flooded in through their living room windows.

"Go on, sweetheart. Give this old guy a reason to hurry home."

She giggled, closed her eyes for a second, then opened them wide to stare intently at him. She stood up and stepped back from the phone, slowly untying the dressing gown cord and letting it begin to fall open, but not too far. When she judged that she had teased him long enough, she let it drop from her shoulders to the floor. Ingvar felt an ache deep inside as she cupped her breasts, pinching her nipples for a moment and covering them with her slender hands.

He wanted to moan with longing, but stopped himself as she pirouetted once for him, awkwardly, and sat down again in front of the phone.

"So how was that, old man?" she purred. "Is that a good reason to hurry home?"

Sitting in the detectives' coffee room, flicking through the pages with a frown on her face that melded her eyebrows into a single perplexed line, Gunna skimmed through Örlygur Sveinsson's report a second time, wondering where the hell Ívar Laxdal had got to.

"Gunnhildur. Looking for me?" He appeared on silent feet. "What's the position with the Áskell Hafberg case? Any problems there?"

"I don't have a problem as such with Áskell Hafberg," she replied slowly, choosing her words and wondering how to present her doubts about Örlygur Sveinsson's report. "I have a problem with his wife."

"Birna Bergthórsdóttir?"

"That's her. I thought you said you didn't know anything about the man's personal life?"

"I didn't yesterday, but I know a lot more now," he said smoothly. "And I notice that you've been doing some digging in the archives as well. So tell me what this is about."

Gunna put the now dog-eared printout, scattered with red question marks, on the desk.

Ívar Laxdal looked at the huge Thermos on the table. "But first you'd better give me a coffee. The stuff here is always better than the gunk that comes out of the machine upstairs."

Gunna handed him a mug, and he poured for himself, sipped and sat back.

"So, Gunnhildur. What's your problem?"

"Örlygur's my problem right now."

"He's retired, so he's not our problem."

Gunna winced at the accuracy of his point. "True. I don't think any of us miss him. But there's something else that's bothering me."

"And that is?"

"Áskell Hafberg's wife died five years ago. Apparently it was an accident. Örlygur carried out the investigation."

Ívar Laxdal sipped his coffee and looked at her from beneath brows that she saw furrowing.

"And?"

"It's riddled with holes. I don't know what Örlygur did, but there's plenty he didn't do. There's no record of an interview with Áskell or any other potential witnesses other than the man who found the body. There's no forensics from the scene. It's as if he took a quick look, decided the woman fell in the lake and drowned, job done."

"And?"

"Judging from what I hear from Áskell Hafberg's neighbour and from Birna Bergthórsdóttir's daughter, who will probably be here tomorrow, there were questions that Örlygur should have asked."

"They don't believe it was an accident?"

"No."

Ívar Laxdal drained his mug and placed it on the table thoughtfully, as if deciding where the most aesthetically pleasing position for it might be. He sucked his teeth briefly and looked at Gunna.

"If you think there's something to investigate, then you'd better investigate it," he said softly, picking up the printout. "And now I think I have a little homework to do."

"I'm not interested in starting a witch hunt against someone who's no longer on the force," Gunna said, feeling awkward. "But there are things that need to be dealt with here."

"Then deal with them."

"That's official?"

"As official as it can be."

"This isn't going to come back and bite me in the arse, is it?"

Ívar Laxdal stood up. He looked quizzical, and Gunna wondered what was going through his mind.

"Raking over the coals is always dangerous, Gunnhildur. You know that as well as anyone," he said with a vague hint of a smile. "But it makes life interesting."

"For you or for me?"

"That depends on what you find out, doesn't it? And I have to admit I'm intrigued, not least because of the Áskell Hafberg angle. What is it about this that's eating you? Surely you could just sign off your report on the man's death as a suicide, which is undoubtedly the case, and get back to your caseload?"

"That would be the easy way out."

"So why?" he asked amiably. "I'm intrigued. We don't have the time or resources to be looking at cold cases."

"Partly because there's something here that's very wrong," Gunna said. "And getting it wrong often comes back to haunt us. And also because I remember Birna."

"You do? How?"

"She was from Vestureyri. I remember her from when I was a child. She was quite a flamboyant character, a single parent who was the butt of a huge amount of gossip, and she left town quite suddenly. My mother and hers still live in the same street. I didn't realise until yesterday, when I saw a picture of her on file."

Ívar Laxdal nodded to himself, standing with one hand behind his back and the other cupping his chin.

"Interesting. Let me know what you find out. But be discreet, won't you? We don't want to wake too many sleeping dogs. And tread carefully."

"You think I hadn't worked that bit out already?"

Jónatan had tears in his eyes by the time Gunna had finished with him. A long-divorced man whose children lived abroad, he was a lonely figure failing badly in his attempt to hide his loneliness. He answered all of her questions without hesitation, explaining once again how he had discovered Áskell Hafberg's body in the workshop.

"Áskell had been drinking heavily for long?"

Jónatan nodded. "For a long time. More and more," he said, and cleared his throat. "Since Birna died, he drank steadily. Every few weeks he'd sober up and visit the booze shop in Mosfellsbær to stock up. That's about as far as he'd go. Sometimes he'd remember to buy food as well. If he didn't, I'd go shopping for him."

"How about the materials he needed for his work? Canvases, paints, all that kind of stuff?"

"He called a supplier when he needed anything and they'd deliver. That was never a problem."

"So he was drinking all the time?"

"Pretty much. He wouldn't exactly be drunk, but he'd just keep himself numb. He wouldn't sleep if he didn't have a couple of drams to send him off."

"Birna's death must have hit him extremely hard," Gunna said.

"It did. No doubt."

"And it must have been terrible for him being alone there at the time."

"Alone?" Jónatan stared.

"I understood there was nobody else about. Or am I mistaken?"

"The place was packed with people that night. I was here. It was the neighbour on the other side who found Birna in the morning," he said, and looked uncomfortable for a moment, a frown passing across his face.

"Go on," Gunna said, sensing that he had something new to say. "Tell me."

Jónatan sat back for a second, and she had the feeling he was choosing his words with some care.

"Don't get me wrong," he said at last. "I'm as broad-minded as anyone. But sometimes when Áskell and Birna's arty friends gathered, it was a bit . . . erm . . . it could be on the wild side. I mean," he added, casting around for words, "they were like a crowd of teenagers. Except that they were all in their forties and fifties, or older."

"You mean drinking and suchlike? Drugs?"

"And the rest," Jónatan said. "Midnight skinny-dipping in the lake, al fresco fucking in the long grass. One time I went for a leak outside and there was a couple at it right there over the bonnet of a car. I recognised the woman because she used to read the news on TV years ago, and she didn't miss a beat when I appeared. Then there'd be white powder and pills, all sorts," he said, and his voice died away to silence.

"So this was quite a party?"

"This one was pretty modest, not more than a dozen or so people. It was August and a lot of their friends were in Tuscany or somewhere. Anyway, I wasn't entirely sober myself, and I wasn't keeping a head count."

"Were gatherings like this a regular event?"

Jónatan shook his head.

"Normally once a year Birna liked to invite a crowd of people. Áskell didn't enjoy company, but he'd put a smile on his face and get quietly legless. The time before that had been a few years earlier, and that ended up with three or four of us spending the evening in his workshop with a couple of bottles of rum while the arty crowd did their stuff in the garden."

"Could you give me a list?"

"Of what? The people who were there?"

"Yes. As far as you remember."

"It was a while ago, you know." Jónatan scratched his head. "Sure. I'll have to think about it."

Gunna closed her folder and placed it on her lap.

"Did anyone speak to you?" she asked. "Anyone from the police?"

"No. I saw the guy who came to see what had happened, after the body had been taken away. A little fat chap with a face like he'd eaten a kilo of lemons for breakfast, if I recall correctly. Not that he spoke to me."

"I see. And Úlfur? Have you heard from him?"

Once more, Jónatan shook his head. "I've been trying to contact him. The phone number I had for him doesn't work any more and he hasn't answered any emails yet. He doesn't believe in being easily contactable. The only one your colleague spoke to was the fellow who found Birna. That's Óttar Gunnarsson. He went bankrupt a few years ago and the bank repossessed his summer house. I haven't seen him since then. He's the kind who always bounces back, so he'll be involved in some business that's just about to go stellar," he added with a wintry smile.

"You've got a fucking nerve," Arnar Geir growled as he dropped into the passenger seat. He glared though the windscreen at the wind whipping up the water of Reykjavík's harbour.

A squall hurled a sudden handful of snow against the glass in front of them, as if the weather was deciding if it ought to go for the full storm or keep it for the rush hour, when the city would be packed with traffic.

"Lovely to see you as well," Ingvar said.

Arnar Geir turned his head to face his brother.

"I hope nobody sees us here. I'll be right in the shit if I'm noticed."

"You'll be all right. There's nobody about. You might be seen, but not by anyone who'll know who you are."

"All right," Arnar Geir conceded. "Good to see you, but let's keep it quick, shall we? Why the hell are you here?"

"My boy's in prison," Ingvar said through gritted teeth. "How did that happen? You said you'd look out for him."

"I did look out for him. I did what I could, but I don't work miracles. He got in with a bunch of shitbags and you know what youngsters are like. They won't be told. Your lad's like you. He has to find things out for himself."

"Couldn't you have kept him out of Litla-Hraun?" Ingvar said, staring at the snow collecting on the windscreen.

"Believe me, I tried," Arnar Geir said. "But there's only so much I can do. We're in opposition, and I'm on the city council, not in Parliament. I don't have a hotline to the Minister of Justice, and even if I did, he wouldn't take any notice of me. In any case, your lad's in the new prison at Hólmsheiði now, and he's better off there."

Ingvar turned and glared.

"Why? He's a junkie?"

Arnar Geir sighed.

"Yeah. Pretty much. I saw him just before he was put away and he was a wreck then. So time in Hólmsheiði is more likely to do him good, as long as he can keep his nose clean. Oh, and you're a grandad, by the way. In case you didn't know."

Ingvar felt his heart lurch.

"What?"

"I thought you knew? You're a grandfather. Congratulations."

"Helgi Svavarsson, city police," he said, showing his ID.

The woman sighed, turned and went to hammer with one fist on a door.

"Aron!" she yelled. "Get up, will you? Someone to see you!"

She turned back to Helgi.

"He'll be right with you," she said, and vanished into the bathroom at the end of the short hallway, clicking the lock shut behind her.

Helgi stood in the hall, glanced at his watch and leaned against the wall as he checked his emails on his phone. He replied to one, and decided he couldn't be bothered to write any more messages on such a tiny screen.

He hammered on the boy's door himself, rattling it in its frame.

"What?" a voice inside groaned.

"Aron! It's the police. You come out here, or I'm coming in."

The door swung open and a bleary young man appeared in the doorway, one hand rubbing his face.

"Who are you?"

"Helgi Svavarsson, city police. Don't worry, we've probably met before." Helgi held up a copy of the receipt he had been given the previous day. "Recognise this?"

"I don't know. What is it?"

The lad stopped rubbing his eyes and his right hand plunged down the waistband of his jogging bottoms to scratch his crotch.

"It's a receipt for a purchase made using your debit card on the tenth of this month. In Vogar."

"Not me, pal."

Helgi felt a surge of irritation.

"So who was using your card?"

Aron shrugged. "Don't know."

"And driving your mum's car?"

He shrugged again. "Don't know."

"Where were you on the tenth?"

"You expect me to know? That was weeks ago."

"It was a Friday. Were you at work?"

"I'm off work at the moment. Depression."

"How long have you been off?"

"Since Christmas."

"And you're still depressed?"

"Yeah. A bit," he said, and his face brightened. "Hey, I do know. I wasn't here."

"Where were you?"

"I was away all weekend. My sister's kid was christened that Saturday. I was in the east, in Egilsstaðir."

Helgi nodded. "How did you travel? Bus?"

"Fuck, no. Flight," he said and disappeared back into his room. A moment later he reappeared brandishing a smartphone with a cracked screen and scrolled through it. "Here's the boarding pass," he said, holding it out to show Helgi.

"And someone will confirm that you were out of town that day?"

"Yeah," he said, nodding eagerly. "My sister. All weekend, Friday morning flight and back on Monday."

"In that case, I reckon I could do with a word with your mother."

"Eiríkur, you worked with Örlygur for a while, didn't you?"

"Our glorious leader? Indeed I did. Why d'you ask?"

"Just wondering. A few years ago a woman drowned in the lake at Hafravatn. Do you remember that?"

"Vaguely," Eiríkur said, scratching his head thoughtfully. "Why? Anything to do with . . ."

He stopped as Gunna's phone rang and she picked it up.

"Gunnhildur."

"Ah, good afternoon, my name's Róbert Simoni. You're the officer investigating Áskell Hafberg's death?" a suave voice asked.

"I am," Gunna replied. "Do you have anything to tell me?"

A bass chuckle echoed down the phone. "Actually, no. I was hoping you could tell me what the situation is."

"You're a relative, are you?"

"Not quite. I've known Áskell for forty years and I handle his work in a professional capacity. I understand there's a lot of his work at his house and I was wondering when I can retrieve it."

Gunna stared at the phone in her hand for a moment before putting it back to her ear.

"I'm afraid that unless you're among the deceased's immediate family, I can't tell you anything at all."

"Oh." The voice sounded surprised and put out at being rebuffed. "I'm sorry, maybe I haven't made myself clear. I represent Áskell Hafberg and have done so for a long time. Our business relationship goes back more than thirty years and I've known him for longer than that. We have a contract under which I represent his work and handle his sales." It continued, less suave now, "I understand that the police have a number of canvases of his, and of course I'm contracted to place them with galleries."

Gunna sat back in her chair and winked at Eiríkur, who was pretending not to listen.

"If I understand you correctly, your contract is with Áskell Hafberg, right?"

"That's quite right."

"Well, regrettably, Áskell Hafberg is no longer with us, so I'll have to assume that your contract is therefore defunct."

"But —"

"His estate automatically passes to his next of kin," Gunna continued, "and as you aren't an immediate relative, that's about all I can tell you."

There was silence for a moment.

"Officer," the voice said with an effort to be patient, "I seem to have failed to make myself clear —"

"On the contrary. You've made it clear that you're not a relative and I appear to have failed to make it crystal clear that I therefore can't tell you anything," Gunna interrupted. "But as you seem to have known him so well, I'm wondering if you can shed any light on his death."

"What do you mean?"

"What was your name again?"

"Róbert Simoni."

"And you're the deceased's agent?"

"I am."

"You were," Gunna corrected. "And where can I find you?"

"I run Gallerí 9."

"Where's that?"

"It's on Mýrargata."

"And you're there now, are you? Don't go away, because I have some questions to ask you," Gunna said and put the phone down.

"Another satisfied customer, chief?" Eiríkur asked brightly.

"We always aim to please. Now, Eiríkur. You were saying, before I was so rudely interrupted?"

"Boy or a girl? When was this?"

"A girl," Arnar Geir said. "She's a sweet little thing. Stulli was allowed out under escort for an afternoon for the christening. I was there as well. I think I'm the only one from our side of the family Katla invited."

"What's her name?" Ingvar asked.

"María Vala."

Ingvar nodded.

"María Vala," he muttered to himself. "María Vala. And the girl? I mean the child's mother? What about her? Where's she?"

Arnar Geir scowled.

"Inga Lára. I've only seen her once, and that was at the christening. She's as thin as a rake and has a ring in her nose. She's a couple of years older than Stulli and had another kid before, but that one lives with its father. Seems she was a bit of a wild child at one point, had that first kid very young."

"Does she work?"

"She works on some help desk, as far as I know. She's pretty much living with Katla now, and your wife spends a lot of time cooing over her granddaughter."

"Wife . . ." Ingvar said absently. He ran a hand over the top of his head and felt the rasp of stubble.

"I wonder . . ." he began. "I'd love to see the little one."

"Don't. Don't even think about it." Arnar Geir shook his head. "You said goodbye to all that once before and you can't just walk in again now. I'll get you pictures and you'll just have to dote on her from a distance. Anyway, how's Spain?"

"Spain's all right. Peaceful, warm."

"Work?"

"Work's fine. The old man persuaded the family to sell me a share, so I have a five per cent stake in the company. That comes with conditions, though. To be honest, they didn't need much persuasion. If five per cent gives me an incentive to keep their ships at sea and stops me looking for greener grass elsewhere, then they've got a good deal."

"And how's things at home? Same girlfriend? Louise?"

"Loulou? That was a long time ago," Ingvar said, and fumbled for his phone. He tapped it into life, found the photo he was looking for and passed it across. "That's Lizzie."

Arnar Geir whistled.

"Fucking hell, man. Legs all the way. You've fallen on your feet for such an ugly bastard. Where did you find her?"

"In an airport."

"Really?"

Ingvar grinned.

"She works for KLM. So she's away a couple of days a week. Always pleased to come back, and it keeps things fresh, y'know?"

Arnar Geir peered at the photo of the laughing blonde woman in a white cotton dress that showed nothing but promised everything.

"Just how tall is this girl?" he said. "Does a fat slob like you have to stand on a chair to kiss her?"

"Two metres exactly. We're eyeball to eyeball."

Before the district had become fashionable, Galleri 9 had been a workshop. Gunna found the contrast between the rough walls and the polished cement floor as incongruous as the piped sound of plucked strings that she didn't immediately associate with music.

Róbert Simoni glowered at her from behind a glass desk. He wore a dark suit of understatedly expensive cut in the same colour as the carefully trimmed circle of beard that surrounded a mouth with heavy lips. He hurried across, hiding his scowl as he forced a smile.

"You're the officer I spoke to just now?"

"I am. Gunnhildur Gísladóttir. I'm with the serious crime squad."

Róbert looked stunned. "Has a crime taken place?"

"That's what I need to figure out."

"I thought it was suicide. That's what I was told."

"Who told you that?"

"I just heard it somewhere."

Gunna looked around the gallery, the walls striped with the irregular imprints of the planks used years before to hold the concrete in place as it hardened, now scrubbed, whitewashed and hung with tiny paintings.

"Any of Áskell Hafberg's canvases here?" she asked, peering at one small, dark image and struggling to make anything out.

"No," Róbert said, as if it should be obvious. "These are all by Hanna Krüger."

"Of course. I'm sure anyone would have known that. You said you knew Áskell for forty years. When did you last see him?"

"A month ago, maybe longer. We haven't been close for a while."

Gunna moved along the wall and leaned forward to squint into the shadows of another painting that looked very similar to the first one. "Any particular reason?"

Róbert followed, as if worried that she might swiftly put a painting under her coat and walk out.

"We were very good friends years ago, when we were both students. Áskell had a real talent," he said almost wistfully.

"And you didn't?" Gunna said, and immediately regretted being so brutal.

"He was far and away the most talented student the place had seen for years." Róbert smiled. "I have talent as well. Just not for the same things. I found myself more at home in commerce, which is why I have a gallery in the most fashionable part of the city while Áskell lived in a shack drinking himself to death."

"Except that he didn't."

"Didn't what?"

"He didn't drink himself to death. He hanged himself from a beam in his workshop roof. So what was his problem?"

Róbert's face went pale. "I . . . I had no idea. I was told he'd killed himself and I assumed he'd swallowed a bottle of pills. That would have been more like him."

"Who told you that?" Gunna asked, looking him in the eyes until his gaze dropped.

"I don't remember. Maybe the shop that sells . . ." He gulped and corrected himself. "Sold him his canvases and paints. They do our framing and I spoke to the manager there yesterday."

"Which shop is that?"

"It's just called Artshop. It's a small place on Klapparstígur."

"My next stop, in that case. When did you last see Áskell? What was his state of mind?"

Róbert groaned. "Disturbed. He was very disturbed."

"Had he always been like that, or just since his wife died?"

This time Róbert shuddered and his heavy-lidded eyes snapped open.

"You knew her?" Gunna asked.

He gazed over Gunna's shoulder into the middle distance and his face softened. "Knew her? Of course I did. That night she died, terrible. Áskell was devastated. He never stopped being devastated, but he produced some of his best work after that. Very intense, very different to what he had done before."

"How so?"

Róbert looked up as if awakening from a reverie. "Right after Birna's death, he painted a series of canvases, mostly of her, which were inspired. There were twenty-eight of them, done over maybe three months."

"And where are these canvases now?"

Róbert looked down his nose with something approaching pity. "There's one in the City Museum of Art. The rest were all sold privately, immediately, for the asking price. Áskell has always been in demand, but these canvases were something special. The torment he was going through just jumped out of his work — deeply moving and very personal work," he said with satisfaction.

"So Áskell wasn't a poor man?"

Róbert shrugged. "I have no idea. He bought his materials, crates of booze and occasionally some food. He never went anywhere, didn't own a car and never bought clothes, plus he lived in a cottage that he bought for next to nothing forty years ago. So I guess he ought to have been worth something, if that's what you mean." He glared and adjusted his tie. "You're surely not insinuating that someone murdered him to get hold of whatever's in his bank book?"

"I've no idea, but I have to ask," Gunna replied. "You said the night Birna died was a terrible one. So you were there?"

Róbert's mouth opened and shut again.

"I was," he said eventually. "There were a few of us there."

"Explain."

"Áskell had finished a series. He'd been playing with industrial sculpture. You know, things made from old tools and pieces of metal," he said in response to Gunna's questioning look. "All right, they didn't turn out to be great, but he enjoyed himself making them. Anyhow, he'd finished it all, sold the welding equipment he'd learned to use for it, and some of the pieces were in my old gallery on Lindargata. He and Birna decided to throw a party out there at Hafravatn."

"A party? So there were plenty of people about?"

"A dozen of us, I guess. Close friends of theirs, me included."

"And?"

"I was in the house most of the time, as far as I recall, but there were people enjoying themselves under the trees. Some of them were going to camp there for the night. I actually left quite early and then someone called me the next morning to say that a body had been discovered in the water under the jetty." Róbert looked older, as if the lines on his face had deepened at the memory. He sighed. "It was Birna."

"I need to get back," Arnar Geir said, glancing at an expensive wristwatch. "They'll be wondering where I've disappeared to."

"Fair enough," Ingvar said. "Good to see you. How are Tryggvi and Brynjar?"

Arnar Geir sniffed.

"Same as usual. Brynjar skippers the boat, Tryggvi looks after everything ashore and takes a relief trip now and then to keep his hand in. There's enough quota to make a decent living, but not enough for a new boat. We'll need one in a few years, if Brynjar's lad decides he wants to make a go of fishing. If he does, then we'll have to find some money somewhere."

"To build new?"

"Or buy something fairly new. And quota. That's the expensive part. A new boat has to work harder, so we'd need enough quota to fish nine, ten months instead of seven or eight."

"What do they know? I mean Brynjar and Tryggvi."

"Know?" Arnar Geir asked. "Or suspect?"

"You tell me."

"They don't know anything. But they're pretty sure that you've been alive and well somewhere all these years. Brynjar would start by boxing your ears if you were to turn up on his doorstep, and you'd deserve it, but you know once he'd done that it would all be in the past. Tryggvi's more laid-back, especially as his health hasn't been great."

"Brynjar's angry?"

"He would be if he knew for certain that you were alive. It's not something we've talked about for a very long time." Arnar Geir paused. "You know, it was hardest when the old man died. That was when we could have done with you being here with us. That was tough. It wasn't so bad when the old lady went, but she spent most of that last couple of years in the old folk's home wondering what had happened to her missing son. If there had been a body, then it would have been easier for her. But there was nothing to bury next to the old man, and as far as she was concerned, there was a huge Ingvar-shaped hole in her last few years."

Ingvar stared through the windscreen and felt tears prick at his eyes for the first time since he had been bullied at school, as the guilt welled up inside him.

"Still," Arnar Geir said. "All over now. It's not as if you're planning to run up north and say hello, are you?"

"No," Ingvar said eventually, shaking his head and wiping his face with the back of one hand. "Nothing like that. Do they come down south much?"

"Brynjar's here right now. The boat's on the slipway in Njarðvík, so you might want to keep clear of the place. Just in case."

"And Tryggvi?"

"He'll be down next week when the boat comes off the slip. Like I said, keep away." Arnar Geir glanced again at the expensive watch. "Look, I really do have to run. Give me a call, yeah? Or send me a text and we can try and meet up somewhere a bit safer."

He opened the car door and shivered as the force of the wind almost pulled it from his hand.

"Yeah. I'll do that," Ingvar said, and turned to his brother, placing a hand on his arm. "But the boy. Do your best, won't you?"

"I'll find out what I can," Arnar Geir said with resignation. "I'm not that high up the pecking order yet. I'll see what I can do, but I'm not promising anything."

"How about you tell me about the tenth?"

Gréta looked bewildered, while her son quietly slipped away and shut his bedroom door behind him.

"What do you mean?"

Helgi sat down on the edge of the sofa without waiting to be invited. A band with eighties quiffs played silently on a vast television in the corner, and Gréta's eyes flitted from the screen to Helgi and back as he checked his notes and read out the car's registration.

"Blue VW Polo, that's yours, right?"

"Yeah, that's my car."

"Can you tell me why it was in Vogar on the tenth of this month, and who was driving?"

"I don't know. That's weeks ago." She glanced at her watch. "Is this going to take long? I have to go to work."

"Let me help you refresh your memory," Helgi said, ignoring her question. "That was the weekend your son was away in the east. He had an early flight that day and came home on the following Monday, so who was driving your car?"

"I don't remember lending it to anyone. Aron uses it sometimes, when his car's broken down like it usually is. I use it to go to work. That's it. I'll probably have to get rid of it anyway, can't afford to run a car on what I earn."

A bitterness had crept into her voice, and Helgi glanced at the huge television screen, wondering how much it had cost.

"So you're telling me you have no explanation as to what your car was doing in Vogar that day?" he said.

Gréta shrugged. Her jaw jutted and she shook her head.

"I don't know. Maybe you've made a mistake."

"That's a possibility," Helgi said. "But there isn't another dark blue Polo on the vehicle registry with a similar number, so I don't think so. Where do you work?"

"Hagkaup. The one at Faxafen. Evening shift this week."

"So you drive to work, or walk?"

"Yeah, sometimes I walk. When it's not raining, anyway. If it's an evening shift I'll walk there and someone will always give me a lift home."

"Then the car's left here? Who has access to it? And what was your shift that day?"

100

Gréta reluctantly reached for a phone, the same recent type as Helgi had just seen in her son's hands, but minus the cracked screen. She went through the entries with her lips pursed.

"Tenth. I was at work from ten until six."

"And someone can confirm that?"

"You're not going to call my supervisor, are you?"

This time there was panic in her voice.

"I don't know yet. Did you drive that day?"

"Probably. I don't know."

"But if the car was left here, who could have had access to it, considering your son was away?"

"Well, nobody."

"You didn't go to the christening that weekend? Why did you stay in Reykjavík?"

Gréta's eyes flashed with anger.

"Because I wasn't invited, and even if I had been, I wouldn't have gone near the place. She's Aron's half-sister, not my daughter. Same father. Is that enough family history for you?"

"That's more than enough, thanks," Helgi said, making notes as he spoke. "But I still want to know who drove your car that day."

"I've no idea," Gréta snapped, getting to her feet. "All I can tell you is that if it was me, it went from here to work and back again." She went out to the hall and came back wearing a coat. "If you don't mind, my shift starts in twenty minutes, and I can't afford to be late."

It was a moment Gunna had not been looking forward to. She knocked at the front door of a house so smart it could have been made from Lego. It creaked open and a colourless woman in an apron answered. Gunna assumed she was Örlygur's wife.

"He's round the back," the woman said in a monotone, seeing the uniform before she saw Gunna.

"In the garden?"

"Or the garage. Go round the side and you'll find him," she said, pointing vaguely.

A clattering came from the garage, followed by the sound of hammering, then silence. Gunna stood in the door and watched for a moment as retired Chief Inspector Örlygur Sveinsson, dressed in a faded blue overall, tapped at a small engine that had been clamped to his workbench. He tapped again and dropped the hammer, and Gunna took the opportunity to draw attention to herself.

"G'day, Örlygur."

He spun and stared. "Gunnhildur? What brings you here?"

"Passing by and thought I'd see how you are."

"Ach, y'know," he said, wiping his hands on a rag and gesturing at the engine on the bench. "Father-in-law's lawnmower. He's too old to walk without a stick but he's determined to mow the lawn the moment there's five minutes of sunshine."

"How's your back, and how's retirement?"

"My back still hurts like hell." Örlygur winced. "Retirement's all right for a while, but it makes you lazy. How's law enforcement?"

"Fine. The usual and more of the usual. But that's not really what I came to see you about."

Örlygur looked at her sideways, suspiciously. "What, then?"

"Five and a half years ago a woman drowned in the lake at Hafravatn. You investigated it and signed it off as an accidental death."

"I remember," he said with a vague sense of unease in his voice. "That was a long time ago. Why are you interested in it now?"

"Two days ago the woman's husband committed suicide, hanged himself in his workshop. There are a lot of things I don't understand and I'm hoping you can tell me more about the wife's death. I'm after anything that might have a bearing on the husband in particular. He was quite a well-known artist, it seems, so there's already interest from the press. I read through your report," Gunna told him and was rewarded with a sour look. "I was wondering if there's anything you remember that might shed some light on Áskell Hafberg's suicide. You didn't speak to him, did you?"

"I tried." Örlygur looked glum. "But the wretched man was out of his skull and then he was carted off to hospital under sedation. Mind you, it was clear enough. She was drunk, went for a midnight swim and drowned."

"Do you remember what the post-mortem results were?"

"Off the top of my head, no. I just recall that she had alcohol in her system."

"Nothing suspicious?"

Örlygur's eyes narrowed. "Am I being interrogated here, Gunnhildur?"

"Of course not. I'm just trying to get a handle on the background from someone who was there."

"Fair enough," he grunted.

"You spoke to the neighbours?"

"There weren't any neighbours there when the incident took place. No witnesses. No evidence of anyone else having anything to do with it. Look, Gunnhildur, it's very straightforward. I know you're ambitious and I know you're efficient. But there's nothing suspicious about this. This artist guy drank himself unconscious and his wife was probably not much better. She went skinny-dipping in the middle of the night after too much to drink. The cold got to her and she drowned. Simple."

"Where was the body found? By the jetty, wasn't it?"

"It was under the jetty, caught up around one of the posts."

"No marks or anything?"

Örlygur shrugged. "Nope. There were scratches on her legs consistent with being rolled around in the shingle, but that's it. Listen. Go back to Hverfisgata and have a word with the Laxdal. He'll put you right on this."

There was something familiar about the woman's face that gave him a shock of the kind he had least expected. Gréta Valdemarsdóttir had changed a lot since he had last seen her. That was probably the best part of thirty years ago, when she had been one of the girls Katla had hung around the city's nightspots with, and he felt a moment's sadness seeing how she had aged. Her face

104

had become lined and she seemed stooped, as if the world had heaped endless burdens on her thin shoulders. He wondered if she could still knock back shots of neat vodka as enthusiastically as she had done all those years ago.

Ingvar watched from the car as Gréta huddled deeper into her parka, hands thrust into pockets, and trudged away from the building to disappear around a corner. It was a grey morning and a few flakes of snow fluttered down through the ice-cold air to join the scattering that had fallen overnight.

In the lobby of the block of flats, he studied the line of buzzers, found one marked *Gréta Vald & Aron Stef*, and held his thumb to the button for five seconds, then another ten. There was no response, so he tried again, this time holding the buzzer button down until there was a reply.

"What?" a sleepy voice asked through the intercom.

"Delivery for you."

"Put it in the postbox. I'll pick it up later."

"It's too big, and it needs to be signed for," Ingvar mumbled.

"What is it?"

"Couldn't say, mate. It's a box for Gréta Valdemarsdóttir. This is her place, isn't it?"

"You think I'm going to come down there and get it?"

"Buzz me in and I'll bring it up, no problem. Third floor?"

The heavy door clicked open and Ingvar shouldered it aside. He didn't hurry up the flights of narrow stairs, and cracked his knuckles as he arrived at the door he wanted before knocking.

As soon as he saw one of Aron's eyes peering at him through the crack in the doorway, he put his shoulder to it. The door crashed into the wall behind it, and Aron tumbled backwards to sprawl on the floor. Ingvar kicked the door shut behind him and stepped forward, planting one boot on Aron's wrist to pin him to the ugly hall carpet.

"You're going to start by keeping your mouth shut," he said in a low voice that dripped menace. "Understand?"

"I don't have anything. There's nothing here," Aron yelped.

Ingvar leaned forward and stared into Aron's eyes.

"I haven't even told you why I'm here, and you're squealing already? Brave boy. Roll over. Hands behind your back. Don't fuck about or I'll break both your arms."

He took a roll of parcel tape from one pocket of his coat and wrapped a thick binding around Aron's wrists, then hauled him to his feet and dragged him to the kitchen, where he dropped him onto a kitchen chair.

"What are you doing? What do you want?" Aron asked in a voice that trembled. "Who are you?"

"You don't need to know. Now you're going to answer a few questions."

Aron's mouth stayed resolutely shut.

Ingvar's open palm landed with a slap on Aron's cheek that echoed from the bare walls and left him staring in shock. The chair teetered, about to fall backwards until Ingvar caught hold of it and steadied it.

"Tell me all about Erling Larsen, and why Sturlaugur is in prison and you aren't. No ifs, no buts," he said quietly.

Without glancing at Aron, he opened kitchen drawers one at a time. He placed a meat hammer and a carving knife on the worktop where Aron could see both. He put a thumb to the blade of the carving knife and shook his head.

"So blunt it wouldn't cut wet shit," he said dismissively, and looked into Aron's eyes. "But you know what that means, don't you?"

"No . . ."

"It means it's just going to hurt more when I cut bits off," he said with a sad smile. "Now, start telling me the story."

Gunna and Eiríkur were nowhere to be seen when Helgi dropped his fleece over the back of his chair. The day had been unsatisfactory so far. The young man and his mother he had spent half the morning with had provided no convincing explanation for how anyone could have driven Gréta Valdemarsdóttir's car, while the boy had no apparent idea that his debit card had been used, adding that it was linked to an account he had stopped using. He had dug into a pocket to show Helgi the card he claimed to use now, which carried the logo of another bank, as if that were some kind of proof. He nudged his computer into life, searched for a phone number and reached for the desk phone.

"Customer services. Kristín speaking," the cheerful voice said.

"Hello, Helgi Svavarsson, City Police. I hope you can help me, I need to check a departure."

"Sure, what's the date you're looking for?"

"The passenger's name is Aron Stefánsson and he had a flight to Egilsstaðir on the tenth. Could you confirm he caught the flight?"

He waited, listening to Kristín suck her teeth and tap at a distant keyboard while he wondered if she looked as pleasant as she sounded.

"Hello?"

"Still here," Helgi said.

"The passenger caught the flight, but it wasn't on the tenth. It was cancelled because of weather and it didn't actually depart until the following morning."

"So he flew on the eleventh? And he was on the flight?"

"He was, and returned on the thirteenth."

"That's great, thanks for your help."

"You're welcome, any time. Bye," Kristín said and the line went dead.

Helgi wanted to grind his teeth in frustration. The man had told a childish lie that was so easily disproved, and now he would have to go back and confront him again, or bring him down to the police station for some more serious questioning. He pondered whether to go back right away, or leave it until later in the day. He clicked to open a browser on his computer and then thought better of using a work machine, deciding instead to use his phone, peering at the screen as he searched. It took a while to find the film on the internet, after trying a couple of search terms that finally took him to what he was looking for.

He remembered it well. Ingvar Sturlaugsson's disappearance had overshadowed any other news related to the tsunami that had wrecked communities from Indonesia to East Africa. The media in Iceland had zoomed in on one man's death as if the rest of the devastation and the other fatalities were almost incidental.

Ingvar's family had been on the fourth floor of their hotel and had been unharmed. Nobody knew where Ingvar had gone, and no body had been identified among the many others. The assumption had been that he had been washed out to sea as the wave had surged back.

Thorkatla Einarsdóttir had become almost a celebrity overnight, immediately known to everyone in the country simply as Katla. As the family had eventually returned home when it had become apparent that Ingvar was not likely to be found, they had been greeted at Keflavík airport by a press mob and the clattering of flashing cameras. The tearful widow and her three small children had been on every front page and every TV news bulletin. Over the next few weeks, the family's life had been under a microscope, as Katla was interviewed on television, radio and in a dozen magazines, describing the family's heartbreak. A fund had been set up for people to contribute cash towards a search for Ingvar's remains, and once the furore had died away, the media and the gossips having found other targets, the whole affair had been catapulted into the television spotlight.

Eight months after the tsunami, by which time Ingvar Sturlaugsson had been pronounced deceased and his life insurance had paid out, Katla had spoken tearfully of her relief that at least the family's home was now secure, all the while twisting the fat gold wedding ring on her finger as she told the camera how she would sacrifice everything if only it could bring him back.

Helgi watched the sequence on his phone as the camera panned and zoomed out from Katla sitting in the shade of the hotel's veranda, wearing a floral skirt and a black bikini top, looking wistfully at the sun-kissed blue sea beyond.

It had been that bikini top that had triggered the backlash, setting evil tongues wagging. It had shown off her ample cleavage and this had become everyone's abiding memory of the film, this ninety-second opening sequence from an hour-long documentary that had taken Katla back to Thailand with a camera crew to make an effort to find out what might have become of Ingvar Sturlaugsson.

Helgi couldn't help admiring the chasm of Katla's cleavage, and wondered why the producer hadn't asked her to put on a shirt just as she was being tearful about the loss of her beloved husband.

The documentary had been completely inconclusive. The last sighting of Ingvar had been on the evening of Christmas Day, when a porter had seen him sauntering out of the hotel.

110

All the same, the film also marked the end of the public's love affair with Katla, not least when it emerged that a new man had accompanied her on the trip to Thailand, and rumours had begun to circulate that maybe the grieving widow wasn't mourning her husband all that much, especially as it seemed the relationship had been a stormy one, with rumours of numerous infidelities on both sides.

For Helgi, there was also a personal element to the whole thing. Ingvar's parents had been prominent figures in the community where he had grown up, while his older brothers still ran one of the few fishing boats still working there, with no ambitions beyond getting through the next winter with the books in the black. The younger two, Arnar Geir and Ingvar, had both moved away — one south to university and a legal career before putting his foot on the lower rungs of the political ladder, and Ingvar to work on big ships, first in Iceland, then Greenland and finally Africa.

Helgi rocked in his chair as the documentary played out on his phone, with a few stills and a couple of quaintly pre-digital home movie clips of Katla, Ingvar and their small children with a half-built house in the background.

Back when Ingvar had disappeared, Helgi had still been a uniformed officer in the rural north, before his own marriage had come to grief and he had moved to Reykjavík with his belongings piled on the back seat of a barely legal wreck of a borrowed car, his wife having kept hold of the smart family Subaru. He thought back to the silence of Brynjar, Tryggvi and their sister

111

Magga, curtly declining invitations to speak to the media, preferring to leave all that unpleasantness to Arnar Geir, and how they had done their best to shield their elderly parents from media intrusion and the worst of the speculation as to what had become of Ingvar.

He wondered if things had changed up there, if there had been any shift in mood. But most of all he wondered if the man he had stood next to at the airport had been in touch with his brothers. He knew who to ask, but felt himself uncharacteristically nervous at the prospect.

Ingvar treated himself to old-fashioned meat and potatoes at the bus station, washed down with a can of malt and followed with a mug of coffee as he flipped through a couple of two-day-old newspapers.

Not much changes, he decided. He had followed events back home in Iceland from a distance, but had mainly paid attention to business matters that were of interest for almost sentimental reasons, and kept an eye on social media to scavenge details of the lives of his family. He was still wondering how he had missed the news that he had become a grandfather.

Now that he was here, watching the news and speaking to people, he realised just how large the gaps were in what he had been able to pick up. All the news of his family had come through the social media profiles of the younger generation, rather than from those of his own age, and the politics had passed him by.

112

He had known that Arnar Geir had paused his legal career to take a detour into politics, but he hadn't noticed that his brother had abandoned his long adherence to the Progressive Party, which every family member was believed to have voted for going back as far as anyone could remember. Instead, Arnar Geir had seen an opportunity and thrown in his lot with the breakaway Moderate Alliance, and Vilberg Sveinsson, the fledgling party's charismatic chairman, and Ingvar guessed there would be no shortage of ill-feeling and recrimination at family gatherings.

He reflected that it was fortunate that the family trait was for anger that flared furiously but quickly burned itself out. So arguments would be loud and angry but mercifully short, he decided, and would probably take place behind closed doors.

To everyone's surprise — especially his own — Arnar Geir had found himself elected as a Reykjavík city councillor, scraping in courtesy of a handful of votes. Now it seemed he was in the news every few days, as he was regarded as the less colourful but also the less gaffe-prone of the party's two representatives, always available to give a comment or an interview, and energetic in chairing committees as he fought to make himself noticeable and indispensable.

Ingvar counted three pictures of his brother in two newspapers, and decided that it was just as well that Arnar Geir had taken after their mother's family, with thick dark hair and fine features instead of the sandy hair and heavy build the rest of them had inherited from old Sturlaugur. So nobody, he hoped, would take a look at him and remark on his resemblance to the Moderate Alliance's rising star.

Arnar Geir wouldn't be long on the city council, that was for sure. Barring a scandal of some kind, it was almost a foregone conclusion that he would be in Parliament after the next election, and his roots on the north coast — of which he never failed to remind every interviewer — meant that he was already being spoken of as a future minister with responsibility for fishing or something else rural.

Ingvar fetched a second mug of coffee from the urn and wondered what to do with himself. He toyed with the idea of a walk around the Kringlan shopping centre, where Katla had her shop — which his life insurance had presumably gone a long way towards financing. But that would be too risky. His former wife was probably the last person he would want to run into. He was tempted to mooch around his old haunts at the quaysides, checking out the boats and trawlers that he had lived and breathed since he had been able to walk, but that was also too dangerous. Too many old shipmates from years gone by could be ready to slap him on the back and ask where the hell he'd been hiding all these years.

He gulped down the rest of his coffee and patted his pockets for the keys to the car.

"Welcome to the big city, young lady," Helgi said. "But you had better be careful around these smooth cosmopolitan types."

114

"Hey, Helgi!" There was a real delight in Anna Björg's grin as she put a leather-clad arm around him and squeezed, making him gasp. "I've been looking out for you. Where have you been?"

"On holiday. Only just got back."

"Had a good time? How's the family?"

"The tribe's fine. Nothing but trouble, but they're fine."

Her eyes narrowed. "And an addition on the way, I'm told?"

"Yeah," Helgi said, wishing he could sound more enthusiastic, and keen to change the subject. "When did you turn up here?"

"A couple of weeks ago. Starting to get used to it now."

"And traffic? Why would anyone want to work in traffic? I've done my time with a speed camera, and dealing with motorists is my idea of hell."

Anna Björg eased open her heavy leather jacket.

"There was a vacancy, and I applied for it. Motorcycles, Helgi. Who wouldn't want to be paid to ride a motorbike all day? It's something I always wanted to try, and I wanted to do it before they could tell me I'm too old."

"What do you mean? You're a youngster."

"Helgi, I'm thirty-six. That may sound young to you, but try getting into traffic when you're forty and female."

"Really? I still think of you as the innocent young farm girl who joined us in Blönduós all those years

115

ago," he said, his brow furrowing. "Hell, it was a while back, wasn't it?"

"It's ten years since you moved south. Or more. Halli's the chief inspector up there now, and he's not going to retire for another ten years at least, so I figured the chances of promotion were pretty much zero."

"So you decided to chance it with us city types?"

"Exactly."

"Are you . . ." Helgi began. "Is Björn Leví moving south as well?"

"Nope. He's staying up there, for the time being at least."

"So you're still together?"

"Yeah. It's a sort of long-distance thing now. He'll come down here every other weekend, I'll go up north between shifts."

Helgi felt a twinge of regret, at the same time as a reassuring relief. He and Anna Björg had always got on well, had worked together for a few years, but the last time he had seen her had coincided with a rift with Björn Leví, which had unexpectedly developed into a brief illicit fling. He knew that Halla had her suspicions. More worryingly, he was aware that Gunna had sensed something, without having been told anything. But that was one of the things that made working for Gunna interesting; her instincts and intuition were rarely far from the mark.

"I . . . er, there's something I wanted to pick your brains about, if you have a spare ten minutes."

Anna Björg nodded and led the way into the building. In the briefing room the traffic department

116

used, empty at this time of day, she collected a bottle of water and a mug of coffee, and poured one for Helgi, who was unable to stop himself admiring the snug fit of her motorcycle leathers.

He told himself to stop it, to be professional, just as she handed him his mug.

"What's it about?" she said, shaking off the heavy jacket and hanging it on a chair before sitting down. "Something back home?"

"Yeah. Look, this isn't an official investigation at all, at least not yet," he began, wondering how much to say. "I'm interested in the family from Vesturhæli. Brynjar, Tryggvi and Magga, old Sturlaugur's family."

Anna Björg sat back with a look of surprise.

"Why? I can't think of anyone more law-abiding. They go fishing, never land a kilo over their quota, pay their taxes on time, the boat's always in perfect order. I gave Arnar Geir a speeding ticket once, but that's all."

"Well," Helgi said slowly, "I'm really interested to know if you had sensed any changes there, anything that might be going on in the background somewhere."

"Not at all. I saw Tryggvi not long before I moved down here. I even had a cup of coffee with him and Brynjar in their net shed. They haven't changed a bit, and I hope they never will. Brynjar's lad is on the boat with his father now, so I imagine there'll be a handover there sooner or later. So what's this about? Come on, Helgi. Is it Arnar Geir? He's the slippery one of that family, I reckon."

"Yeah, he's in politics now, and that's no profession for an honest man."

"And for the Moderate Alliance as well."

"Right. It doesn't get much worse than that."

"Only if you're a dyed-in-the-wool Progressive like you, you mean?"

"There is that," Helgi admitted.

"So what's there to be suspicious about?"

Helgi scratched his chin with a thumbnail.

"Strictly between you and me . . ."

"Don't worry, Helgi. We can keep things strictly between ourselves," Anna Björg said with a low laugh, and Helgi blanched for a second.

"OK, well like I said, strictly between you and me, I'm curious to know if there's something spooky going on relating to Ingvar. You remember, the brother who disappeared."

Anna Björg's eyes widened in astonishment.

"Really? You think —"

"I don't think anything right now," he interrupted. "And I absolutely don't want to start any rumours. I was just wondering. Mainly because I've noticed a few things that don't quite add up."

"You think he's alive?"

Helgi shrugged.

"I've no idea. Just hunches and intuition so far."

"I see," Anna Björg said, nodding slowly. "Y'know, if Brynjar or Tryggvi knew anything, I don't imagine they'd keep a secret easily, especially in a little place like that. So I reckon if there's anything to know, it would be Arnar Geir. Like I said, he's in politics and so lying should come as easily as breathing to him."

118

"And he left to join Vilberg Sveinsson's party," Helgi said. "A man who can go to the dark side like that is capable of anything."

He knew what she looked like these days. He had spent long enough hunting the three of them on social media, though it was becoming apparent to him that he had only been seeing the edited, filtered side of their lives that they put online.

Unsurprisingly, Sturlaugur's presence had stopped as soon as he had been arrested. Einar interacted with a tight group of friends in an almost monosyllabic way, and clearly much of his online activity was kept behind closed doors. Tekla was the one he had managed to stalk most closely, and a friend request from a fake profile with a teenage girl's photo randomly plucked from the internet had been accepted without question, giving him an insight into his daughter's circle of friends.

Best of all, it meant that he had been able to keep abreast of how she was doing at school, where she spent her time and who she hung out with between school and home. Now that she was twenty, a lot of growing up had been done in a few short years and she was about to graduate from college. Ingvar knew she was considering what to do at university, hoping that her grades would be good enough to get herself into medicine, but also tempted by business.

He sat in the car, lying back in the seat, watching students leaving in twos and threes. He had almost given up, was about to start the car and drive back to

119

the hotel to wonder what to do with himself for an evening in this city that had become a stranger to him, when she appeared, alone, and strode down the path towards the street.

Ingvar froze. He had seen her and didn't know exactly what to do. Just watch and let her walk away?

He got out of the car, clicked the lock and set off after her, keeping her in sight, but not too close. It was as she approached the main road that he realised where she had to be heading. The shopping centre was a few hundred metres away, beyond six busy lanes of traffic, and this presented another obstacle. She had stopped at the crossing, waiting for the lights to change. Did he dare go and stand behind her and risk being recognised? If he were to let her cross, and then wait for the lights to change again, he would lose her in the distance, and he didn't relish the thought of braving Kringlan with Katla somewhere inside.

He couldn't recall ever having felt this nervous. Ingvar had never had a problem dealing with people. He had a knack of somehow gauging instantly how he should come across and how to speak. This had helped him deal with colleagues, crew, suppliers, officials and even the occasional minister over the years as he had worked out within a few seconds what the right tone would be, how to adjust his voice and body language.

He felt a tide of frustration inside; for the first time since he had been a teenager, he was at a loss, not sure how to approach this young woman and unable to predict what her reaction would be. Anger? More than likely, he decided, especially if she had turned out as fiery as her mother could be when the mood took her.

He took slow steps towards the crossing, where Tekla stood bouncing on the balls of her feet. He hadn't realised how tall she was, how grown-up she looked, with a determined expression on her face as she glanced left and right, checking the traffic as if she was about to risk crossing before the green light.

"Hæ, Tekla," he said quietly, standing next to her, his heart pounding as he waited for a reaction.

She stopped, looked sideways at him with a suspicious frown.

"Hæ." Her voice was gruff and stern. "Who are you?"

"You wouldn't remember me. It's a long time since you've seen me."

"Try me." The lights turned green, but she made no move to cross the road.

Ingvar opened his mouth to speak. Tekla stood and stared calmly at him, arms folded, her head cocked on one side.

"I'm . . ." he said, and swallowed.

"You're Ingvar Sturlaugsson," she said softly as the lights changed again and the traffic roared past once more. "You're Ingvar fucking Sturlaugsson. You're my dad."

"Yeah."

He watched as her eyes widened, sharp eyes the same shade of sea green as his own. The serious look remained on her face as she surveyed him, taking him in from head to toe.

"Y'know," she said at last, "somehow I always knew that you'd show up again one day, sooner or later. I always thought you'd turn up at Mum's funeral, or maybe at my wedding, standing at the back of the church. I didn't think you'd materialise like a stalker outside Kringlan."

Birna Bergthórsdóttir's daughter wasn't hard to spot among the travellers emerging at the arrivals gate. Purple hair on a woman close to two metres tall was striking, Gunna decided as Ursula strode through. She waved her across.

"Gunnhildur?"

"That's me. And you're Ursula. Do you speak Icelandic, or shall we stick to English?"

"I always spoke Icelandic with my mother, but it's really rusty. So English, eh? Unless you speak some Swedish."

"Unfortunately not, and my schoolroom Danish has long disappeared, so it'll have to be English," Gunna decided. "Shall we go?"

She ushered Ursula out and into a patrol car that she had twisted an arm to borrow purely so she could avoid having to use the airport car park. Her passenger looked appreciatively at the dashboard array.

"It's a while since I've sat in one of these," she said.

"Really?"

"But I never got to sit in the front," she added brightly. "I was what they call a problem teenager."

"Ah. I can understand. I have a couple of those of my own. Well, not teenagers any more, but they're still a handful. Good flight?" Gunna asked, preferring to change the subject away from children.

"As usual." Ursula shrugged. "Lousy food and not enough space for your legs, otherwise fine. This place has changed," she said with a little wonder in her voice as the patrol car swept out of the airport and towards the main road. "It's been a long day, rushing around to get a flight and sort out childcare. Anyway, I'm here now."

"When were you here last?"

"When Mum died. I came for the funeral."

"Five years ago?"

"It was five years in September. Tell me about Áskell. What happened?"

"We were called out. A neighbour raised the alarm."

"The old guy next door? Jónatan?"

"That's him," Gunna said, eyes on the road and a fully loaded van ahead of them that was making heavy weather of the slope as the road took them past Keflavík and into open country. "He went to borrow a can of petrol, found Áskell in the barn and cut him down. He'd already been dead for a good few hours by then, but Jónatan wasn't to know that."

"I guess Áskell had been hitting the bottle?"

"So I gather. Did you have much contact?"

"He'd call and we'd talk a couple of times in a week, and then he might not call again for a month or so. The last time, I was busy with the kids and didn't have time to talk. I said I'd call him back the next day, and when I did, there was no answer."

"When was that?"

"Ten days ago, a week. Something like that."

"And how did he sound the last time you spoke?"

Ursula sighed and settled back in the passenger seat. "He seemed OK, I suppose. Depressed."

"Any more than usual?"

"You mean was he suicidal?"

"That's about it."

"Áskell had been suicidal since Mum died. It was only a matter of time," she said in a matter-of-fact voice. "If he hadn't done it himself, he'd have drunk himself to death or fallen asleep somewhere outside in the snow."

"Don't imagine that I'm not pissed off with you," Tekla said. "I'm fucking furious. But that can wait. Right now I have a zillion questions."

Ingvar walked docilely at her side as she strode across the road, around a couple of corners and towards the shopping centre.

"Hey, your mother's place is here, isn't it?" he said. "I'd prefer to keep clear of her."

"Don't worry, Dad," she said, savouring the word as much as he relished hearing it spoken. "We're going to the last place Mum would ever show her face. Come on."

A group of seven-year-olds in the children's section of the library chattered at the tops of their voices, so there was no need to be quiet. Even so, they spoke in undertones, sitting in a corner. Tekla unslung her backpack and sat with it at her feet.

"Why are you here?"

124

"Why did you think I'd be back?"

"I asked first."

Ingvar sighed and felt a spark of joy inside. The girl was clearly a ball-breaker.

"Your brother," he said at last. "I heard he's in prison. I have no idea why I'm here because there's not a single thing I can do. But I couldn't keep away. It's been a long time."

"You haven't been back at all? Since 2004?"

"Not once."

"Tell me, then. I know Mum's story. She's told me a million times what an arsehole you were. I want your side of it. I reckon you owe us that."

"There's his story and her story," Ingvar said. "Somewhere between the two you'll find the truth."

"I can figure that out for myself. Go on, talk."

Ingvar groaned.

"Your mother was . . . is," he corrected himself, "demanding."

"You're telling me something I don't know?"

"I was away a lot, earning to pay for the house, the car, the leather sofa, the big TV, all that shit. I was away too much; we drifted apart. It happens. Then there was that trip to Thailand for Christmas. If your grandmother hadn't decided to tag along as well, it would probably have been fine. We'd have made up and sorted ourselves out. But that was the last straw. Couldn't take it any longer."

"So? What happened?"

"The tsunami. It was a split-second decision, an opportunity that would never come again. I just walked."

Tekla shook her head.

"I mean . . . how? How could you do it?"

"It's easy enough when you have a pocketful of cash. I bought all the paperwork I needed when everything had quietened down. Nobody was asking too many questions back then."

"No, Dad," she said, and he felt another fizz of excitement at the word. "I mean, how could you walk away from us? You couldn't have known whether we were safe, surely?"

"I knew you were on the fourth floor. So you had to be safe. I watched the whole thing on TV, from a bar; they showed the same clip again and again." Ingvar felt a solid lump of emotion grow in his chest. "Once it was done, there was no going back. There wasn't any way to just show up again as if nothing had happened."

"Didn't you miss us?"

"You have no idea," he said with a sigh that came all the way from deep down. "You can't imagine how much I missed you and the boys. I couldn't have imagined it either. It was so much tougher than I could ever have believed. But it wasn't as if you weren't in good hands. You mum's a crazy wife but she's a good mother. I knew you wouldn't starve or be mistreated."

Tekla sat hunched forward at his side, her chin in her hand. Ingvar sat back on the bench in the corner of the library, hardly able to keep his eyes off her. She had Katla's sharp nose and full lips, the look of determination that declared this was not someone who would be easily trifled with, but those were his eyes and he recognised the kink in the eyebrows as they lifted in disbelief, something the brothers all shared.

"I'm not staying for long," he said abruptly. "How's Stulli? Have you been to see him?"

"Up at Hólmsheiði? Not for a while."

"Why not?"

"You want the long answer or the short one?"

"The short one first."

Tekla drew a long breath and her eyes closed for a moment as she weighed her words.

"He's turned into an evil bastard. It's as simple as that. I hardly recognise him at all as the brother I grew up with."

Ingvar frowned and stared.

"How? What happened?"

"He's what? Twenty-three now? He's been trouble since he was fifteen. I told Mum when I noticed the dope stink, and I was only a kid then, thirteen or something. I knew what he was up to. She wouldn't believe it, refused to accept that he was doing anything the other kids weren't doing, and she might have been right up to a point."

"No job, nothing like that?"

"He's never been out of work for long. He's a strong guy and he can graft when he puts his mind to it, but he'd get sacked and then go off on one for a couple of days. He'd find a grunt job somewhere else and everything would be fine for a few months, and then he'd fuck things up again." Tekla was looking into the distance. "Then he met Inga Lára and for about a year he calmed down, really seemed to get things together."

"And?"

"Well," she said with a scowl, "before he met Inga Lára, he and a couple of others had this dope farm running. They'd rented a crappy old place right out on the edge of town, practically a wreck of a building, and they rigged it up, about a thousand plants. They were a few days away from their second harvest when the police jumped them."

Ingvar held his head in his hands.

"So what happened?"

"They all got a slap on the wrist. Stulli was the only one who did time for it, and because the system is so slow, by the time he actually went to prison, he was already shacked up with Inga Lára, so he wasn't very happy. But he kept out of trouble and they let him out after a month or two."

"But now he's back inside again? Fourteen years?"

"The bastard that Stulli and his pals are in hock to does all kinds of horrible stuff, including collecting debts. Stulli and that shithead Aron were sent to give some guy a beating, but it turned out the guy was more of a handful than they expected. One of them pulled a knife and ended up carving half the man's face off. Whether he did it or not, I really don't know. But my brother is the one who has ended up doing the time for it."

The banner took up most of the floor of Steini's workshop. Gunna found him sitting on a stool in the corner, ignoring the chatter around him. He looked up with the slow smile that made her heart soften as he saw her come in, shaking snow from her coat before hanging it up. This was Steini's domain, and the workshop in one of the units near the Njarðvík quay had been his long before she had met him.

She looked around and reflected that normally the workshop was tidier than the house, tools in rows on the walls, benches clean and spotless, with maybe the radio burbling in one corner, but today it was full of people who seemed to be a collection of gangly arms and legs in denim and wool as they crowded around their handiwork.

"What does that say?" Gunna asked, frowning at the message on the white canvas spread out on the floor.

"Hey, Mum." Laufey got up to greet her. "It says 'We all breathe the same air' in English and Chinese," Laufey said, getting up from the floor, while a whisper had gone through the group kneeling down, paintbrushes in their hands, at the sight of Gunna's uniform trousers and official shirt.

"It's all right," Laufey said quickly. "It's only my mum."

"Are you sure that's what it says?" Steini asked.

"Yep. We checked with the Oriental languages department," Laufey said.

"You're sure it doesn't say 'Used washing machine going cheap' or something like that?"

Laufey shook her head.

"I hope not," she whispered. "We'll find out to-morrow," she added brightly.

Gunna sat on an upturned crate next to Steini's stool and took the coffee mug from his hand. She took a gulp and passed it back.

"What's going on tomorrow?" she asked.

"Protest," Laufey replied shortly.

"And just where is this protest taking place? As if I can't guess."

"Outside the Chinese Embassy. There should be fifty or sixty of us. We're protesting about environmental crimes taking place in China. Did you know that China, Russia and the US are responsible for more greenhouse gas emissions than the rest of the world put together?"

"Outside the Chinese Embassy?"

"Well, yeah. There's no point protesting outside Parliament, is there?"

"True," Gunna agreed with a heavy heart. "Though I'd be a lot happier if you were protesting outside Parliament. At least Austurvöllur isn't right next to where your old mum works."

Laufey grinned.

"It's a peaceful protest, Mum. We'll be there for an hour or two, then we'll be on our way home again. No trouble."

"What kind of a protest is it if there's no trouble?" Steini asked. "You want people to notice this, don't you?"

"We can make our point and get the message across without getting in anyone's way."

One of the group got to his feet, standing back and admiring the banner.

"That's it, I reckon."

The English lettering was bold and solid, while the Chinese characters beneath looked less confident. A rainbow border had been added to each end of the banner.

"That's cool, thanks, Finnur," Laufey said, taking the pot of paint and a brush from him. "Where do you want these, Steini?"

"Just put the lid on the can and stick it under the bench. Get one of those bags from over there and put the brush in it, and wrap it around the handle. That way it won't dry out and I can use it tomorrow."

"Are you Jón Hagalin's son?" Gunna asked, catching the boy's eye and wanting to laugh as he quailed.

"Yeah. That's me."

"And your dad knows you're part of this protest tomorrow?"

"Well," Finnur muttered. "Not exactly."

"You mean he doesn't?"

"No."

"All right. Make sure it goes off peacefully and nobody needs to tell him," she said. "And I'll be looking out of the window to keep an eye on you all."

"Inga Lára goes to see him regularly, and so does Mum. She has to because Inga Lára doesn't drive and it's a bit of a way out to Hólmsheiði. She goes to see him, takes the baby, María Vala."

"My granddaughter," Ingvar said absently.

"Yeah. You're a grandad."

"What's she like?"

Tekla's face softened into a smile of delight.

"She's lovely. They're pretty much living with us now, and Mum spends a lot of time with her. Inga

131

Lára's a sweet enough girl, but I can see some tension there before too long. She's not quick on the uptake, but I reckon sooner or later she's going to resent Mum wanting to run her life for her. And eventually Stulli will be out and I suppose they'll want to pick up where they left off, if Inga Lára can wait that long for him." She shrugged. "All the same, their problem. To be honest, I don't really want to be there when Stulli comes out of prison."

"Why's that?"

"He's angry and he's bitter," Tekla said. "He's grown a king-sized chip on his shoulder and nothing's his fault. He blames absolutely everything that's ever gone wrong with his life on everyone else, and most of all on you."

"Me?"

"For getting drowned in that tsunami. He says the moment when everything started to fall apart for him was when his dad disappeared."

Ingvar sat in stunned silence. The group of children had been collected from the library and shepherded out, leaving the place quiet enough to hear the clock on the wall as it ticked away the seconds.

"Personally, I think that's bullshit," Tekla said. "And I've told him so. That he ought to take responsibility for himself and not blame someone who disappeared back when he was only what? Seven?"

"Yeah," Ingvar said. "He was just seven. His birthday's the ninth of October."

"And when's mine?" Tekla asked.

"Fourteenth of November. Einar's is the first of September. All autumn kids."

Tekla glanced at the clock on the wall and stood up.

"Look, I have to go. Mum's expecting me about now and she'll sulk if I'm late."

"At this shop she owns?"

"Yeah," Tekla said with a grin. "It's called Essentialz. That's sort of ironic, because there's not a single thing in there that anyone would actually ever need. It's all overpriced junk. I'm telling you that so you can keep clear of it. How long are you staying?"

"Here in Iceland? Not long. A few more days."

She opened her mouth, ready to speak, and shut it again as a barrier appeared between them.

"You want to see me again?" he asked, breaking the deadlock.

Tekla paused and looked into his eyes, her eyebrow kinking as she met his gaze.

"Oh yes," she said quietly. "There's so much more we have to talk about."

"You're going out?" Gunna asked as Laufey laced her boots.

"Yeah. I'll stay at Finnur's place in Kópavogur tonight so we can be ready for an early start in the morning."

"Really?"

"What do you mean?"

Gunna tried to look innocent.

"I mean, getting up early isn't something that comes naturally to you. Normally you need your old mum

133

banging on the door a couple of times before you wake up."

Laufey glared.

"I'm a grown-up, Mum. I can do this stuff, you know. Anyway, there'll be a few of us staying at Finnur's, so maybe *his* mum will bang on the door to get us all up."

"Fine," Gunna said. "I hope it all goes well for you tomorrow. Just don't get arrested, all right?"

"I'll try not to."

"I won't be there to bail you out of a cell."

"Mum, I wouldn't expect you to."

The door closed behind her and Gunna wondered what had happened to the quiet, introverted Laufey of a few years ago.

Steini looked up from the sofa where he lay with a book in his hand.

"That's you told, isn't it?"

"Yep. I'd better keep my nose out of it."

"Not that I expect you will," Steini said. "But you can be discreet. Do you think she'll get into trouble?"

"Not with us, I don't expect. But I imagine they'll have her name on a file somewhere, if they haven't already."

"Are you concerned?"

Gunna shrugged.

"Not exactly. But what am I supposed to do? Laufey's a big girl now so I can't ban her from doing this even if I wanted to. It was the same with Gísli, and you had it with your boys too, didn't you? All you can

134

do is try and steer them in the right direction, then sit back and watch them make their own mistakes."

Steini closed the book and put it aside.

"True," he said. "Though with the boys it was more about watching them do silly things because that was what all their friends were up to, and I suppose it was the same with Gísli. But Laufey doesn't seem to have that problem. She seems impervious to peer pressure. If anything, she's setting the lead for the others to follow. Did you see how that Finnur hangs on her every word? The lad's besotted."

"You're right. She's a force to be reckoned with. I just hope I don't run into her on the stairs tomorrow being bundled into a cell. If that happens, I've no intention of getting involved."

"Quite right. She'd never forgive you if you did. But are you worried about her?"

"Of course I am. I can't not be. All the same . . ." Her voice tailed off.

"All the same what?" Steini asked.

"I can't help being proud of her," Gunna said. "She's standing up for what she thinks is right, and I would never in a million years tell her not to do that."

Eaten in a hurry, the overcooked fish and greasy chips sat in his belly like a lead weight.

Ingvar took a shower at the hotel, then wrapped himself in a towel. He wasn't sure what he missed most, the swimming pool and his habitual forty lengths, Lizzie or the dog. He decided it had to be Lizzie, with

135

her knowing smile and legs that seemed to go on forever, but the pool and the dog vied for second place.

He lay back on the bed with his iPad, and once it had logged into the hotel network, he searched until he found what he was looking for and set the video to play.

A couple of times he bit his lip as emotion welled up inside him at the sight of Sturlaugur, Tekla and Einar as he had last seen them, shaky home video clips he had taken of his pretty fair-haired children playing in the garden behind the house he had built. No doubt Katla had found the tapes and given them to the film's producers as they put the documentary together.

He knew the whole film inside out. He had watched it a dozen times before over the years, growling to himself at the sight of Katla pretending to grieve the loss of the husband she had already become tired of as she was interviewed on the terrace of the hotel in Thailand where it had all happened.

He had been lucky. In all the chaos, it hadn't been difficult to cover his tracks. He had sobered up on the long, slow nightmare bus ride to Bangkok. Things had improved as soon as he had got to a hotel with a phone, a computer and access to cash, and from that point it had all become easier and more comfortable. Avoiding airports, where he would have to give his name and ID would be asked for, from Bangkok there had been buses, a ferry and then more bus rides until he had reached a crewing agent he knew in Ho Chi Minh City, who had asked no questions but looked at him quizzically and taken him out to dinner. He had graciously accepted a handful of cash and a promise of future business, and put Ingvar in touch with people who could help out with the right papers.

He had left Vietnam a month later. Ingvar Sturlaugsson had disappeared and Chris Stevens, with his dog-eared New Zealand passport, boarded the first of several flights that took him from Ho Chi Minh City to West Africa, where he felt at home and where there was plenty of work, and nobody cared too much what his real name was as long as he could run a tight ship and fill an old but sound trawler with fish.

He realised that he had been lost in thoughts of that nervous, exciting month in Vietnam when he had thought seriously of just staying in the Far East. The last few minutes of the TV documentary were playing on the iPad balanced against his knees, and he saw Katla shedding a tear that he reckoned she must have worked hard to force out as she gazed over the blueness of the tranquil Andaman Sea.

CHAPTER
FOUR

Strong easterly wind, rising to near gale later in the day. Cloud cover. Snow or sleet on high ground. Wind backing north-easterly overnight and possible snowfall. Widespread sub-zero temperatures.

It was almost too easy, Ingvar thought as he strode through the heather. The car was a few hundred metres behind him, far enough from the place he was heading towards for it to remain unseen. It was a bright, starlit night with remnants of a showing of Northern Lights fading from the sky, but he still took care to tread carefully through the tussocks until his feet crunched on gravel.

The house was a long, low building on the outskirts of a village that had once been busy but which now had become a quiet backwater as the neighbouring port had grown. It had been many things over the years: a farmhouse, an equestrian society's clubhouse, and for many years a commune with a reputation for attracting eccentric oddballs, who came and went but were never inclined to do any maintenance, until it had fallen into disrepair. Then Erling Larsen had seen it and decided it was where he could conduct his business at a comfortable distance from the city, a forty-minute drive away.

Ingvar picked his way through the building site around the place, where holes had been dug, some of them already sporting the two-metre-high posts clearly intended to form an impenetrable security fence to maintain the occupants' privacy and freedom from disturbance.

There were no lights anywhere and the silence was absolute. The only sound was the creaking of his leather jacket beneath the overalls he had pulled on, his breath in the cold night air forming clouds in the moonlight.

It was a disappointment that there was nobody home. He used the torch in his phone to light his way once he had kicked in the door at the back of the house with surprising ease.

The place was half furnished already with an odd mixture of ultra-modern and antique. Boxes had been stacked in the split-level living room, between the vast black sofa and a couple of armchairs deep enough to swallow someone up. Pictures had been placed on a long ornate sideboard and Ingvar examined them one by one in the light of his torch, checking them against the few images of Erling Larsen he had been able to find online. The photo of the laughing man standing in front of a white Range Rover and another with his arm around the shoulders of one of Iceland's best-known rockers left him in no doubt that this was the same person who stared out from a police mugshot that had been released to the press in the distant past, back when Erling Larsen had done his own dirty work. The dark hair had gone from lapping at his shoulders to being swept back from a high forehead, but the resemblance was there in the cold, deep-set eyes, and there was no doubt in Ingvar's mind that this was the same man.

The lower end of the long living room was occupied by a tangle of stacked steelwork, the frames and weights of an expensive home gym ready to be assembled.

He wanted to be quick, and didn't bother to check what lay behind the doors in the shadows at the far end of the room. The place was clearly being partly used while it was being prepared for its owner to move in, presumably as soon as the security fence around the edge had been completed. The sink was full of dishes and there were bottles and glasses on the kitchen table, a couple of empty takeaway boxes and remnants of meals, as well as an ashtray and the detritus of tobacco and cigarette papers around it.

Someone had been shopping, Ingvar saw as he searched the kitchen. He switched on the largest of the hotplates of the electric stove, holding his hand to it until it was too hot to keep it there.

He emptied a five-litre can of cooking oil into the biggest of the steel saucepans and placed it on the hotplate. He found a plastic jug and half filled it with water, then put it on top of the extractor unit directly above the stove.

Then he stood back and watched the pan until the oil started to boil.

As it began to seethe, he retreated. Leaving the back door of the house open behind him and looking over his shoulder occasionally, he walked through the frozen moorland back to the road. He wanted to see the

140

fireball, hoping that the jug of water would melt to hit the hot oil, but decided that it would be better not to be too near when it happened.

As he started the engine, he peered into the darkness and grinned with satisfaction as he saw a flickering pinpoint of orange in the blackness.

In the hour between Hvalvík and the hostel where Ursula had a room for a few nights, Gunna ran through her mind the conversation with Ívar Laxdal. She thought over what both Jónatan and Róbert had told her. Determined to concentrate on work, she wondered why Örlygur Sveinsson's investigation had been so rapid. But the thought of Drífa's concerns and growing belly repeatedly pushed their way to the forefront of her mind.

Snug inside the Pajero that had once been Gísli's, a pleasure to drive but an uncomfortably thirsty car for a regular commuter still looking forward to a pay rise, she was shielded from the morning's buffeting wind that occasionally bullied the heavy car with wild gusts. She could see the lamp posts along the sides of the main road shivering in the wind, and white horses danced on the sea, flinging the smell and taste of brine landwards.

She shivered as she thought of Gísli at sea in this weather, but reminded herself as so often before that he was working on a comfortable, modern ship and was as safe as she was.

She admitted to herself that she missed Gísli. They had always been close, first as the two of them had been a tiny single-parent family, and then during the few happy years with Raggi before he was snatched away only a year after Laufey's arrival and the long return to some semblance of normality, when her closeness to her growing son had been her greatest support. She wondered if he realised just how important he had been, before she brushed the thoughts aside and the traffic started to move again.

Ursula waited outside the guesthouse wrapped in a thick parka, her blonde-and-purple hair awry in the strong wind.

"Good morning. Sleep well?"

"Not really. I miss the kids. I didn't think I would, but I do."

"How many?" Gunna asked, pulling away into the traffic.

"Three. A boy, then twin girls. They drive me nuts most of the time."

"Tell me about it," Gunna said with feeling, but refrained from further comment.

"Where are we going?"

"To the station. I need to take a formal statement from you about your stepfather's death, even though you weren't here. It seems that there's a lot of value in his paintings, and if Áskell's son doesn't show up, then I'd imagine it all goes to you. I spoke to a dealer yesterday, someone who knew Áskell and your mother. He's desperately keen to get hold of those paintings."

"That creep Róbert Simoni?"

"You know him?"

Ursula's lip curled in derision. "Yeah, of course I know him. He'd been friends with Áskell since they

142

were kids, or some time way back in the Stone Age. Not that it stopped him trying to get out of paying the right percentage when he sold any of the old man's work, and it didn't stop him trying to get Birna into the sack whenever there was an opportunity. He was like that with everyone. The old perv never left me alone the moment I turned fifteen."

Gunna pulled up at the lights on Snorrabraut. "Your mother knew about this?"

"She must have guessed. She'd have had his nuts for breakfast if she'd seen him try," Ursula snarled as Gunna swore to herself. An old Ford Escort stalled at the second set of lights and she beat a tattoo on the wheel as the driver started it and accelerated away in a cloud of black smoke. Gunna drove through the gate and parked behind the Hverfisgata police station next to Ívar Laxdal's black Volvo.

"I have to speak to one of my colleagues, so if you don't mind, I'll leave you in my office," she said as they crossed the car park and went up the back stairs. She nodded to colleagues on the way, and Ursula looked appreciatively at two burly officers in motorcycle gear as they emerged from the traffic department's meeting room.

"I like it here already," she said with a grin, easily keeping up with Gunna's long stride.

"One of the perks of police work," Gunna assured her. "This is my colleague Eiríkur Thór," she said. Eiríkur looked up from his desk. Gunna saw the black bags under his eyes. "Bad night?"

"And how. One with a temperature and the other one throwing up," he said. "The joys of parenthood."

"You don't have to tell me, Eiríkur. Been there and done that, thanks very much, and I have a cupboard stacked high with the T-shirts to prove it. This lady is Ursula Birnudóttir, and she's here to make a statement, but I need to have a word with the Laxdal first."

"He was upstairs five minutes ago."

"Fine, I'll see if I can track him down," Gunna said, turning to Ursula and pointing to the next room. "Do you mind if I leave you in the coffee room for a while? I really need to get my colleague's approval for something before we go any further."

Ursula shrugged and unzipped her parka to reveal a white T-shirt and a knitted cardigan as purple as the streaks in her hair. Gunna caught Eiríkur's beetle-browed look of suspicion as she made for the door.

"Make the lady a cup of coffee, would you, Eiríkur? I'll be back in a minute."

"Were you in close contact with your mother at the time of her death?"

"You mean were we on speaking terms? Yes. We got on fine."

"You were at Hafravatn the night she died?"

"I was."

"And you weren't aware of any problems?"

"Not at all. She was in good spirits, happier than I'd seen her for a long time."

"Were you staying at the house with Áskell and Birna?"

144

"No, we had a camper van and we had parked it about three hundred metres away, outside the neighbour's chalet. We thought it would be quieter there."

"Tell me what happened that day."

Ursula leaned forward and hugged her arms around herself, frowning as she thought. She spoke slowly and carefully for the microphone, slipping into hesitant Icelandic with a lilting accent. "It was a really lovely day. Áskell could be an awkward bastard, but that day he was all smiles, telling jokes and laughing. It had been Birna's birthday not long before and he organised a party for her, which was totally unlike him."

"How so? Áskell having a party was unusual?"

"Absolutely. He didn't do it often and he didn't like visitors. He was all right with me and Úlfur, but normally he liked solitude. Once or twice each summer they'd have a barbecue by the lake for his neighbours, or at least the ones he got on well with, and some friends from Reykjavík who would sometimes arrive and sometimes wouldn't."

"You remember who was at the party the night your mother died?"

Ursula looked to the ceiling and put her hands behind her head. "Now I'll need to think hard. Áskell and Birna, obviously. I was there with Lasse."

"Your husband?"

"Yep. No Úlfur, as usual. I'm not sure if he'd disappeared at that time, but at any rate he didn't show up. There was the man from next door, the insurance guy. There were half a dozen people from the neighbourhood, people with summer houses at Hafravatn, but none of those people stayed long."

"These weren't particular friends of Áskell and Birna's?"

"Birna got on better with the neighbours. Áskell always said the best time to be there was in the spring, when it was still too cold for the Reykjavík crowd and the place stayed quiet. He got on all right with the insurance guy. They had nothing in common except fishing, and I guess it amused Áskell that this guy couldn't care less that he was a great artist," she said, making ironic quotation marks in the air with her fingers. "They talked about fishing and stuff like that, and they'd spend hours on the lake in that little boat of Jónatan's, trying to catch a few charr."

"Do you remember who else was there that night?"

"A whole bunch who came from Reykjavík. Róbert Simoni was there, along with his latest girlfriend or wife or whatever. Not that it stopped him from grabbing a handful of my arse when he had the opportunity."

"How did you react?"

"I just told him to keep his wandering hands to himself and next time I'd punch him."

"His reaction to that?"

"He laughed. I don't imagine he thought I was serious."

"They stayed the night?"

"I'm not sure. Lasse and I were tired out after travelling and were asleep before midnight. It's not that far back to town, so I imagine they would have gone home, unless they had both been too drunk to drive."

146

"You remember the girlfriend's name?"

"Ey-something. Eyrún or Eydís. Something like that. Tall, willowy, blonde. The art world is full of them and I think she worked at his gallery."

"Who else was at the party that night?"

Ursula's cheeks puffed and she shook her head. "I can't remember. The morning is absolutely engraved on my memory, but the evening before is a blur."

"You had been drinking as well?"

"Hell, no. I was four months pregnant and it was strictly fruit juice for me. I was shattered. We'd taken the ferry to Iceland and driven all the way from the east in two days because Lasse wanted to see the landscape. I thought it was going to be all right, but it was exhausting." She sat back and thought. "There were a couple of the theatrical types that Birna knew, Mímir Sveinsson, Magnea Briem, Gústaf, the actor."

"Gústaf Bóasson?"

"Yeah. Mum knew him from years ago. He was on TV back when it was in black and white and he was at the National Theatre a few times, but I think he'd dropped out of sight. Mímir was involved in some film venture and Magnea had got herself a part on TV in Norway. Then there was Lind Ákadóttir."

"Another artist?"

"She calls herself a critic. She's the one who encouraged Áskell to do all that weird metalwork. She had some guy with her, which was awkward because I recall her ex-husband was there too."

"It sounds like a who's who of Reykjavík's cultural mafia."

147

"Róbert hadn't been impressed with Áskell dabbling in sculpture, quirky animals and figures made from worn-out tools and scrap metal." Ursula shrugged. "They'd had an argument the day before and it ended with Áskell getting a lump hammer and smashing up a lot of the sculptures he had made, right in front of him."

"I know Áskell had a stormy relationship with Róbert Simoni. But how about Birna? They were happy together? Your mother's death was judged at the time to be suicide. Was there any indication that the balance of her mind was disturbed?"

"None whatsoever. She was buzzing with enthusiasm and making plans to come to Sweden to see us after the baby was born. She definitely wasn't suicidal, so I felt it had to have been accidental." Ursula scratched her chin and then put her hands on the table as if exasperated by her own fidgeting. "They were devoted to each other but that didn't mean neither of them strayed. I know Áskell had occasional affairs, normally with the young women trailing around Róbert's gallery, and it tortured him. But there had been no recent adventures as far as I know."

"And your mother? It must have hurt her?"

"I'm not sure. If it did, she never said a word."

"Did she do the same?"

"Affairs? I think there were a few, but a long time ago. She resisted Róbert on principle, plus she simply didn't like him. He always chased after her when he had an opportunity, but I know she hated the way he pressured Áskell."

"To produce more work, or what?"

"Partly. He also applied emotional pressure. Mum said once that Róbert had told her she should leave Áskell because the emotional turmoil would drive him to produce better work. You can feel the sadness in those paintings after Birna died and I can hardly bear to look at them."

The journey was eerily familiar, but shorter than he remembered. So much had changed since he had last been here, almost two decades ago. The roads were better, that was sure enough. North of the pass there were patches of fresh snow on the ground, crisp under the car's wheels.

At the top of the heath he stopped and brooded at the view opening up far below, winding down the window to gaze at the twisting blue ribbon of Hrútafjörður as it snaked seawards between hillsides dusted with white. This felt like home, despite the fact that he had left home at seventeen and that even while he had lived in Reykjavík, a trip to the north was a rarity. Katla's family were city people going back a couple of generations, with nothing more than some vague connections to a farm in a now long-abandoned fjord in the west. While Katla had fretted with boredom every time they had ventured out of the city, the children had always enjoyed the occasional trip north, with hot dogs and fizzy drinks on the way and the freedom of village life for a few days at the far end. His parents had loved seeing their grandchildren, who had regarded the old couple as representatives of some ancient age and had never been able to connect properly with people who lived in this far-flung place with only one shop and where the filling station kiosk was the hub of the local social scene.

At the bottom of the pass on the north side, the old café at Brú had gone; as far as he could make out, the new road had been rolled out right over the top of where the shabby but colourful burger joint had been. The road had been rerouted, which took him by surprise, and a sandwich and coffee at the new place that had replaced the old truck stop left a sour taste in his mouth. He could even see the old place up on the hillside where the road used to run, and mourned the old-fashioned food that had been served there: stews and meat soups, and coffee that came from an urn and not a machine that hissed and fizzed.

He drove slowly along the winding strip of road that twisted and turned beside the coast after leaving the main highway. The landscape was familiar, a little sunshine breaking through the clouds to gleam on the white-sided hillsides on one side, the black rocks of the stony shoreline on the other. The strip of land between the two extremes was dotted with farms with familiar names, and he felt a stab of memory as he passed Vesturhæli, the farm between the rocks where his grandparents had toiled their whole lives to keep sheep and a modest herd of cows in the barn that the old man had built with his own hands, using planks sawn from the driftwood trunks delivered to the beaches by every winter storm.

150

He stopped the car at the turnoff to the village, turning over in his mind whether to go down there, to chance driving unobtrusively down to the harbour, taking a quick look at the quayside and rolling back the way he had come.

Instead he took the gravel track in the other direction and brought the car to a halt in front of iron gates. There were no other cars there, and as he killed the engine and opened the door, the silence hit him. There was no sound to be heard other than the breath of a wind so cold it made him gasp and huddle deeper into his coat.

The iron gates groaned as he pushed one of them open.

He turned up his collar and strode through the half-inch layer of pristine snow between the rows of silent graves.

It took him a long time to find what he was looking for. Eventually, after backtracking and criss-crossing his own footsteps more than once, he stood in front of two names on a polished black headstone.

Sturlaugur Th. Jóhannsson
22 March 1942-8 September 2010
Fjóla Karlsdóttir
30 June 1946-25 January 2012

He stood for a long time with his head bowed as the wind snatched at his jacket. He had not seen either of his parents to their graves. Both had ended their lives not knowing what had become of the fourth of their

151

five children. He had known they had died, and both times the tug had been so strong that he had been barely able to resist it, the call to stand at the side of the grave as they had been laid to rest at the foot of the mountain looming over the village that had been their home for their whole lives.

Gunna watched from the sidelines. She had no business being there but hadn't been able to resist taking a look. She caught Laufey's eye and gave her a discreet thumbs-up. Laufey grinned back at her, a mischievous look in her eye.

Around forty people had congregated in front of the Chinese Embassy, a black-fronted building festooned with security cameras that watched every movement. Gunna had no doubt that everything was being carefully recorded for future reference. It was unnerving to think that facial recognition technology would more than likely be in use and that the identity of most of those present would probably be known by now inside the building.

She shivered in the brisk wind and walked over to two burly uniformed officers standing close to the demonstration, but not too close.

"Everything all right, Geiri?"

"No problem. This lot are harmless enough. They'll all troop off home when they've finished putting the world to rights."

"I thought so. Any response from inside?"

Geiri shook his head and rubbed some warmth into his hands.

"Nothing so far. The Laxdal had a meeting in there earlier, but they let him out again."

"So he's convinced them not to worry about this lot?"

"I suppose so," Geiri said and looked up. "Aha, the press are here."

A white van emblazoned with the state broadcaster's logo rolled to a halt and a team with cameras and tripods unfolded themselves. A reporter whose face everyone in the country could recognise stood hunched in his heavy coat as he puffed a cloud of cigarette smoke into the cold air, while an assistant spoke to the demonstrators.

There was nothing to be seen at the embassy building. The doors were shut and every window was a dark pool of black glass, although Gunna had no doubt that people inside were also watching the demonstration unfold.

The assistant walked back over to the famous face from the television and had a brief conversation. As they set up a tripod with a camera on it and the sound man checked his levels, Gunna decided she had seen enough. It was time to get back to work.

There wasn't a single thing in the shop that Helgi could see had any practical use. Winsome faces on a row of porcelain puppies begged him to give them a safe home on a shelf in an overheated apartment, while a stack of electronic picture frames winked at him as the image on each one changed every few seconds.

The woman behind the counter ignored him as he spent a couple of minutes browsing the goods in the window, still vainly trying to locate something that could be of more than decorative use.

"Katla?" he said, approaching the counter where the woman was painstakingly packing items into gift boxes and tying them with ribbon.

"That's me," she said. "Can I help you? Looking for something special?"

She tightened a bow, cut the ribbon, then ran the blade of her scissors along inside it so that it rolled itself into curls.

"My name's Helgi Svavarsson and I'm a police officer, city force," he said. He watched Katla's face turn to stone as she glared at him.

"Is this about Sturlaugur?" she snapped. "If it is, then you know as well as I do where to find him."

"Not at all, this isn't about your son," Helgi assured her. "I wasn't involved in that case."

"What then?"

Her movements were as deft as before, but sharp and quick instead of fluid.

"It's your husband I'm interested in," Helgi said, eyes on her face. "Ingvar, I mean."

"Fucking hell." Katla put a finger to her mouth and a single drop of blood spotted her blouse. "Look what you've made me do," she snarled.

She looked around, pursed her lips in irritation and dropped the scissors.

"Can I get you anything?" Helgi asked as a second drop of crimson joined the first on her cream-coloured top.

154

"The best thing you can do is get out of here, right now."

"I'm sorry I gave you a fright. I didn't mean to upset you."

Katla paused and took a deep breath through her nose, held it for a second and breathed out through her mouth, lips forming a perfect circle.

"Do you have a first aid box?" Helgi said.

"Through here," she replied, pushing open a door behind the counter with one elbow.

He dried her forefinger where the scissors had nipped the tip, mopped a drop of blood with a tissue, then, as she held out the damaged finger, eyes narrow with suspicion, neatly wrapped a plaster over the wound.

She wedged open the door so the shop's interior could be seen, and looked down at the row of crimson drops across her blouse.

"Fuck," she growled to herself. "Wait. And keep an eye on the shop for me, will you?" she ordered, fingers popping buttons as she disappeared behind a door into a cubicle. A moment later she was back, the blood-spotted blouse replaced with a black T-shirt.

Katla was a striking-looking woman, Helgi decided. The T-shirt was a snug fit and he couldn't stop himself from admiring her figure as she lifted her hands to her head, pulling her fair hair back into a thick ponytail and snapping a band onto it from around her wrist.

"Sorry about that," he said again.

"What's this about?" Katla pulled out a stool from under the table and sat down, leaving Helgi leaning against the sink.

Helgi shrugged.

"Routine," he said. "Just going over old ground, as we do now and again."

"Don't give me that. Ingvar's been dead fifteen years and the only people interested are journalists, not the police." She glared. "I know you, don't I? Aren't you one of Arnar Geir's friends?"

"Not exactly," Helgi said. "I'm from up north myself and I suppose I've a bit of an interest as I went to school with Tryggvi's son. We had an enquiry from an overseas police force as Ingvar's name had popped up somewhere, probably on some old document, I guess. This really is nothing more than a routine enquiry so I can say I've asked a few questions and there's nothing new."

He watched as she thought over his words, wondering whether or not to believe what he knew was a thin lie.

"I take it you've —"

"Of course I haven't. I don't know any more about what happened to Ingvar than I did the day he disappeared," Katla interrupted a little too quickly for Helgi's liking. "If my first husband had suddenly come back from the dead, don't you think I'd be shouting about it?"

"Mum? You there?" A face appeared at the door, cheeks rosy from the fresh wind outside. "Oh, sorry."

"It's all right, sweetheart," Katla said. "This gentleman is from the police, but don't worry. It's nothing to do with your brother. And he's just leaving."

Helgi nodded to the girl; the broad jaw and chin had told him right away that this had to be Ingvar's daughter.

"Thanks for your time, and sorry to disturb you," he said.

"My daughter, Tekla," Katla told him.

"I thought so," Helgi said to the girl as she stepped to one side. "There's a Vesturhæli look about you."

Gunna drove in silence out of town through afternoon traffic. She swung the unmarked car off the main road and suddenly they were in bleak winter countryside. Ursula had looked about her with interest as they drove through the city, but as the suburbs vanished behind them, she looked more thoughtful.

"This is familiar. We must be almost there."

"Not far. Just along here, and a right turn."

"The last time I came here was when Mum died. That was in summer and it was all trees and green grass. It looks weird now, like the place is asleep."

"I suppose it is," Gunna said. "Hardly anyone lives out here through the winter. Most of them return to town and only go near Hafravatn during the summer."

"Yeah. Except for weirdos like Áskell Hafberg."

"Where did he and your mother meet?"

"Gothenburg," Ursula said. "Look, there's some complex history there. Birna turned up in Sweden with me when I was about five. It was just the two of us. My father's identity was off-limits, and the more I pushed for answers as a teenager, the harder she dug her heels in. Anyway, when I was growing up, we lived in

157

Gothenburg in a place that was almost a commune, and she worked for the postal service. Then after a few years, Áskell washed up there. I don't know if he swept her off her feet or if it was the other way around. But it was pretty sudden and at the time I resented him. The problem teen thing began not long after that, I think," she said with a lopsided smile. "I was an early rebel."

"And then they came back to Iceland?"

"Áskell had never really left Iceland. He just spent extended spells of time in Sweden or Spain, or wherever, and after I went off to university, they both more or less stayed here. He always found his way back here," she said as the car crunched along the gravel road. "You can see why, can't you?"

The steel-grey water of Hafravatn glinted in the muted sunlight as Gunna eased the car down a track and towards the cluster of cottages among the trees overlooking the water.

"Did you find anything out about Úlfur?" Ursula asked. Gunna had slowed down outside Jónatan's place, checking to see if he was there.

"No luck so far. His registered domicile is Holland, but that doesn't mean he lives there. He hasn't been registered in Iceland for ten years. Do you know if Áskell had any contact with him?"

Ursula shook her head. "They never got on well. Úlfur got on better with my mother than with his own father."

"How did you get on with him?"

"We were close as young teens. But then he got into booze and drugs."

"And you didn't? I thought you said you were a problem teenager?"

"So I was. But I grew out of it. Úlfur was never going to grow out of it."

The pull of the village was too strong, but he didn't take the direct route that approached it from the main road, instead driving a little further on the gravel track that carried on along the coast. He turned off to take an even narrower track that curled past the farm nestling closest to the village and a couple of outlying houses, and down to the harbour huddled in the shelter of the brooding outcrop of basalt that gave the place its name.

He drove carefully, as the fresh covering of snow hid the road's surface. This would be the worst place in the world to end up in a ditch or even a snowdrift. He would have no option but to seek help, and anyone coming to help him here could recognise him as Sturlaugur and Fjóla's long-absent son. That would be a disaster. The nature of village gossip would mean that his secret would spread from house to house within minutes and would probably reach Reykjavík before he did.

The quayside was deserted. A couple of small boats, white fibreglass hulls shining in the rays of the low-hanging sun, nuzzled the pontoons on the far side as the wind buffeted them. The ninety-foot boat that Tryggvi and Brynjar ran was absent. Ingvar knew that the family boat was one of the last of its kind in the village. The couple of larger trawlers that had kept the local fish plant supplied, providing employment for around half of the village's working population, had long ago been snapped up by a larger company that had made some fine promises to keep things unchanged. Naturally those promises had proved to be worthless, but a lot of equity had been created for the investors down south who had been behind the deal.

Ingvar remembered vividly the futile anger and betrayal as first *Sæthór* and then *Arnthór* had been steamed away to be laid up. Their real value lay in the quotas and not in the serviceable but practically worthless steelwork and machinery. The same went for the factory, which soon shut its doors, after which there had been an exodus from the village as people moved to places where there were employment opportunities and colleges for their children to attend.

He stopped the car on the dock where he and Arnar Geir had played as youngsters, back when Tryggvi and Brynjar were already working the boat on their own, the pair of them barely out of their teens but by then already both solid married men with responsibilities on their broad shoulders.

As a black pickup nosed its way around the corner of the long-closed factory with its blank windows, Ingvar started the engine, slid on a pair of dark glasses and pulled away.

He drove slowly along the curve of the bay to the village itself, past the single shop, the filling station that backed onto the one remaining bank, and the tiny church. He saw Tryggvi's house, a warm glow of light in the kitchen window, and he couldn't help thinking of his eldest brother sitting by the window, his feet in thick wool socks on a stool as he listened to the lunchtime news and sipped coffee through a lump of hard sugar.

With a pang, he saw the place where he had grown up, where Brynjar and his wife now lived, the rambling house divided into a couple of flats so that upstairs could be rented to tourists in the summer.

It was time to go. He had seen enough. The sun hung low in the sky, now behind a thin veil of cloud that dulled its brightness. He wanted to make at least some of the journey back to Reykjavík in daylight. He put his foot down as he took the road past the last of the houses and the sprawl of stables by the junction, and out of the village, wondering if he would ever see the place again.

"Someone's been here," Gunna said. There was no obvious sign of activity other than the disturbed grass, flattened by heavy feet, and an instinct that told her something wasn't right. "Let me take a look before you come inside," she instructed as Ursula got out of the passenger door.

She stalked towards the house, pulling on a pair of gloves as she went and easing open the front door. The place was filled with a brooding silence disturbed only by the flat tinkling notes of a home-made wind chime outside. The floor creaked under her feet and the walls seemed to hold their breath as she went along the passageway. Nothing seemed to be out of place and she relaxed after checking the couple of rooms.

Ursula towered over her in the entrance. "Everything all right? Shit, this place gives me the creeps."

"It's not comfortable, is it? Maybe the door just hadn't been shut properly. Let's check the barn."

Behind the house, last year's grass swayed in the breeze under the gnarled trees.

Gunna stood in front of the workshop and lifted the chain loosely looped through the twin doors. Fresh saw marks shone on one of the black links. She stood back and surveyed the scene.

"Not a professional job," she said, stooping to pick up a broken hacksaw blade from the ground. "Someone had a go and didn't have the sense to bring a spare blade. Stay where you are, please."

She checked around the doors, making sure that none of the rusting steel plates had been forced to make an entrance, then went back to the car, returning with a fingerprint kit. Ursula watched as she dusted the lock.

"Why are you doing that?"

"Let's call it old-fashioned curiosity. I'd be interested to know who wanted to get in here, but it's not certain that our would-be intruder's prints will actually be on our system, considering this looks like a strictly amateur piece of work."

She finished, satisfied with one fairly clear print taken from the back of the heavy padlock, then took the key from her pocket and clicked it open.

The doors creaked apart. Ursula switched on the lights and shivered as they flickered. "It was always cold in here. Sometimes Áskell used to paint with the doors

162

wide open so he could get natural light. So it was never warm even when that stove glowed red hot."

Gunna looked around carefully, but nothing seemed to have been disturbed. "You'd best take a look through the paintings," she said, gesturing to the stacks of canvases against the walls.

"Was he preparing for an exhibition?" Ursula asked.

"I've no idea. Not that I know of. Did he show his work?"

"Of course. But not often in Iceland."

"Not appreciated here?"

"He was appreciated all right. But his work fetched better prices abroad and he normally had an exhibition in Copenhagen or Gothenburg. There are quite a few Hafbergs in collections," Ursula explained, lifting painting after painting up to the light.

"I hadn't realised he was so respected."

"His name has been growing in Europe for quite a few years. The consensus is that his work has a raw energy to it, combined with a sophistication that makes it unique," she said seriously.

"You know a bit about this stuff?"

Ursula smiled for the first time. "I dabbled myself, but didn't have the talent to get anywhere near Áskell. There's something that an artist has," she said absently. She paused, looking intently at a small canvas, the steel stud in her tongue clicking against her teeth as she stood deep in thought. "I trained as a conservator and work at the Gothenburg Museum of Art. So yes. I do know something about all this."

163

"Right. What sort of value are we talking about here?"

Ursula put the canvas gently back in the stack and walked her fingers over the tops of the crude frames.

"Twenty-five here. About the same here, and that stack over there is maybe thirty. I didn't expect there would be so many. So around eighty canvases at let's say six thousand each as a conservative estimate." She counted on her fingers. "That comes to close to half a million."

Gunna frowned suspiciously. "Half a million what? Swedish crowns?"

"Euros."

"What? So what's that in Icelandic krónur?"

The stud in Ursula's tongue again clicked against her teeth as she thought. "Around seventy-five, eighty million."

Gunna's jaw dropped. "Seventy-five million?" she echoed. "Fucking hell. I had no idea."

Ursula shrugged. "You might want to think about somewhere a little more secure for these than a shed in the countryside."

"Especially one that someone's already tried to get into," Gunna said, reaching for her phone.

"Where've you been?"

Tekla returned her mother's baleful glare.

"At the library, as usual. Exams are coming up and I need to pass these."

Katla sniffed and retreated. A confrontation with her daughter could always be dangerous. The girl had quick wits and knew how to use them. It was different with the boys, she thought, but admitted to herself that Sturlaugur had hardly drawn a breath for the last ten years that hadn't been polluted by some drug or other, while Einar lived in his own world and rarely emerged.

"I'm going up to Hólmsheiði tomorrow to visit your brother. Inga Lára wants to come as well, so could you look after María Vala for a couple of hours?"

"Sure," Tekla said. "When are you going?"

"We'll need to be there at one. Can you be home by twelve?"

"I can if I can get out of English class in the afternoon. I'll just have to promise to do extra homework to make it up."

"Please," Katla said with an effort. "I wish Inga Lára could go by herself, but she doesn't seem to be able to pass her driving test."

Or have enough money to afford a car, Tekla thought, but said nothing.

"You're going out again?" Katla asked as Tekla dropped her school bag inside her bedroom door and hung a sports bag on her shoulder.

"Yeah. Judo tonight. Had you forgotten?"

"Sorry. Get yourself a snack now and we can have dinner when you're back."

"Don't worry, Mum," Tekla said, helping herself to a banana and an apple from the fruit bowl in the window. "If you feed Inga Lára and Einar, just leave a few leftovers then I can get something for myself after the class."

"If you like," Katla said.

"Just trying to make things easier for you. You don't need to worry. I'm not going to waste away if I miss a meal or two."

"If you say so." Katla stood with pursed lips and folded arms, an infallible indicator that there was something on her mind.

"What's the problem, Mum?"

"Problem? What do you mean? Does there have to be a problem?"

"Yeah. You're jumping right down my throat. That says problem loud and clear."

"Who's the man?" Katla demanded.

"Man? What man?"

"The other day, when you came to the shop late. Stella from FastFlower said she'd seen you with a man."

Tekla stopped in her tracks and stared.

"What? What has Stella been drinking?"

"Stella doesn't make things up," Katla snapped. "She said she saw you with a man, and you hugged him."

"Mum, please," Tekla said. "A couple of weeks ago you were worried sick I might be a lesbian because Stella saw me with some of the girls from the basketball team. Now you're worried I'm seeing some imaginary man. Which is it going to be?"

"An older man. Stella told me," Katla said sharply. "Old enough to be your father, she said."

Two uniformed officers, one of whom had been there the day Áskell Hafberg had been found, arrived in a van and started the long job of carrying the paintings out of

166

the workshop and down the overgrown path to the road.

Gunna photographed each picture as it left while Ursula went carefully through the last stack, each painting containing an image of the same woman.

"I've never seen any of these before." She studied them one by one. "These were all painted after Birna died."

"That's her in the pictures?"

Ursula nodded and sighed. "She was very striking, wasn't she?"

"She was when she was young as well," Gunna said.

Ursula looked at her sharply. "You knew her?" she asked in surprise.

"Not really. Your mother grew up in Ósvík and I'm from Vestureyri. I remember seeing her about; she could hardly be missed because fire-engine-red hair really wasn't the done thing back then. I remember the old women clucking about her leaving town in a hurry."

"I don't know much about her background," Ursula said. "I rarely saw my grandparents and I don't think they much wanted to see us. I went to Ósvík once when I was a kid, for a funeral, I guess. Mum never spoke about the place, never had any inclination to go back there."

"She had a rough time, I gather," Gunna said. "She was different to most of the single mothers. The gossip went on endlessly."

"Because she never named my father?" Ursula shrugged her broad shoulders. "There are a few clues, but not enough to figure it out. I just reckoned he was probably married." She lifted a painting up and looked at it intently. "I'm sure Áskell knew, but I never asked him."

The painting was of Birna in profile, black hair in a fringe to just above her eyes, the black collar of a coat folded up to her chin and with her visible eye flickering to one side as if aware of the artist. It was executed in broad strokes in shades of grey; almost a monochrome portrait. Ursula ran a finger gently across the area of deep shade behind the figure's head where the dark hair merged into the background.

"See here?" she said, pointing to a darker mass within the grey and holding it up to the light. The faint image of a man could be made out almost concealed within the shadow. The painting was not a happy one. The sitter looked nervous and the artist had captured the tension in her face, while the shadow of the man behind looked distant but menacing.

Gunna squinted and nodded.

"I noticed that when I was going through the pictures yesterday," she said. "I thought I was seeing things, but if you can see it as well, then there must be something there."

Ursula lifted another canvas, a smiling portrait of Birna sitting cross-legged on a rock. She examined it through half-closed eyes, then shook her head and put it back in the stack, lifting out the next one, a monochrome portrait in charcoal.

"There," she breathed, pointing at the mane of hair that swept back from the sitter's head and whirled across two thirds of the paper.

Gunna looked closely and made out the same man's features cleverly hidden within the tendrils: sharp nose and eyes, and a jaw-line that looked familiar. She glanced quickly at Ursula and then back at the portrait, checking for a resemblance, but could not be sure without a closer and longer look.

"I think it's Áskell himself," she said at last. "Watching over her. Or wishing he had watched over her that night? We'll never know now, will we?"

"Excuse me? Are you done?" One of the two uniformed officers appeared in the doorway. "We've packed up all the others. Wondering if we can we put these in the van now?"

"Helgi, my old friend. What can I do for you?"

Arnar Geir took a seat behind a desk that was at least one size too small for the volume of paperwork stacked on it and waved Helgi to the only other chair.

"Partly a social call, partly work. Just a formality, though. Nothing serious."

Arnar Geir half closed one eye and squinted at Helgi as he rocked his chair back on two legs.

"The Blönduós mafia at work?"

"Your late brother Ingvar," Helgi said, deciding to stick with the same lie as before. "We had an enquiry from a foreign police authority, probably because his name turned up on some piece of paperwork. I've already told them that he died in 2004, so that should be an end to it. But I have to ask a few questions," he added with a bored shrug. "Formalities, y'know."

Arnar Geir's eyes widened. He tried to hide his astonishment, and was almost successful. His phone chiming in his pocket came to his rescue. He answered it without looking to see who was calling, and Helgi listened with interest to one side of the conversation.

"Yeah, hæ," he heard Arnar Geir say. "Who? . . . Oh, right, sure. Of course . . . What was that? . . . Really?" He looked up at Helgi and mimed holding a cup to his lips.

Helgi gave him a thumbs-up in response and Arnar Geir got up from behind his packed desk and ushered him out into the corridor, beckoning him to follow as he strode along.

"I see. I'm sorry, but you've caught me at a really awkward moment and I can't say much right now . . . Yes, in a meeting." He showed Helgi into a small kitchen, where he pointed to mugs hanging from hooks and a heavy flask on the table. "Absolutely. Yes. Thanks for calling, Villi . . . No, no problem. Call you back once I'm out of the meeting . . . Cool, thanks. Bye."

He ended the call and dropped his phone into his pocket while Helgi poured half a mug of coffee.

"Sorry, Helgi. It's like this all the time."

"I know how you feel. I just leave the work phone on silent most of the time and figure that if it's important, they'll call back."

"What's this about Ingvar?" Arnar Geir asked as he sat down on the far side of the table and helped himself to coffee. He glanced at his watch and grimaced. "I've a meeting in twenty minutes. That's to say, I have a meeting in fifteen minutes but I can stretch things a bit."

"Like I said," Helgi tried to sound casual, "his name came up in a routine enquiry, something to do with a bank account or a mortgage overseas. I've told them the man they're interested in was declared deceased fifteen years ago. But I have to go through the motions." He sipped his coffee and caught Arnar Geir's eye as he gazed over the rim of his mug. "There's nothing new, is there?"

"New? Hell, no. Not since Ingvar was declared legally deceased. Normally it takes seven years, but for Katla's sake we were able to push for the formalities to be waived, taking into account the circumstances. If she'd had to wait seven years for Ingvar's life insurance to pay out, she'd have been bankrupt."

"So there's absolutely no chance that he's alive and well somewhere?"

Arnar Geir sat back with a humourless smile.

"You want me to be straight with you?"

Helgi nodded. "Go on. Considering you're a lawyer and a member of the Moderate Alliance, that's a stretch of the imagination, but try me."

"Get away with you, Helgi. You know as well as I do how politics works in this country, and the Alliance is no more or less crooked than any of the others."

"I'll accept that's arguably quite true. You could hardly be more crooked than —"

"Anyway. Let's not go there," Arnar Geir cut in. "Look, Ingvar vanished in 2004. No sign of him, no body. Nothing. Things had been rocky between him and Katla."

"Really? I wasn't aware of that," Helgi lied. "But I was still in uniform up north back then."

"Yeah, it's true. He'd been away a lot, fishing off Africa. She'd had a fling with one of their neighbours. The trip to Thailand was to patch things up."

"So you're telling me that not everything in the garden was rosy?"

"Far from it," Arnar Geir said. "All the same, Ingvar would never have been capable of cutting off contact with his children. He could be a hard bastard sometimes, but that would have been too much, even for him."

"Busy, Gunnhildur?"

Gunna looked up to see the brooding presence of Ívar Laxdal with his black eyebrows knitted into a tight frown.

"We're always busy," she replied. "Never a dull moment. Anything the matter?"

Ívar Laxdal sat in Helgi's chair and looked around.

"Erling Larsen," he said slowly. "Does the name ring a bell?"

"How could it not? Half the city's dealers are working for him in one way or another. He's been in a cell here once or twice, but not for a few years."

"Just so you know, his house burned down last night."

"And it couldn't happen to a more deserving person," Gunna said.

172

"He'd bought a house out near Hveragerði, a place with the delightful name of Saurbær, a former commune of some kind that it seems he was in the process of fixing up before moving there permanently. Less than an hour from Reykjavík, but far enough away to keep a distance from all the crap he deals with, is what I'm given to understand. Mundi Grétarsson's sons and a few others have moved out of town, but they planted themselves in Reykjanes instead."

"Do we need to get involved?"

"We'll see. The place is a wreck, pretty much burned out. We'll probably be involved if there's a suspicion it's arson rather than a straightforward chip-pan fire, which is a possibility."

Gunna nodded, her mind already ticking over.

"Could this be someone repaying a favour?"

Ívar Laxdal shrugged.

"Who knows?" he said. "Right now Erling Larsen is shouting from the rooftops that the police ought to be doing their jobs and tracking down the bastard who vandalised his property. Which is a little rich from a career criminal."

"And you're telling me because you reckon this might be the start of a little tit-for-tat turf war between Erling Larsen and whoever he thinks did it, and we can expect to see some heads cracked in retaliation?"

"Precisely. If this was deliberate, then you're right, it could be payback from someone he's done a bad turn, and there's no shortage of them. Or else it's someone giving him a warning that there are others who are

173

prepared to play hardball. But the fun part is that there's a corpse in the house."

"So things will get serious now?"

Ívar Laxdal ran a thumb through his short black beard.

"Maybe. According to Erling Larsen, the person at the house was Aron Stefánsson. He'd stayed behind there because he had been drinking all day and passed out."

"And his mates just left him? Aron Stefánsson is the deadbeat Helgi has been trying to track down for the last couple of days. He's . . . was fond of breaking elbows and knees."

"So we have an interest in this," Ívar Laxdal said. "We're waiting for the investigators to decide whether he set fire to the place himself by accident or if someone did it for him. But I reckon we'll be taking a hand in this before long. That's why I asked if you're busy."

"Like I said, we're always busy."

"Nothing personal, Gunnhildur," Ívar Laxal said with a grin. "This isn't going to call for a sensitive approach, so it's right up Sævaldur's street."

Darkness had fallen as Ingvar drove out of the long tunnel beneath Hvalfjörður. The tunnel still seemed unreal. Back when he had travelled regularly back and forth between home and Reykjavík all those years ago, there hadn't been a tunnel, and the old road had followed the shoreline, past the old whaling station and the truck-stop café at the deepest point of the fjord.

Back then the winters had also been heavy, and drifts of snow on the Hvalfjörður road could mean having to turn back, or a detour to Akranes in the hope of catching the ferry that used to run across the bay. Now he sailed through. He hadn't even realised there wasn't a toll to pay any more; that morning he had slowed down, looking to see where he had to deposit his thousand krónur.

The tourist information centre at the base of Mount Esja, where on a brighter day hikers would gather before heading up the slopes of the hulking mountain that faced Reykjavík from across the bay, stood dark, shuttered and locked. The car park was deserted as he got out of the rental car, He took the opportunity to piss against one of the back wheels, then walked back and forth in the gloom until his cheap phone buzzed in his pocket.

Tomorrow, 1300. There's a cake shop on Bæjarlind called Kaffihorn. I'll be there with María Vala if you want to see her.

He read the message, smiled to himself and replied with *OK*, before stuffing the phone back in his pocket.

Traffic hurtled past along the main road below, the wind bringing a scattering of snow with it. He narrowed his eyes and peered down at the road, checked his watch and nodded to himself as a crew cab pickup roared a little too fast into the car park, scattering slush, and stopped next to his hired car.

"Hey, little brother," Ingvar said as he made himself comfortable in the passenger seat.

Arnar Geir grunted a greeting, opened the window and lit a cigarette, blowing smoke out into the wind.

"Where've you been?"

"Home."

"Shit. I hope nobody saw you."

"Come on," Ingvar said. "If anyone had seen me there, you'd have heard about it by now."

"Yeah. I suppose you're right. Never underestimate the power of the jungle drums."

"It doesn't look like it's changed much."

"It's changed a lot," Arnar Geir said, dropping his half-smoked cigarette into the slush. "The place is poorer now. *Sæthór* and *Arnthór* went when Aldan bought the whole lot out and sold it all again within a year. No fish and no work. You wonder why people are voting for us?"

"I don't wonder," Ingvar said. "I don't spend a lot of time keeping up with politics here. But you can see why they're disillusioned. The village has gone from gold town to ghost town."

"There isn't anyone under forty living there these days, and you can understand why, can't you?"

"And this is where your voters are coming from?"

Arnar Geir nodded. "Pretty much. They don't know what the hell they want. They just know they don't like what they have, and they imagine things used to be better."

"Weren't they?"

Arnar Geir's laughter was chillingly hollow.

"Not a bit of it. Some things are a disappointment. In other ways they're better off than they ever have

176

been. The difference is that these days they have the internet and social media feeding them all kinds of shit, and that's all they notice — the bad stuff. They don't see cheaper food, more choice, tarmac roads. They forget there aren't power cuts every five minutes like there used to be. Remember that?"

Ingvar laughed. "Yeah. I remember we had Christmas dinner on the boat one year when the power was off for the best part of a day, the old folks and five kids crammed into the galley. You remember that?"

"Yeah, and then we were all upset when the power came back on and we had to go home again."

"How's politics?" Ingvar asked.

Arnar Geir snorted.

"Politics is shit. Endless wrangling over things that make no difference, empire-building on a grand scale, endless horse-trading and favours for old pals. You know how it works. And it's not only the old parties. The new ones are just as enthusiastic, though they're not as good at it yet."

"So are you going to keep it up?"

Arnar Geir sighed.

"There'll be an election in a year or so. Two years at the outside. I'll be selected, that's a given. Should have a reasonable chance of getting into Parliament. A couple of years there, then I'll engineer some reason to stand down, resign on a point of principle, and that'll do me, I can go back to the law. Two or three years in Parliament sets you up for all kinds of good stuff: directorships, consultancies. It's a great career move. Plus I can always go back if I feel like it."

"That's as cynical as hell."

"Says the man who faked his own death."

"Well, there is that," Ingvar admitted. "Can you get away with it? And you reckon they'd let you make a comeback?"

Arnar Geir's face broke into a chillingly cold smile that bared his teeth.

"I have a gold-plated insurance. You've no idea how much Vilberg owes me. They can't afford to not let me come back. I know where too many bodies are buried," he said, his eyes glittering. "Some of them quite literally."

"Vilberg's the big man?"

"That's him. Our glorious leader," Arnar Geir said, not troubling to keep the disdain from his voice.

"And you're sure you'll get in?"

"Yeah. A new government gets swept in on a tide of misery. We're already making promises we don't have a hope in hell of keeping. The plan is to get out before we're rumbled as being the same as the previous bunch of crooks and incompetents."

"So not much changes?"

"Nothing changes," Arnar Geir said, and turned in his seat. "And you want to know what's really interesting?"

"Go on."

"I had a visit from Helgi Svavarsson. Remember him? Svavar from Efstibær's son? Used to be a copper in Blönduós years ago. He's a detective down here now. Guess what he was fishing for?"

★ ★ ★

Gunna opened her iPad, scrolling through messages she knew she would have to deal with in the morning, and then switching to take a look at that morning's newspaper.

She was scratching her head, trying to work out if one of the subjects of the day's obituaries had been a distant relative, when Steini's hoarse call broke through to her.

"Gunna! Quick!"

"What?"

"Come here, quickly!"

As she strode towards the sofa, Steini dropped his book and fumbled for the remote control, increasing the volume. Laufey's voice boomed into the room and Gunna felt a pang as she saw her daughter facing the camera with a microphone held out towards her.

"What is it you and your friends are complaining about this time?"

The well-known TV presenter's lazy voice sparked a glint in Laufey's eye that Gunna recognised instantly, just as the words *Laufey Ragnarsdóttir, activist* appeared across the bottom of the screen.

"Well, Jörundur. We're here to draw attention to the environmental disaster that's facing the world today. It's as simple as that."

"What makes you say that? There are plenty of people who believe this stuff about global warming is just a hoax."

Gunna saw a muscle twitch in Laufey's cheek.

"That's quite true. There are also people who believe the world is flat, despite irrefutable evidence to the contrary. There are people who deny that the Holocaust took place, when there are people alive today who witnessed it. So there are also climate change deniers, and you have to accept that they are divided into several camps. There are those who deny anything is wrong, even though the Greenland ice caps are melting fast, the North Atlantic pump is demonstrably slowing down, desertification is increasing. Then there are others who say that this isn't due to human action and is a natural process. But that's almost beside the point. The key point is that it is happening right now, the process is becoming faster, and the weight of recognised, reliable scientific evidence is very much against those who don't want to face the fact that the roof of our house is on fire."

Laufey spoke in a clear, measured voice, with a quiet emphasis that seemed to punch the interviewer. The microphone began to wobble in his hand.

"And why is this protest taking place here, outside the Chinese Embassy in Reykjavík? Why involve the Chinese in this?"

"Because China is one of the world's four major polluters. This is something that affects the whole world, but nations such as China, Russia, India and especially the United States need to know that the rest of us are looking to them to take action."

"Right, I see. So why isn't this protest taking place outside the US Embassy?"

"Maybe the next one will."

"And what is it you're trying to say? Do you have a message for Icelanders on this?"

Laufey shook her head without taking her eyes off the camera.

"I don't have a message for Icelanders. Iceland is already doing a lot of what can be done, although that's not to say we can't do better," she said. "The message needs to reach the major industrial nations and their leaders."

"And what do you expect them to do?"

Laufey shrugged and her gaze moved from the interviewer to the camera, looking into it with clear grey eyes.

"It would be a step in the right direction if they would listen," she said. "The message is in fact pretty simple, and if I were speaking to the leaders of these nations, I would simply say to these extremely wealthy men — and they are all men — that we are genuinely all in this together. We all breathe the same air and we all drink the same water. This isn't something that only affects the poor people they only see occasionally in the distance. If humans continue to poison the earth, then these men in their ivory towers are going to suffer in exactly the same way as everyone else. Wealth and status may defer things a little while for them. But wealth and status won't protect them or their children, or their grandchildren, who won't thank them for the legacy they are leaving. That's it, that's the message."

"A powerful message from a committed activist there in front of the Chinese Embassy during today's protest," Jörundur said, his dark brows knitted as the camera swung away from Laufey to zoom in on him. "Not everyone will agree with what this young woman has had to say, but few will be able to deny that the message is a passionate one. And now, back to the studio."

By now Steini was sitting up, and he shot a glance at Gunna.

"Well, you can't say Laufey doesn't say exactly what she thinks, can you?"

Gunna dropped onto the sofa next to him.

"She wouldn't be Ragnar Sæmundsson's daughter if she didn't have strong views," Gunna said. "He might not have agreed with everything she says, although I reckon he would. But he'd have been properly proud of her for standing up to that patronising idiot."

Steini dipped each piece of catfish in beaten egg and then in breadcrumbs before dropping them in the pan one by one to sizzle.

"The seasoning is mixed in with the egg, not the breadcrumbs," he explained to Drífa, who waddled between the table and the cupboard while listening to Steini's every word. Gunna half listened, her attention on her iPad as she and Kjartan giggled over an old Tom and Jerry cartoon.

"Don't give away too many secrets, Steini," she called, and looked up to see him start to flip the fish. Drífa leaned against the kitchen cupboard, her vast belly in both hands, exhausted and with a trickle of sweat running down the side of her head. The inky black of her hair had long grown back to its natural brown, and the goth clothing had been replaced with forgiving tracksuit trousers to accommodate her expanding girth.

Steini turned off the heat under the pot of rice simmering at the back of the stove and turned the fish a second time.

"How long does it cook for?" Drífa asked.

"Depends how thick the pieces are. But normally it's done about a minute before you think it's cooked."

"Right. That's easy then."

"And as these are thin pieces, it'll be ready in a few seconds." He raised his voice. "Gunna! Food! Drífa, drain the rice, please."

Drífa tucked her hair away in an untidy ponytail as she waited for Gunna to come to the table.

"Drífa, have you heard from your dad recently?" Gunna asked, thoughtfully spooning rice onto her plate and breaking down a piece of fish to feed to Kjartan as he perched on her knee.

"Svanur, you mean? No. Why?"

"Just wondering. I could do with a word with him," Gunna said, struggling to keep up with Kjartan. "This one's going to be a strong lad," she said. "That's a fisherman's appetite."

After they had eaten, Drífa put Kjartan in the bath and splashes and whoops could be heard, while Gunna lay back on the sofa with the iPad, searching for auctions of Áskell Hafberg's paintings. She was taken by surprise by the prices quoted on American and European dealers' websites.

"Would you pay that much for a picture to go on the wall?" she asked Steini as he sat next to her, showing him a picture from an American gallery on the screen.

183

"I don't think I'd pay that much for a car, let alone a pretty picture. Is that really how much those things cost?"

"Unbelievable, isn't it?"

He nodded and settled himself with a book and his head on her shoulder. "Why the sudden interest in modern art, if I may ask? Something work-related, I'd imagine."

"It is. Not something I can say much about. But if you look at the artist's name, and compare it to the obituary in today's paper, you'll know what I'm investigating."

"You mean Áskell Hafberg?" Drífa asked, lowering herself gently into a chair with Kjartan in her arms wrapped in a towel. "His wife was from Vestureyri, wasn't she? Wasn't there something about her a couple of years ago?"

"She was from Ósvík. She drowned."

"Oh, right. I was sure I heard Mum say something about her. I think she knew her years ago."

"Could be," Gunna said. "Have you heard from your mum?"

"Not today," Drífa said with a smile. "But she's not going to give up."

"She's worried about you."

"I know," Drífa sighed. "She can't seem to accept that I'm staying here with Gísli. I don't want to go back and have everyone talking about me again."

"They'll be talking anyway, whether you're there or not."

"I know. But I'd just prefer them to chatter without me being there," Drífa said firmly.

184

CHAPTER
FIVE

*North-easterly gale, gaining strength towards
evening. Gusts overnight could exceed 30 m/sec.
Heavy cloud cover and widespread snowfalls
expected. Temperatures 0--4°C. Heavy
snowfalls expected on high ground. Snowfalls in
coastal areas, possible heavy snow overnight.
Severe weather warning from 1800 onwards.
Road closures expected.*

"His name's Erik Petter Tallaksen," Helgi said with
satisfaction as he started the day by scrolling through
his emails.

"Who?" Gunna asked.

"Mr Mystery. The airport guy."

"Ah. So he's no longer a mystery man?"

Helgi looked at his screen again.

"Judging by his date of birth, he's about the right age
— a couple of years older than Ingvar."

Gunna came around to his side of the desk to peer at
the screen.

"That doesn't mean much, does it? If he's masquerading
as someone else, he'd hardly be likely to use his original
date of birth, would he?"

"True. Look, Danish passport, resident in Spain,"
Helgi said. "A bit of a globetrotter."

"By the way, that deadbeat you were looking for," Gunna said.

"Aron?"

"Yep. He's dead. Erling Larsen's country pad burned down."

"That's going to stir things up a bit."

"It could be a straightforward house fire, or it could turn into a murder inquiry. It's on the Southern District's patch, so they'll need all the info they can get. Could you liaise with them?"

"It'll be our headache if it turns into a murder inquiry. Or does Sævaldur get that pleasure?"

Gunna gave him a sideways look and shrugged.

"It's Sævaldur's baby, I hope. We're busy enough already, and he loves that kind of stuff."

"What are you up to today? Are you working on this now?"

"I'm still tied up with the late artist, and I have to go out for an hour or so," Gunna said. "By the way, there's a break-in that needs checking out. Can you take a look?"

Lind Ákadóttir greeted Gunna with barely controlled impatience in her apartment so close to central Reykjavík that it was only a short walk from the Hverfisgata police station. The fourth-floor windows gave a panoramic view of the bay and Esja beyond it, or would have done if the cloud level had not dropped so low as to obscure all but the base of the mountain in the distance.

186

"It's very early," she said dubiously. "What is it you want exactly?"

"You were at Áskell Hafberg's place on the night Birna Bergthórsdóttir died?"

Gunna could see a network of fine lines around Lind's mouth as she frowned, the corners of those sharp-cut lips pulled out of shape as she tapped a foot on the wooden floor.

"And just why are you asking?"

"Because I'm looking for answers to something that doesn't add up."

Lind scowled. "And why are you asking now, all these years after Birna died?"

"Let's call it curiosity."

"I was at the party in the summer house, as you know. I had already been there most of the day, helping Birna get everything ready."

"You drove up there?"

"Birna came and collected me. I don't drive."

"How was she? Was there anything that rang alarm bells?"

"Quite the opposite. Her daughter was there and Birna had got used to the idea of being a grandmother. She was looking forward to it."

"Who else was there?"

"Áskell, being grand."

"Grand?"

Lind hesitated. "Not grand exactly. He was happy, and that was unusual. He'd been through an awkward patch, depressed and miserable. He'd been doing sculpture in metal, and while it was imaginative and

187

quite startling, it didn't go down well. His agent hated it."

"You mean Róbert Simoni?"

"Róbert was not impressed," Lind said, suppressing a grimace.

"You don't get on with him?"

"Not any more. Not since the divorce."

"You were married to Róbert Simoni?"

"No, he lived with my sister for a few years, a long time ago. It was acrimonious, to say the least. Róbert has a Latin temper he inherited from his father, and a Mediterranean attitude to fidelity."

"Go on," Gunna prompted. "What's his background?"

"Róbert's father came from somewhere in southern France, near the Italian border. He washed up in Iceland sometime in the seventies and was a salesman for a long time, selling saltfish to people in Portugal and Spain, I believe. I don't know any details but I gather he wasn't welcome back where he came from. He had a ferociously quick temper, so maybe that's why he was happy to hide out on this little island in the north."

"I see. But Róbert was brought up here?"

"He was. He's as Icelandic as you or me, except for the name and the fact that he's an insufferable snob."

"The night of the party. What happened? When did you last see Birna?"

Lind sat back and her forehead under its thick owl-grey curls creased as she thought. "I've been over it hundreds of times in my mind. I'm not completely sure but I spent a lot of the evening with Birna and I think

188

the last time I was conscious of her nearby was when we were clearing up after the meal. Most of the garbage just went into the fire or into rubbish bags, but I think . . ." She paused and frowned. "I'm sure she went back into the house to get some glasses and I don't recall seeing her after that."

"When was this?"

"Around ten, I think. Not later. Between nine and ten, I'd say."

"Do you recall who was still there?"

"Mímir was snoring on the couch inside. He was dead to the world. Magnea was holding court in the garden with that old fool Gussi. I don't know about Róbert. There was an argument," she added in a faint voice. "I . . . was there with a companion. He and Róbert had a disagreement, over a young woman."

"Interesting. Róbert didn't mention this when I spoke to him. Tell me more."

"I . . ." She faltered, then recovered her composure and took a deep breath. "It's something I've tried to put behind me. Tolli was beautiful, but he was a mistake."

"Tolli?"

"His name's Thorlákur Thráinsson."

"The musician?"

"That's him."

"What happened?"

"He punched Róbert. Quite hard." Gunna raised an eyebrow and saw that Lind noticed. "Tolli wasn't about, so I went to see where he was. It wasn't quite dark, so around eight. Something like that. Anyway, I

189

heard voices from behind Áskell's workshop, went to see what was going on and saw Tolli punch Róbert, twice. Left, right. It was just like in a movie, but it was shocking."

"If you're not used to seeing violence it can be," Gunna murmured. "And then?"

"Róbert howled like a child. I could see Tolli was going to hit him again, so I put myself in between them." Lind lapsed into silence and wrung her hands before continuing, choking back a sob. "Róbert's assistant, Eyrún, just hung onto Tolli. I couldn't believe it at first."

"What had happened? Did you see what the fight was about?"

"No. But it all came out in bits and pieces. Tolli and Eyrún had been whispering to each other all evening. She told him to meet her behind the workshop, and he's a man, so he didn't need telling twice. But when he went round there a few minutes after her, he found Róbert already there. It seemed Róbert thought she was waiting for him, and he was, what shall I say? Insistent. As she wasn't wearing a lot, he assumed he was invited."

Lind's mouth set into a hard, narrow line.

"Eyrún was pushing Róbert off as Tolli came round the corner, so Tolli punched him."

"Ah. Undignified. I'm not surprised Róbert didn't mention that episode."

"I'm not surprised either. He has an ego the size of a small country and the thought of a woman turning him down isn't something he'd comprehend."

"So he left?"

"First Eyrún disappeared in tears, comforted by Tolli. Then Róbert leered at me and said that as his intended fuck and my toyboy had run off with each other, did I fancy taking up the slack at his place? Needless to say, I didn't."

"So you stayed?"

"Until the morning, when the neighbour came hammering on the door to say that he'd found Birna by the shore."

"Nobody had noticed she was missing before? How come? Why hadn't Áskell or Ursula noticed?"

"Look, there was a lot to drink that night and some of us were upset. There were a few lines done as well. The world could have ended and Áskell was so wasted he wouldn't have noticed. Magnea was curled up with Mímir on the sofa. I suppose I had assumed Birna had gone off to her own bed."

"And where were you?"

"In the tent in the garden that Tolli and I had brought with us. I haven't seen him or Eyrún since, except the time Tolli came to return the keys to this flat, and even then we didn't speak. He just put them in my hand and walked away."

There were patches of ice on the road and snow was falling from a heavy sky that seemed to be almost close enough to reach out and touch. The mass of Hólmsheiði prison appeared from the grey gloom. Slowing down as much as he dared, Ingvar glanced sideways to see the prison's gate facing him, while the rest of the sprawling building was hidden in the murk.

He drove a little further, then pulled over and turned the car round, but sat for a while staring out through the windscreen at the landscape that was disappearing under a fresh white covering.

He felt his phone buzz in his pocket, but ignored it. Whatever it was, it could wait.

It was chilling to think that his elder son was so close to him, but so far away. For a few seconds he had considered applying for a visit, but had rejected that thought almost immediately. There was no knowing how Sturlaugur would react, or even if an application would be accepted, and drawing attention to himself was the last thing a man in his precarious position should be doing.

All the same, he felt an endless depth of sadness that the boy was probably no more than a few hundred metres from where he sat, but he might as well be on the far side of the world.

Ingvar shook himself. This way insanity lies, he told himself. He would have to face the reality that there was very little he could do for the son he had abandoned all those years ago. That monumental weight of water had crashed over the beach in Thailand and he had stayed in that scruffy bar to watch it on television, mesmerised as the same clip had been shown again and again.

He pulled the car back onto the road and drove back past the prison and towards the city.

He was angry and restless. He knew he ought to feel satisfied that he had destroyed Erling Larsen's house — not that four walls and a roof could ever equate to the

years his son would lose staring at the inside of a cell —
but not being able to see the boy or do anything that
might help him out of his situation filled him with a
frustrated emptiness.

That young hooligan he had intimidated so easily
was just small fry, hardly worth bothering with, he
decided as he pulled up at a filling station on the city
outskirts. He pumped fuel into the little 4x4's tank and
stared moodily at the sky over the rooftops as the snow
thickened. The wind had eased, and instead of the
sharp, dry flakes it had hurled at him an hour before,
fat snowflakes fell softly to collect on the ground.

Inside the filling station, he paid, fetched himself a
cup of coffee and a sandwich and sat at a bench by the
window to leaf through the previous day's newspaper while
headlines scrolled past on a screen high on one wall.

He froze with a chunk of prawn sandwich in his
mouth, and had to thump his own chest as he began to
cough.

A grainy picture of the burned-out house taken from
some distance away filled the screen, and inset into it
was an old passport-style photo of a man with a smile
that showed bad teeth. A ribbon of text rolled across
the lower edge of the picture.

*Police have identified the body of the man found in
the house fire at Saurbær in Flóahreppur as Aron
Stefánsson, aged 30, who had recently been . . .*

Ingvar sat and stared at the blackened timbers of
what had been the roof of the house. The words
relatives have been informed jumped out at him. His
fingers had gone numb and he had to shake himself to

193

wrench his eyes from a much younger version of Aron's face as it smiled goofily at him.

It was time to go, he told himself. He had outstayed his welcome.

He made himself look away from the TV, leaf through the rest of the newspaper and close it. The coffee in his paper cup was cool, but he needed the jolt its bitterness gave him.

He dropped the cup and the newspaper in the nearest bin. As he fumbled in his pockets for car keys, he found his phone. Sitting in the car, he opened the message he had ignored earlier, peering at the screen to make out the picture that Lizzie had sent him.

It was another grainy image, this time a monochrome moonscape that he frowned at before he felt his fingers freeze again in shock.

A little Lizzie or a little Erik? read the message below the ultrasound scan. *9 weeks. See you soon . . . xxx*

The corners of Ívar Laxdal's mouth were pulled down in the absolute reverse of a smile. Not that she had seen the man smile too often, Gunna reflected as he stood with brawny arms folded over his barrel chest and stared out of the window at the flurries of snow pattering against the glass.

"What do you have, Gunnhildur?"

"A list of people who were at Áskell Hafberg's house the night Birna died," she said. Ívar Laxdal squinted at the chart she unfolded on the desk in front of him. Gunna ran a finger along the names as she gave her report. "Mímir Sveinsson and Magnea Briem didn't

194

leave the house the entire time. I can account for Jónatan and Gústaf, but it's less clear where others were at various times," she said.

"There's no estimated time of death for Birna?"

"No. The last sighting of her was around ten that evening, roughly nightfall," Gunna said, and Ívar Laxdal followed her finger. "Áskell himself didn't leave the garden around the house, according to Ursula. Thorlákur and Eyrún left soon after nightfall. That leaves these." She tapped two names at the end of the list. "One isn't accounted for, and what the second has said doesn't tie in with other witness statements."

"Why's there no estimated time of death?"

"No mention of it in Örlygur's report."

"Nothing, you say, Gunnhildur?"

"No forensic evidence either, and hardly any witness statements."

"I can't believe there was no full post-mortem."

"All I can find is a blood test."

"Not a high enough alcohol level to make her pass out?"

"Nothing conclusive. It doesn't add up."

"It stinks, Gunnhildur. Why didn't Örlygur carry out a proper investigation?"

Gunna shrugged. "I don't have a clue. Maybe because it was the bank holiday weekend and we were even more short-handed than usual?"

"That's no damned excuse," Ívar Laxdal rumbled and cupped his chin in one hand as he stared at the floor in thought. "Gunnhildur," he said sharply, looking up and into her eyes. "Are you after Örlygur's head?"

She stopped herself from stepping back in surprise. "No," she said after a second's thought. "No, of course not. The man's retired. I'm not interested in starting a witch hunt against someone who's no longer even on the force."

"Even if you have evidence of incompetence, or that he overlooked evidence?"

"If I come across anything along those lines, then it goes without saying that I'd flag it up. But that's not my department, I'm delighted to say."

Ívar Laxdal nodded. "Right enough. If you show that Örlygur screwed up that investigation, then you've a good chance of being branded a back-stabbing bitch with a grudge against an officer who retired with a blameless record."

"I'm aware of that," Gunna said. "If I were the cynical type, I could suggest that Örlygur was blameless because he didn't do a great deal and didn't allow himself all that much opportunity to be in the firing line."

"Unlike you, you mean?"

"Unlike you and me, I mean," she said.

Ingvar fidgeted as he sat in the car. It wasn't like him. Normally he was confident and assertive, all of which was part of the persona that came with his working life, having to be quick with his wits and fast on his feet.

Now he felt at a loss, a fish on dry land even though this was the country where he had grown up. The place felt alien to him now that so much had changed. Reykjavík had gone from being a quiet backwater where not a lot happened most of the time to this brash city where everyone was in too much of a hurry for their own good.

He scowled to himself as he watched Kaffihorn from the car park through the snow that fluttered down. There was half an inch on the road and he thanked his lucky stars that he had made his pilgrimage to the north before the weather had started to close in. That morning's news on the radio had told him that the road over the heath where he had stopped to admire the view was open only to heavy vehicles. Even with its four-wheel drive, this little runaround would have struggled, and he would have run the risk of being stranded on the north side of the mountains by nightfall.

Tekla had already arrived. He had watched her from a distance as she strode effortlessly through the gathering snow, twisting to push open the coffee house's door with one shoulder, pulling the stroller containing his granddaughter in behind her. His granddaughter . . . Ingvar shook his head at the idea, and the thought of the picture Lizzie had sent came rushing back to him.

He slammed the car door, huddled deep into his jacket and took a deep breath.

Outside the door he stood for a moment and closed his eyes, on the point of turning around and disappearing into the winter afternoon. He growled to himself under his breath that walking out on his family once was enough, and this time he needed to get a grip on himself.

Learning that he had a grandchild had hit him harder than he had expected. Now he wondered whether once he had seen the little girl he would be able to walk away, although he knew inside that there was every likelihood this would be his only chance ever to see her.

The sky had turned the sinister silver of molten lead and the wind had dropped to a breeze, but an ice-cold breeze that had snow on its breath. Helgi shivered as he inspected the ransacked workshop that had been stripped of every single power tool during the night by a thief who had let himself in by wriggling through a tiny bathroom window.

"Asian, I'm telling you. It'd have to be some midget to get through that window," the workshop's red-faced owner blustered.

"Or some youngster. Any ideas?" Helgi said. "Disgruntled former staff, dissatisfied customers? Anything like that?"

"We don't have dissatisfied customers," the man said through gritted teeth. "That's why we're busy, and that's why I can't be without all this gear. I've two teams out today, and it's just as well one of them had all the stuff they needed at the site."

"What else is missing? Anything from the office?"

"No, just here in the store."

"Stolen to order, probably," Helgi said. "If I were you, I'd get an alarm. Now they know about this place, I reckon they'll be back."

"I'm going to get a fucking dog and leave it here every night," the man said.

"That's your decision. Officially, if someone gets hurt, then it's your responsibility, so take care. Between ourselves, make it a big, angry dog."

"I'll tell you what else is missing. They even stole a fucking wheelbarrow to take it all away," the man fumed, and held up his phone as it began to ring. "What?" he demanded, putting it to one ear and walking away.

Helgi inspected the toilet window and its surroundings, scowling to himself. He checked it again from outside the building, and then cast around until he found the erratic track of a single wheel flanked by boot prints across a patch of grass at the back of the building. The overnight frost had left the grass stiff and pristine, and the wheel's track stood out clearly until it disappeared as it crossed the tarmac yard. When it reappeared on another grass verge, it wasn't so easy to follow. He was able to pick it up again as it crossed patches of snow, until he came to a halt by a verge in a quiet cul-de-sac of old wooden houses on one side and a terrace still under construction on the other, the new concrete of the walls a pearly grey in the morning light.

A dented green wheelbarrow had been thrown onto a heap of rubbish outside the new terrace, its wheel in the air as if waving forlornly to him.

Helgi rubbed his hands and looked around as he walked along the street, checking out buildings on both sides.

Close to where the quiet backwater joined a main road, he pushed open the doors of a pizza place that had just opened for the day.

"Morning," he said as a sleepy young man looked questioningly at him from behind the counter. "I'm a police officer and I need to check your CCTV."

★　★　★

"A match made in heaven, my darling."

Gunna stared at Albert as if he had lost his mind. "Would you care to elaborate?" she asked, knowing that something worth hearing would be bound to come of it. "Just who is a match made in heaven? Or are you making some kind of roundabout proposal? If so, I want Hallgrímskirkja, the bishop to run the show, a huge white dress, a Mercedes bigger than Ívar Laxdal's Volvo and a month's honeymoon in the Caribbean. And that's just for starters."

"Absolutely. I'm sure my girlfriend won't mind," Albert said. "She'll understand totally that I've dumped her for you."

"Precisely, Albert. What man wouldn't fall over himself to snap up a glamorous grandmother with stretch marks and a bad temper? So before we go any further, I'd best give you the opportunity to back out, or at least to explain."

"The prints you brought in. We have a perfect match."

"Prints?"

"The ones you asked me to check yesterday? Remember? Have thoughts of white dresses and bridesmaids scrambled your mind for a moment?"

"Yes. Sorry. I was thinking about our honeymoon on a sun-kissed beach and all the piña coladas I was going to have for breakfast. The prints from the place at Hafravatn, that's right."

"The guy's name's Ellert Ásgrímsson. I've emailed you the details."

"Certain?"

Albert glared and put a hand theatrically on one hip. "How often do I give you bullshit?"

200

"All the time, Albert. All the time," Gunna assured him. "But you very rarely get anything wrong."

"Could I have that in writing?"

Gunna checked Ellert Ásgrímsson's records and found that rather than a hardened criminal, she was looking at a photo of a fresh-faced boy barely out of his teens. A minor brush with the law over possession of a small amount of grass had given him a police record, placing his fingerprints conveniently on file to be matched against the practically textbook print from the padlock on Áskell Hafberg's workshop.

Not a professional housebreaker, Gunna decided, and in a few minutes she had turned up a Facebook page scattered with pictures of the fresh-faced young man looking the worse for wear among groups of similar young men and a few girls, plus a more recent photo than the one on his driving licence showing him looking thinner, gaunt, and with a ring through his lower lip.

The address given as his legal residence turned out to be a large detached house in Kópavogur, on the older side of the suburb among established trees now heavy with snow and hedge-bordered gardens. Presumably the Ásgrímur Ellertsson who paid the municipal tax for the property was the young man's father.

Gunna pressed the button and heard a bell chime deep inside the house. When nobody had opened the door after thirty seconds, she hammered on it with the heel of her hand and listened to the echo. Then she wiped snow from the frosted glass panel, hoping to see a sign of life.

A figure moved rapidly in the distance, stepping across the hall, looking directly at Gunna's face then disappearing through another door. The sound of it banging closed reached her and she hammered a second time. She decided that the figure must have gone through a back door and hurried round the side of the house just as an engine roared into life around a corner.

She threw herself out of the path of the motorbike as it hurtled past, landing in an undignified heap in the clean snow of a flower bed. The bike accelerated away, spitting gravel from under its back wheel until it gripped the road surface and vanished from sight.

Lips pursed with anger, Gunna clicked her communicator. "Control, ninety-five fifty."

"Ninety-five fifty, control. What can I do for you, Gunna?"

"Something for traffic," she said, breathing heavily. "A lad on a motorbike has just narrowly avoided running me down. It's a smallish bike, yellow, driver wearing a black jacket and a silver helmet. I didn't catch the full number but there's an AX in there and it ends with a three."

"Understood. I'll see if I can get it located. Where are you and where was he headed?"

"Kópavogur, on the old side, Kópavör 66. He'll probably be on the main road to town, and he must be insane trying to ride a motorbike in this weather."

"No problem. There's a patrol not far away from there and I'll get Hafnarfjördur to watch out for him at their end as well. You have the driver's identity?"

"It's probably a young idiot called Ellert Ásgrímsson."

"Leave it with us. I'll let you know what we find."

Gunna sat up and checked if anything had been broken in the tumble, but found that only her pride had taken a knock. As she dusted mud from her trousers, she saw that one leg had been ripped. The shoulder she had landed on was stiff and caked with snow and black earth, while a rose bush had left her with scratches across the back of one hand that oozed blood.

She stood up and limped back to the car. Sitting inside it, pressing a tissue to the stinging scratches, she recovered her breath and calmed down, wondering where Ellert Ásgrímsson had disappeared to. As she started the engine and pulled away, turning onto the main road back towards the centre of Kópavogur, her communicator buzzed into life.

"Ninety-five fifty, control. You there, Gunna?"

"Battered and bruised, but here. Go ahead."

"We have your man. Anna Björg caught up with him on Digranesvegur just now. You want to go to the location yourself?"

"That was quick. So the little bastard didn't get far?"

"Hit a patch of ice and fell off his bike. His dignity's bruised but otherwise he's unhurt. What do you want us to do with him?"

"If you'd be so kind, sling him in a cell at Hverfisgata. Assaulting a police officer means he gets to stay over and enjoy a little hospitality."

Róbert Simoni stared at Gunna, his eyes bulging slightly as he took in the rip in her trousers and the mud-caked shoulder of her uniform.

"You spoke to my colleague who carried out the investigation?" she asked.

"Not as far as I recall, no."

"Not as far as you recall? What's that supposed to mean? Either you were interviewed by a police officer or you weren't."

"I didn't speak to a police officer."

"And the woman who was with you at the party the night Birna died?" Gunna prompted.

"Her name's Eyrún. She used to work here."

"She doesn't now?"

"No."

"Where is she, and what's her full name?"

"Eyrún Njálsdóttir. I don't know where she is these days. She only worked here for a little while."

Gunna nodded grimly and pulled out a notebook. "Good. As she was employed here, you'll have a record of her address and her national identification number, won't you?" She tapped the notebook with her pen as Róbert looked increasingly flustered.

"When I say she worked here, I don't mean she was actually employed. She was here for a while in a voluntary capacity, work experience," he said in triumph, as if that explained everything.

"She was here as some kind of intern, you mean?"

"That's just it. An intern."

"A smart term for unpaid labour?"

"You're trying to be offensive."

"I don't have to try. It comes naturally," Gunna told him. "Especially when people are economical with the truth"

Róbert shrugged. "It's not as if there's anything I could tell you."

"Let's try, shall we?"

He glared at her for a moment and glanced across at a smart couple who were looking at the paintings on the walls, discreetly waiting to catch his eye.

"Will you keep your voice down, please? I have customers."

"You don't have an intern who can deal with them?"

Róbert's smile dripped icicles. "If you'll excuse me for a moment . . ."

"No problem. I'll wait right here."

He shimmered across the gallery floor and the smile he gave the couple was a world away from the glassy-eyed version Gunna had been treated to a moment before. He laughed and chatted and the couple nodded and smiled back, until Róbert finally gestured discreetly towards Gunna with an apologetic shake of the head. Gunna caught the muted words "an old friend has died", and "difficult circumstances", and the couple assured him that they understood perfectly. Róbert almost bowed to them as they left the gallery, promising to return. As the door eased itself shut behind them, his stony expression returned.

"It's not good for business, being interviewed by the police. I may have to examine my options, you know."

"Fine by me. We can do this at Hverfisgata if you prefer. I'll send a car to collect you."

She could almost see Róbert shudder. "That won't be necessary, I assure you."

"Good. In that case, we can return to the night Birna Bergthórsdóttir died. What time did you and Eyrún Njálsdóttir arrive at the house at Hafravatn?"

"This was years ago. Surely you don't expect me to remember details like that?"

"I do, and I'll be checking against everyone else who was there."

"All right." Róbert's shoulders sagged, as if he had been defeated. He pulled a stool from under the desk and sat heavily on it. "We got there around seven, as far as I remember. Eyrún drove as I had already had a few glasses of wine at lunch."

"In your car?"

"In the Mercedes, yes."

"Who was there?"

"Birna, Áskell," Róbert said, blank-faced. "Mímir was there, already disgustingly drunk; that bitch Magnea Briem, Gussi Bóa, Lind Áka and some young stud she had brought with her, even though I think her husband was there as well. There were more people I didn't know, maybe they were neighbours. Áskell used to associate with all sorts of odd people."

"Ursula? Úlfur?"

"Úlfur wasn't there, I'm certain of that. But I think Ursula was."

"Sure?"

Róbert shrugged. "I'm not certain. It was a long time ago now."

"And what did you do? What happened?"

"What do you usually do at parties?" Róbert demanded. "I spoke to my friends and avoided everyone else, especially the petit bourgeois insurance salesman Áskell spent so much of his time with."

"Ah, you mean Jónatan?"

"If that's the man's name, yes. An insufferably dull person with no idea of how special a talent Áskell has. Had, I mean."

"You were inside the house the whole time? Or were you in the garden? Did you go down to the jetty?"

"As far as I recall, I spent half an hour with Áskell and Lind in the workshop and he showed us what he was working on, all that ironmongery he had been wasting his time with."

"And then?"

"We ate. The insurance man —"

"Jónatan."

"Yes, yes. Jónatan. He was behind the barbecue with a chef's hat on and a greasy apron over his belly, handing out scorched food to everyone. We ate in the garden, as far as I remember. Afterwards we sat outside until it started to get cold, and after that I went inside."

"You stayed the night?"

"No, I went home."

"With Eyrún?"

"No. I went home and she . . . went elsewhere."

"Why?"

A sardonic smile played over Róbert's features.

"Because the delightful Eyrún had disappeared with Lind Ákadóttir's toyboy, and when Lind went to look for him, she found him doing his heroic best on top of my decorative but otherwise useless assistant in the long grass. Lind was rather drunk and somewhat upset,

207

and as we had both been stood up, so to speak, I called a taxi and we shared a ride back to town."

"Why didn't you drive?"

"I had been drinking and I like to remain within the law. Anyway, as I told you, Eyrún had driven us up to Hafravatn and she had other things on her mind, namely Lind's toyboy with the body of a Greek god and the mind of a fairly mediocre household pet. She wasn't happy at all. Lind, I mean. I was gallant and offered her the chance to go back to town."

"So you left. At what point did you last see Birna?"

"I'm not entirely sure. As I was leaving I apologised to Áskell for leaving him to deal with Eyrún and the toyboy, but I felt I owed it to Lind to at least offer her a way out so she could return home."

"And she'll verify that, I presume."

"Ask her."

"Don't worry," Gunna said. "I will."

"Hæ, Dad," Tekla said with a smirk.

She leaned over the stroller and gently lifted a bundle from it, crooning as she did so.

"Can you get me a green tea?" she asked. Ingvar watched in fascination as she settled herself with the baby in her arms.

He brought back coffee for himself, tea for her and a couple of pastries on a plate. He sat down in a daze. The little girl opened her eyes, and as she gazed up at him, he felt himself blinking back tears of emotion. He put out a hand and she closed her fingers around the tip of his, which made him look away as he wiped his eyes.

"How old is she?" he muttered in a hoarse voice.

"Ten months. She's almost walking."

"She's a smart kid," Ingvar mumbled. "María Vala. Where's the name come from?"

"Inga Lára's mother's name is Vala. I guess they just liked María," Tekla said and held the baby out to him. "Want a cuddle?"

Instinctively Ingvar rocked as he held the little girl, his shoulders hunched and his head bowed low as he looked into her eyes. He couldn't recall ever having experienced such a feeling of joy and contentment, even when his own children had been born. He looked up and saw Tekla watching him with a wry smile.

"You know, Mum always said you were such a hard-hearted bastard. So I guess she wasn't telling the truth all those years she's been telling us what a slimeball you are."

"Your mother has her moments," Ingvar said gruffly. "How is she? She likes being a grandmother? I have to admit I can't see her in a granny role."

"She's loving it," Tekla said. She sawed one of the pastries in two, dropped the knife back on the plate and munched without much of an appetite. "But she takes care to be a glamorous granny."

"No slippers and rocking chair?"

"Definitely not her style." Tekla held out her hands as the baby began to cry. "She needs her bottle. Do you want to do it, or shall I?"

Ingvar fetched a coffee refill and sat down again, a warmth inside him. María Vala's eyelids drooped as Tekla fed her. He laid his arm on the table, and her little hand found his finger again.

"She's no trouble, then?"

"She's a real sweetie. Feeds, shits, sleeps," Tekla said. "Perfect child."

"You were the same. The boys weren't."

"Really? That's not what Mum says. According to her, we were all a nightmare."

Ingvar shook his head.

"The boys never wanted to go to sleep. You were the good one. I used to lie on the couch in the living room and you'd sleep on my chest."

Tekla looked up at him and stared into his eyes.

"Dad. Didn't you miss us?"

The version of Thorlákur Thráinsson that answered the door was remarkably unlike the public image she had seen on TV. The luxurious head of dark brown hair had been cropped short and the designer stubble had been replaced by a bushy growth. Somewhere behind him a child wailed.

"You're from the police? You called earlier, right?"

His eyes narrowed, more in curiosity than suspicion, Gunna felt, and he stepped aside to usher her into the hallway of the narrow house that seemed to stretch back into the distance.

"Just a moment," he said, disappearing through a doorway, and Gunna could hear a muttered conversation behind it. "Teething," he said, reappearing and pulling on a buttoned sweater knitted in grey and blue shades. "Let's go to the studio. It's quieter there."

The studio had once been a garage, its doors blocked off by a makeshift wall faced with plywood sheets that nobody had ever got round to giving a lick of paint. Three bare concrete walls had been hung with fabric and there were microphone stands, a drum kit and wires that snaked across the floor in every direction.

"You record in here?" Gunna asked, wondering if she had ever heard any of the man's music.

"No, the acoustics are shit. We practise here and go to a proper studio to record." He eyed Gunna curiously as he dropped into a chair. "What can I do for you?"

Gunna put her folder of notes on the table and perched on a stool, preferring it to a shabby armchair that looked ready to collapse.

"I want you to cast your mind back a few years. Almost six years. A party at a summer house at Hafravatn. Does that ring any bells?"

"Yeah." He nodded. "I remember someone died."

"That's right. You were there with Eyrún Njálsdóttir?"

This time he shivered.

"Completely nuts," he said in a grave voice. "Stunning, smart and fun. But crazy."

"And Lind Ákadóttir?"

Thorlákur glared.

"Is this some kind of inquisition into my exes?"

"Not at all," Gunna assured him, taking a sheet of paper from her folder. "Tell me about the party. Why were you there?"

Thorlákur sat back, eyes wide.

"Well, I went because of Lind. She was invited because she knew the people who lived there, and she took me with her. It was a bit weird, because her husband was there as well, but I reckon he must have been a very ex-husband by then. I went with Lind, Mímir, Magnea and a few others. I was studying under Mímir back then, so it wasn't as if I was a stranger."

"Her husband?"

"Yeah. A creepy sort of guy. I can't remember his name; you'd have to ask her."

"Talk me through it," Gunna said. "I'm not looking for secrets. I'm trying to build up a picture of who was there, and roughly how and when they turned up."

"It was years ago! I hardly remember what I was doing last weekend."

"Someone died at this party," Gunna said, her voice turning frosty, and Thorlákur froze. "So I'd have thought it would have been a slightly more memorable gathering than most. You've mentioned a few names already. Let's start with those, shall we? You, Lind, Mímir and Magnea arrived together?"

"Lind was already there. But, yeah. Mímir drove. I can't remember what time, but it was still light."

"And Eyrún was already there?"

Thorlákur shifted uneasily.

"She came with the guy she was working for."

"That's Eyrún and Róbert. Who else?"

"Some old guy who was doing the barbecue. The artist who lived there, Andri, Agnar, whatever his name was, and his wife, the woman who drowned."

"Do you remember who else was present?"

Thorlákur shrugged.

"Those are the ones I know, more or less. There were more people there, and some turned up after it started to get dark, so I couldn't say who. There was a tall girl who was pregnant, really striking, and the guy she was with."

"So, what? A dozen people altogether?"

"No more than that," he said after a moment's thought.

"And you left when?"

"After dark sometime. Eyrún's boss had got sloppy drunk so she took his car and we went back to her place," he said. "Thinking back, I reckon that must have been the last time I saw her. She lives somewhere abroad now."

"And you can't put names to any of these other people?"

He shook his head.

"Nope. They were all pretty old, like Lind." He grinned, and paused. "You want to see the pictures?"

Ingvar had the feeling that it was time to leave, an unconscious hunch that he had spent too long here in the warmth of this almost deserted café with the snow collecting against the windows. Tekla gently lifted the sleeping María Vala back into the stroller, swaddled in a padded pink suit. She lifted one tiny hand at a time and pulled knitted mittens onto them while the little girl slept.

"She's very quiet."

"She's a dream baby."

He watched her, unable to tear his eyes from the soft face that looked so tranquil in sleep. Tekla sat back and sipped what was left of her tea.

"Where's your mother? She doesn't mind you taking María Vala out?"

"She's taken Inga Lára to Hólmsheiði today to see my brother."

"Do you go and see him as well? How is he?"

Tekla grimaced.

"I've been up there once. That was enough."

"Why?" Ingvar asked with a frown.

"Like I told you before," Tekla said with a sigh, "Stulli is all about Stulli. We don't get on. Everything's someone else's fault."

"Mine."

She shrugged.

"That's what he says. But it was his choice to mess around with those idiots and get involved in dope instead of thinking straight. It wasn't something you encouraged him to do."

"Or something I was here to stop him doing."

Tekla shook her head.

"Dad. Don't feel guilty. Stulli was always going to do his own thing, and nobody was ever going to be able to stop him." She grinned. "Vesturhæli people are a pretty hard-headed bunch, you know."

"Born stubborn, every one of us," he said. "Your mother's family are no better."

He shivered as a current of cold air caught his ankles, and he saw Tekla stiffen and look over his shoulder.

214

"I suppose your mother hasn't changed on that score?"

"Fuck." Tekla took a deep breath, and he half turned to follow her eyes. "You can ask her yourself," she said. "She's just walked in."

"You have pictures of the party?"

Thorlákur tapped at the keyboard of a computer on the table.

"Yeah, should do. I never delete anything, though it might take a while to find them," he said slowly, eyes on the screen as he clicked and searched.

"You normally take pictures?"

"Not so much now," he said, attention elsewhere. "But like I said, I was studying under Mímir, and he's a cinematographer, y'know. I was studying film, and I had my first iPhone back then, so I was snapping off pictures of everything and anything."

He swung the computer screen around so they could both see it, and scrolled through the images, muttering names.

"Lind, and Lind again. That's Mímir," he said under his breath. "Don't know who that guy is . . ."

Gunna watched as Áskell, Birna and Jónatan wearing a white apron, tongs in his hand, appeared. In between were shots she presumed had to be artistic: odd details of the house and its surroundings, the bark of one of the gnarled birch trees, smoke rising into the warm summer air.

"That's Eyrún," he said, as a slim young woman with silver hair appeared on the screen, scowling at the lens.

The next shot was of her laughing, head tipped back and mouth wide open, and a glass of wine in one elegant hand.

"She looks like she was having a good time there. That was before the altercation?"

Thorlákur looked awkward.

"Yeah, she was still pretty sober there." He sighed. "She went to take a piss in the grass behind that big old shed, and her boss must have followed her round there. When she didn't come back, I went to see where she had gone and found her pushing the old guy off. So I gave him a smack and he flounced off."

"I see," Gunna said grimly. "Not exactly the version I've heard from other people, but it'll do for now."

"There's some movie files as well," he said. "You want to see those?"

"That's why I'm here."

There were eight clips, from a few seconds up to a couple of minutes for the longest, and Thorlákur sat in silence as each one played through.

"Pause it there," Gunna said as the camera lingered on a man with curly hair sitting on a garden bench talking earnestly to a woman Gunna recognised as Birna. She was surprised to see how slight Birna looked in the film, wearing a woollen cardigan over a summer dress and with her dark hair loose over her shoulders. "Who's that?"

"That's Lind's former husband," Thorlákur said, clicking to set the clip rolling again, just as the man looked up and glared. "He wasn't very happy with me taking pictures," he chuckled. "I don't think he approved of his ex-wife socialising with a younger man."

"I don't doubt it," Gunna said drily, handing him a flash stick. "Can you copy these for me? I need to take a closer look at all this."

"Sure. It's weird seeing these after all this time," Thorlákur said. "I don't think I've ever even looked at them before. It's just as well I didn't delete them, isn't it?"

"G'morning, gentlemen," Helgi breezed. "I'm looking for the driver of the red HiAce outside, TF-289? Anyone?"

The four men in work-stained blue and grey overalls looked at each other. Eventually one stood up. Helgi found himself looking up as a young giant towered over him.

"Yeah? Who's asking?"

Helgi flipped his ID.

"Helgi Svavarsson, city police. And you are?"

"Manni."

Helgi looked though the list of names that Hermann had emailed him.

"Ármann?"

"Yeah."

"I need to take a look at your vehicle."

A bunch of keys flew high in the air and Helgi caught them.

"Help yourself."

"No, I don't think you understand me. The idea is that you show me the vehicle, not that I poke around in it on my own."

"Can't you see I'm busy?"

"Sure, son," Helgi said patiently. "And so am I. So the quicker you do as you're asked, the sooner I can leave you to get back to work."

Outside the building, Helgi took his time rooting through the back of the red van, while Ármann shivered in the cold and fretted as he looked over his shoulder. Snow had piled against one wall of the half-completed building, and the van's windscreen boasted a deep white layer. When he had finished, he leaned against one of the open back doors, sheltered from the wind.

"You normally drive this one?"

"Yeah."

"So you take the van home, and then drive it back to work in the morning? Every night?"

"Yeah, pretty much."

"Last night?" Helgi probed. "And every night this week?"

Ármann nodded. Helgi took out his tablet, turning it round to show Ármann the image he had selected.

"So if the vehicle's your responsibility, can you give me a good reason why it was in a dead-end street a hundred metres down the hill from the company's workshop just after midnight?"

Ármann looked sulky and muttered something. Helgi flipped to a second image.

"Same vehicle, forty minutes later, coming back the other way. Any ideas?"

"I . . . Well . . ."

"All right," Helgi said. "I'll make it easy for you. This is how it looks to me. You went home as usual, and just

218

before midnight you came back, parked the van around the corner, walked to the workshop, let yourself in, heaped the drills and stuff in a wheelbarrow and wheeled the lot to the van. How does that sound?"

Ármann's mouth opened and closed, but he made no sound.

"You opened the window in the toilet to make it look like someone had got in that way. Right?"

"Yeah."

"Where's the gear? Already sold?"

"It's at my place," he said, and smothered a sob.

"Is there a problem with your work? Or are you just short of cash?"

"Hermann takes the piss out of me all the time. I wanted to give him a kick in the balls."

"But without losing your job, and so he'd actually blame someone else?" Helgi suggested. "That's really smart. He's convinced it had to be some Asian midget who squeezed through that little window. So you have a key to the workshop?"

"No. Only the van. I didn't lock up the other night. Just left it on the latch."

"So what are we going to do about this?" Helgi asked, scowling at the young man who perched on the back of the van with his head hanging.

Gunna's head was buzzing as she arrived back at the station on Hverfisgata. She was brooding over the conflicting accounts of the evening six years before, trying to make some sense of what might have happened. She was sure that Róbert was hiding something, reminding herself that a combination of booze, jealousy and frustration could push the mildest of characters to extremes.

She wondered if the new and unexpected side that she had seen of Ívar Laxdal as an art lover was what was keeping him from pulling her back into line right away, but the sight of Ursula sitting in the lobby pushed those thoughts from her mind.

"Hæ," she said. "I wasn't expecting to see you again today. Is everything all right?" She took in the worried lines under the young woman's eyes and noticed that the purple in her hair looked fainter.

"Yeah. I wanted to see how far . . ." Ursula began. "I was wondering if you've found anything out."

"I've found out all kinds of things, including stuff that I can't tell you, but I'm more confused than I was this morning," Gunna admitted. "And right now I have to interview a young thug who tried to run me over earlier today."

"Look, I ought to go. I'm sorry. This is all getting too much for me. I really need to get away, back to the kids. They've never been without me more than a night before."

Helgi's face appeared in the doorway. "Gunna. Ready for you. His lawyer's here."

"Give me a minute, Helgi. And hold on a moment, would you?"

Ursula's eyes shone as she held back tears, and Gunna sensed that this was more than simply missing home.

"What's happened, Ursula?" she asked in a low voice. "What's gone wrong?"

Ursula shook her head and Gunna beckoned to Helgi.

"Helgi, this lady's having a rough time. Could you take her to the canteen and give her something to eat? I'll be as quick as I can with our friend upstairs."

Helgi pulled a tissue from his jacket pocket and handed it to Ursula, who blew her nose.

"In fact, maybe you'd like to take her to see Ívar Laxdal," Gunna added, and saw Helgi flinch at the prospect.

"Who's that?" Ursula asked.

"Ívar Laxdal? He's the man we all walk in fear of, all the days of our lives," Helgi intoned.

"But it seems he's a keen art lover and an admirer of your stepfather's work," Gunna said. "So I don't doubt he'd be delighted to meet you."

Ellert Ásgrímsson sat slouched in a chair, one hand supporting his head as if it were too heavy to stay up of its own accord. Gunna said nothing as she set the computer to record. Eiríkur sat by the door, his face a mask of severity. Gunna was pleased to see the lawyer was an elderly man she had encountered often enough before, and he shook her hand before sitting down to scan a folder of notes.

Gunna glared at Ellert.

"My name's Gunnhildur Gísladóttir and we met briefly earlier today. My colleague is Eiríkur Thór

Jónsson. Everything that happens in this room is recorded, sound and video. Understand?"

The young man grunted and shifted in his chair.

"I'll take that as a yes," Gunna said briskly. "You're Ellert Ásgrímsson?" she asked, rattling off his ten-digit national identification number from the pad in front of her and holding up a printout of his driving licence with a picture of a younger version of him on it.

Ellert grunted again.

"I'll take that as another yes. So where were you two nights ago?"

His eyes widened in surprise. "What?"

"You heard me. Where were you two nights ago, and what were you doing?"

"Excuse me," the lawyer interjected, stifling a yawn with limited success. "Is this relevant? What's it about?"

"It's about an attempted break-in where we identified your client's prints on the lock that he tried and failed to crack open. That's what it's about, until we move on to other things."

"I see," the lawyer said, and scratched his head. "There's proof?"

"His dabs. No question."

"Fine. Go on then. But we are getting to the matter in hand, aren't we?"

"The assault on a police officer?" Gunna asked. "Sure. But let's deal with this first."

"Assault?" Ellert squeaked. "Don't be so fucking stupid! I didn't see you there."

"Ah. So you can talk?"

"I didn't see you there, I swear."

"So that's why you sneaked out the back door when you heard me ring the doorbell at the front, and that's why you revved the bike as soon as you came round the corner?"

"Yeah. I mean, no."

"This is going to be fun, isn't it?" Gunna said wearily. "Look, assaulting a police officer isn't a trivial matter. I could ask our legal team to push for attempted murder, which would be what? Eight years, maybe out in four if you behave?"

"Officer, I'd prefer it if you refrained from speculation," the lawyer admonished with a twinkle in his eye that passed his client by, but Gunna could see that the damage had been done and Ellert's face had gone pale.

"As you prefer," she said as Ellert sat shell-shocked. "The assault on a police officer is something I'll come to in a minute. First I'd like to clear up this little matter of where our friend was two nights ago and why we were able to identify his dabs in a shed out by Hafravatn. After all, that's why I came knocking at his door earlier today and presumably why he was in such a hurry to disappear. Ellert?"

"I just wanted to have a look in there. That's all."

His voice was sulky and guarded, his face long, and Gunna could see that he was bewildered at having been identified.

"Let me get this right. You went for a drive up around Hafravatn and decided that you'd have a look at this place? Not just the house, I notice, but the shed behind it. How come? You didn't find yourself there by accident."

"Yeah. I went for a ride around."

"In the dark? So just for fun?"

"Yeah. Just for fun."

Gunna leaned forward on the desk that separated them and placed her elbows on it with her fists balled together under her chin as she looked at Ellert, unsure but defiant in front of her.

"When you were brought in here, you might remember that your personal effects were handed over. Right?"

"Yeah."

"Including your phone."

"Oh, right."

"Right now one of my colleagues is going through the contents of your phone, and in a while he's going to come up here and tell me exactly what he's found in it: pictures, texts, call records, all that kind of thing. Understand? So if you'd like to come clean right away, it's going to save us all a lot of trouble."

The lawyer nodded as he tapped his teeth with a ballpoint pen.

Ellert stared at him furiously.

"I thought you were on my side," he wailed.

"Could I have a few minutes to confer with my client?" the lawyer asked mildly.

"Sure. I'll go and get myself a coffee and see if my colleague upstairs has finished with your client's phone while you two have a chat," Gunna said. "Interview with Ellert Ásgrímsson suspended at 1420," she announced for the benefit of the recording. "Ten minutes, or do you want longer?"

Katla's hands trembled as she took a seat at the end of the table, sitting bolt upright. Her eyes blazed as she glared at Ingvar.

"Hæ," Ingvar said. "It's been a while. I suppose I ought to say sorry."

"Sorry?" Katla hissed, as if her voice had pent-up pressure behind it. "What the fuck are you doing here?"

Ingvar shrugged and zipped up his fleece.

"A final visit to Iceland. Don't worry. I won't be back."

Katla rattled her knuckles on the table and turned to Tekla.

"And you, how fucking dare you? How could you deceive me?"

"It's not as if there's any easy way to tell you she's been seeing her dead father, is there?" Ingvar said, cutting Tekla off before she could speak. "Don't blame her."

"Fuck . . . There's so much . . ." Katla lapsed into silence, biting her lip in fury. "I knew you were seeing some older man, but never in a million years could I have imagined it was this one."

"Like I said, don't blame the girl. I came and found her. She didn't go looking for me."

"You bastard," Katla snarled, making an effort to keep her voice down but failing to mask the venom. "I knew you couldn't be dead. I just hoped that you'd never show up again."

Ingvar grinned. He could see that a twitch had developed below Katla's left eye, a sign that in the past had been a precursor to flying crockery.

"I always wanted to say sorry," he said, "but I reckoned you'd be better off without me."

"I always knew you were alive somewhere after the bank account was cleaned out two days after you vanished. That was a fucking dirty trick, Ingvar."

"I didn't clean it out. I took half, left the rest for you," he replied smartly. "And there was plenty in there."

"You shit. And now you have the . . ." She spluttered, struggling to get the words out through her fury. "And now you turn up here . . ."

"She's my granddaughter as well."

"You lost all that. You put it all behind you when you walked out."

"One time, Katla. One time. That's all."

Ingvar's eyes flickered between Katla's face, her mouth, drawn into an angry twitching line, and the hand that trembled as it snaked towards the knife lying between two halves of a pastry. He caught her wrist, holding her arm in the air, the blunt blade pointing at him until her hand opened and the knife clattered to the floor.

The blood drained from Tekla's face as her eyes flashed between her parents, and she shrank back, hugging María Vala close.

"You arsehole!" Katla spat. "You bastard!"

"Come on. You've done well enough without me."

"All the shit you did . . . all those women . . ."

"And you didn't exactly keep it to yourself while I was at sea, did you?"

"Ingvar! You fucked the bridesmaid at my sister's wedding!"

There was an immediate silence as the few customers in the place looked up to see what was going on.

"Quiet," Ingvar snarled. "Keep it down, will you?"

Katla howled with fury and slumped back in her chair, cheeks wet with tears as she sobbed. Tekla deftly tucked a blanket around María Vala in the stroller as the manager came over and stood with an uncertain frown on his face.

"Is everything all right?"

"Everything's fine, thanks," Tekla told him.

"Because if there's any trouble, you see, I'll have to call the police," he said, as if in apology.

"No trouble," Tekla told him. "We're leaving anyway."

The man nodded, clearly relieved, and backed away, while Katla wiped her face with the end of her expensive scarf.

"Dad. Go," Tekla snapped. "Go now."

Ellert had a look on his face that didn't inspire confidence.

"Ellert Ásgrímsson interview resumed at 1445," Gunna said, looking at the clock on the wall behind Ellert and the lawyer. "Officers Gunnhildur Gísladóttir and Eiríkur Thór Jónsson present." She smiled broadly

227

at Ellert, gratified to see panic in his eyes. "Hafravatn. The night before last. Explain."

"Well . . ." he mumbled, then stopped, looking at his hands.

"Go on."

"My mate said he'd been asked to check something out and he'd split the cash with me if I'd drive because he's lost his licence."

"And what were you supposed to be looking for out there in the middle of the night?"

"I don't know. I was just the driver."

"Right," Gunna said. "All right, talk me through what you did up there and don't even try to bullshit me. I've caught you out already, don't forget."

"My mate wanted to go out there because he said he'd been asked to by some bloke. I drove and stayed outside when he went into the shed. That's all."

"The lookout man, were you?"

"Yeah. Sort of."

"Wonderful. Just like in the movies," Gunna said, and Ellert flushed. "I take it your mate picked the lock, did he? So it's strange that it's your prints that are on it. But you had nothing to do with the actual break-in? Is that what you're telling me?"

"Yeah. That's it."

Gunna took several sheets of paper from the folder in front of her and looked at them thoughtfully without allowing Ellert to see what was on them. She passed one to Eiríkur, who nodded appreciatively.

"In that case, maybe you can explain these messages we retrieved from your phone just now?"

Ellert looked stunned as Gunna laid them out on the desk.

"Your date of birth, two-five-zero-zero, isn't exactly an ideal code. Now, let's cut the crap and forget about this imaginary friend of yours, shall we? Who sent you up there?"

"Hermann?" Helgi said as he propped his phone between shoulder and chin. "Helgi Svavarsson, city police. We spoke earlier."

"You found the bastard yet, have you?"

"Well, let's say there's progress," Helgi said. "I've asked around the usual places and I'm fairly sure this can be wrapped up quickly."

"Really?" There was clear surprise in the man's voice.

"Yes, really. You have a crime number, so if you want to you can go ahead and make your insurance claim," Helgi said. "But if I were you, I'd hold on for a day or two."

"Why?"

"Just a hunch. I'll give you a call tomorrow and we'll see how things look. All right? Speak to you then."

He ended the call, sat up straight, nudged his computer from sleep and looked with a sinking heart at the long line of unread emails.

"Gunna?" he said after a few minutes of deleting and replying.

"Yes, young man?" she replied without looking up. "Burglary sorted out?"

"Yep, and more information from Denmark about the guy at the airport."

"And?"

"It looks very odd. Erik Petter Tallaksen, born in Hjørring. No criminal record and he hasn't been resident in Denmark for almost thirty years. Passport last renewed at the Danish embassy in Madrid six years ago."

"So he lives in Spain. What's odd about that?"

"Nothing. It's his picture that's odd," Helgi said. "Take a look."

Gunna stood behind him as Helgi flipped between documents on his screen.

"This is the guy at the airport. He's almost two metres tall and a good hundred kilos," he said, calling up another picture. "This is his passport photo. Same guy. And this . . ." he clicked again, "is his driving licence, issued when he was nineteen. Not the same man, is it?"

"There's thirty years between them," Gunna said, squinting at the screen. "Of course he looks different. The guy at the airport has a beard and a buzz cut, and in the old photo he's clean-shaven and has a really bad mullet."

"Yeah, but look at the nose and the shape of the chin," Helgi said. "That's not the same person. And look at this."

He clicked again, and a picture of a square-jawed man with sandy hair and moustache appeared.

"And this is?" Gunna said.

"This is Ingvar Sturlaugsson, a couple of years before he disappeared." He recalled the photo from the airport CCTV so the two were side by side. "And this is Ingvar today, calling himself Erik Petter Tallaksen. I knew I was right. The bastard's alive and well."

230

Everything about the snack bar was uncomfortable, from the too-loud rock music blaring from a tinny speaker to the plastic seats slightly too small for anyone younger than twelve.

"What a dump," Ingvar grunted. "Why here?"

"Because it's not far to walk, and I don't have much time," Tekla told him, lifting the bun on top of her burger to check the contents. "I don't eat this shit often, you know. But once in a while it's all right."

"You OK?" Ingvar asked.

Tekla sighed and chewed a chip.

"No. I'm not. Since you've been here it's been crazy. Mum's acting like she wants to kill someone. Einar's being really weird as well at the moment, so I don't know if he's picked up on some bad vibe, because I haven't said anything to him. Mum's watching me like a hawk. And I'm not sure you have a real idea of just how deep her anger and resentment go. You walked out, Dad. Rejected her and us. I can sort of forgive you, because I was just a kid at the time and hardly remember, but for her it's crystal clear."

"And she's frightened of what'll happen if I show up?"

"Of course. She's married to Valgeir now, and what happens if her long-lost husband reappears, alive and well?"

"She makes a decent living, doesn't she?"

"Between them I think they do all right. That shop of her does OK, but doesn't bring in a fortune. Why do you think I work at weekends? It's not because Mum's raking it in."

"You want me to help you out?"

Tekla's eyes flashed.

"Some kind of a millionaire, are you?"

"No. But I'm not broke either. I can help you out with money if you need it."

Tekla chewed and shook her head.

"It would feel wrong. Anyway, exams are over this year and I can work full time then."

"Not thinking of university?"

"Yeah. But in a year or two. When I know what I want to do."

"And what are you thinking?"

"Maybe the police, or the customs service."

"Really?"

"Sure. Why not? Modest pay, but no chance of being unemployed."

Ingvar toyed with his own burger. There was something about the smell of it that he didn't like, the gritty meat swathed in sauces and pickles to disguise the lack of flavour. He pushed it aside and munched the chips a few at a time.

"Let me know, won't you? I can help you. I'd like to help you, even though —"

"Even though you walked out on us?" Tekla said, and paused as she saw the twitch of suppressed anger on his face. "Talk about something else, won't you?"

"I'd really like you to go and see Sturlaugur."

"And let him know you're alive?" Tekla shook her head. "Stulli couldn't keep a secret if his life depended on it. You might as well appear on TV and tell the world that way."

"He's that bad?"

"He used to be all right, after he came out of prison that first time and got himself straightened out. Not now. He's full of rage, and, like I told you before, most of it's directed against you."

Ingvar flinched.

"When do you think they'll let him out?"

"I don't know. He got fourteen years, and normally they serve about half of that. He's been on remand and then in prison for almost two years now. So another five, maybe. Mum wants to push for a retrial, says he was fitted up and that there's other evidence out there that could prove Stulli was there but didn't commit the murder."

Ingvar leaned forward as Tekla dropped her voice.

"Like what?"

"There were three people present. Veigar Ólafsson, who was the victim, Stulli and a guy called Aron. There were a dozen different fingerprints on the knife, including Stulli's. But not Aron's, and Stulli told Mum that was because Aron wore gloves. Aron was the killer. Sturlaugur was the one who got the blame for it."

Ingvar felt his heart sink.

"So . . . it would mean persuading this Aron to confess?"

"Yeah, that would have been the idea. Not that he ever would have," Tekla said. "But that's not an option now, because Aron died in a house fire the other night. So now the only one who knows the truth is Sturlaugur."

★ ★ ★

233

Helgi knocked, but didn't bother to wait. Arnar Geir looked up from the laptop on the desk in front of him, clearly holding back from an angry response.

"I'm just after a few minutes of your time," Helgi said, sitting himself down in the leather chair that faced Arnar Geir's desk.

"Right. What can I do for you?" Arnar Geir said suavely, closing his laptop and checking his watch. "I have to be out of here in ten minutes."

"Your brother Ingvar is right here in Iceland. You know that as well as I do, so I'd appreciate it if you'd stop playing games."

"I don't know what you're talking about. Ingvar is dead." Arnar Geir looked pointedly at Helgi. "You know that as well as I do."

"We have images that place him at Keflavík a few days ago, arriving on a flight from Amsterdam," Helgi said, getting straight to the point. "No doubt, Addi. It's him. And if there's anyone he was going to keep in touch with after whatever vanishing act he was able to pull, it's you. You two were always close."

Helgi took the sheaf of printouts from his pocket and spread them like playing cards on the desk. He jabbed a finger at the screenshot of Ingvar from the arrivals hall at the airport.

"Are you telling me that's not Ingvar Sturlaugsson?"

Arnar Geir made a show of putting on a pair of glasses, first slowly polishing the lenses with a soft cloth before perching them on his nose.

"I have to admit there's a likeness," he said guardedly.

234

"So Ingvar has a double somewhere, does he? Sorry, too much of a coincidence."

Arnar Geir's face hardened as he busied himself slipping his laptop into a case.

"Look, I haven't seen Ingvar since a couple of weeks before he vanished in Thailand. You may believe he pulled some kind of stunt. I believe he's dead."

"So who is this guy?"

Helgi's forefinger stabbed down on the printout.

Arnar Geir shrugged.

"Search me. How should I know?"

Haddi had always been the toughest of the three of them, the one who could stare down a teacher or browbeat other youngsters with consummate ease. But this time he was sent head-first into the snow piled against the bus shelter, a booted foot planted firmly on his forearm so that he whined with pain and discomfort.

The second of the two men took Einar's arm with a deceptive firmness. There was nothing friendly about this, he realised with a sinking feeling.

"Einar, isn't it?" the man said in a soft voice. "I think you need to come with us."

"Who are you? The police?"

The man's eyes sparkled with amusement.

"Hear that?" he said to his friend, who was ignoring Haddi's whimpers. "He thinks we're the law."

"We are the law," the first man said, finally looking down at Haddi as if surprised to see a gangly teenager under his boot. "But we're not the police."

He shifted his foot and allowed Haddi to sit up, dazed, in the drift of dirty snow, then leaned over and glared at him.

"Listen, son. Your pal is coming with us for a few minutes. There's nothing to worry about, as long as you sit there and keep your mouth shut. We'll be right back."

Haddi nodded, holding his sore forearm in the other hand. Einar looked from one to the other of the two men. They were dressed the same, in dark clothes and black boots, hair cropped as short on their heads as it was on their faces. The differences were in the details. One had a white shirt beneath his leather jacket, the other a black singlet. One had a missing front tooth, the other a ring in one ear, all of which Einar took in instantly as he wondered what they wanted.

They left Haddi sitting in the snow as they shuffled Einar into an anonymous grey people carrier and pushed him into a seat. The man with the missing tooth sat behind the wheel and the car pulled away and cruised gently along the street. Einar looked up and found himself sitting next to the man with the ring in one ear and facing someone new: a short man in a smart overcoat buttoned over a scarf at his throat, with a truculent look on his long face.

"You're Einar, right?"

"Yeah."

"Sturlaugur's little brother, yeah?"

It finally dawned on Einar that these had to be friends of his big brother's, if friends was the right word. Suddenly he doubted that the guys his brother had looked up to were as cool and friendly as he had been told.

"Who's the big guy?"

"What?" Einar asked, frowning.

The man in the smart coat looked first saddened and then pained.

"There's someone been sticking his nose where it's not wanted, asking questions about your brother. Who is he?"

"I don't know anyone like that. Nobody's asked me anything."

The man nodded to his friend with the earring, who turned and put an arm around Einar's shoulders. He shrank away at the man's touch, and the grip tightened around him. With an alarming suddenness, the man's hand fastened itself firmly over his face, squeezing his nose and mouth. Einar struggled, his free arm flailing, as the man leaned sideways into him, pinning him against the door, unable to draw breath.

"That'll do," the man in the smart coat said at last, and the hand was released. Einar took shuddering gulps of air. "Now," the man said, his voice like that of a patient teacher dealing with an unruly troublemaker at the back of the class. "Let's try again."

"I don't know any big guy," Einar said. "Honest I don't."

The man nodded a second time, and this time Einar felt that he was about to black out by the time the hand across his face was removed.

"How about your old lady, any strange visitors?"

Einar was still gasping for breath, but he was able to shake his head.

"Your sister? Or Stulli's girl?"

"I don't know. I haven't seen anyone, and I'm not at home a lot."

Tears were running down his cheeks and he felt faint.

"If he knew anything, he'd have told us by now," the man with the earring said gently.

The man in the coat nodded.

"Take him back where we found him," he said, speaking over their heads to the driver, and Einar made himself as insignificant as he could in the corner of the people carrier.

"Ari here is going to give you a phone number," the man in the coat said, leaning forward as the car drew to a halt by the bus stop, where Haddi still sat in a daze. "The second someone asks a question about your brother, asks how he is, where he is, how he's doing, who his friends are, anything like that, you're going to give Ari a call and let him know. Understood?"

The door slid open and Einar felt the fresh outside chill on his damp cheeks.

"Yeah. Understood."

A square of cardboard was slipped into his pocket.

"There. Don't lose it."

"I won't."

"Good, now get out."

Einar felt himself propelled out of the car. He narrowly managed to stop himself sprawling on the icy pavement, but clattered into the bus shelter. The people carrier was already disappearing around the corner before its side door had even slid fully shut.

Gunna zipped up her coat and peered through the narrow window in the door at the wind whipping up snow in the street outside. A gritting lorry rumbled past, spitting gravel onto the road as it made its way towards the old bus station at Hlemmur, which had now become a food hall, while the handful of street people who had previously used the place as a daytime hangout had dispersed around the city.

She shivered. On the other side of the road, a lonely figure sat hunched on a bench outside the food hall, only a pair of watchful eyes visible in the narrow gap between the collar of his shabby coat and a woollen hat pulled low. Gunna hoped that Siddi had somewhere to go that night.

The lift hissed open and Ursula appeared, a head taller than Ívar Laxdal, who stalked at her side towards Gunna.

"It's been a pleasure to meet you," he said, and Gunna wondered if he was slightly star-struck. "I hope Gunnhildur has been able to make things as painless as possible while you're here."

"She has," Ursula said. "She's been great. It's almost a shame I have to go home. But, you know. Small children."

Ívar Laxdal nodded.

"If there's anything . . ." he said, and hesitated. "If there's anything I can do to help with your stepfather's estate, please feel free to call me." He handed her a card, and Gunna watched in astonishment. "That's my personal number on there. You can reach me at any time."

"Thank you. And if you're ever in Gothenburg, it would be lovely to see you," Ursula said. She glanced at Gunna. "You're waiting for me?"

"We ought to be going," Gunna said.

"I take it you'll look after Ursula?" Ívar Laxdal said, extending a hand for her to shake.

"I will, don't worry."

"Terrible weather," he grunted, and turned to head back to the lift. "Remember. Give me a call if there's anything I can do."

Gunna waited for the lift door to close behind him.

"You're honoured, you know," she said. "I don't have his personal number, and I've been working with him for almost ten years now."

"He's a real admirer," Ursula said. "You meet them now and again. He knows more about Áskell's work than I do."

"Ívar's a very decent guy, even though half the people here are scared stiff of him. You can take him at his word, you know. If he said he's happy to help, then he really means it."

Ursula sighed. She looked tired.

"Where now?"

"Well, I'll have to take you back to the guest house now, as I'm on duty until six. I'll tell you what, if you don't have anything else to do, I'll collect you when I'm finished and you can come to my place this evening. My guy's cooking, so it'll be worth it."

240

"Thanks . . . That would be lovely. I'm flying home early in the morning."

"There's a severe weather warning this evening and it looks like there'll be road closures and flight delays. I live not far from the airport, so how about you stay the night and I'll drop you off for your flight in the morning?"

"You need to disappear," Arnar Geir said as he dropped into the passenger seat. He shivered and slammed the door. "Again."

Ingvar stared into the snow falling in the darkness. In the lights of the buildings across the street he could see drifts piling up, and people bundled in coats and hats trudged along the muddy pathways that feet had made in the white covering.

"I'll see if I can get a flight tonight," he said, still shaken by his encounter with Katla. "You were right. I should have known better."

Arnar Geir pulled off his woollen hat and ran a hand through his hair, sweeping it back from his forehead.

"No you won't," he said gloomily. "You're not going to like this, but they're on to you."

Ingvar turned and stared.

"What?"

"They're looking for you. Believe me, the last place you want to show your face is an airport."

"How do you know?"

"I've had a couple of visits from the police. You remember I told you Helgi Svavars had been to see me? Well, he was in again today."

Ingvar's brow furrowed as he scowled.

"All right. And what does he know?"

"I reckon more than he's letting on," Arnar Geir said with a sigh, shifting in his seat and unbuttoning his coat. "He has a couple of CCTV pictures of you going through immigration at Keflavík. He reckons it's you, but he doesn't have any concrete proof. If he has pictures, then he'll be able to figure out which flight you were on, and that means he can see a passenger list. So there's a good chance he'll be able to work out that you're the mysterious Mr Tallaksen."

"You're sure it's me?"

"Ingvar, he showed me the pictures. Take my word for it. It's you."

"So I'm fucked."

"Not yet. But you're going back to your hotel right now and checking out. And you're going to make a song and dance about how you've had some bad news so you're getting the first flight to wherever; just say anything that'll help put them off the trail."

Ingvar switched on the engine and turned on the heater, rubbing his hands.

"And then what? I'm not staying with you."

"No chance. A prospective Member of Parliament can't be seen to be consorting with the dead." Arnar Geir grinned and fumbled in a pocket of the jacket under his heavy overcoat. He handed across a sheet of paper, roughly torn in two.

"That's where you're going. It's a cheap guest house. Don't check in until after five." He tapped at the sheet of paper. "All the staff will have left by then, so you use

242

that code to get in, and the room key will be in the door. In any case, the staff are all foreigners who won't have heard of the disappearing Ingvar Sturlaugsson. All the same, keep your head down. It's booked for five nights, but hopefully you won't need them all if we can find a way to sneak you back to Spain somehow."

"Fucking hell," Ingvar snarled to himself. He pounded the steering wheel with the palm of one hand. "What are you doing now?"

"Me? I'm going to walk back to City Hall. Then I'm going to go and see if I can head your wife off at the pass." Arnar Geir pulled on his woollen hat and buttoned his coat. "Y'know. Just in case."

The taxi came to a halt at the corner.

"This is as far as I'm going," the driver said, pointing along the street. "That road's not been cleared and I'm not getting stuck in the snow."

"You must be a city boy if you're frightened of a couple of inches of snow," Arnar Geir said, handing over some notes.

The man shook his head.

"I'm from up west so I know what snow looks like, thank you very much. But this old heap's not on nails, so I'm not risking it."

"Fair enough," Arnar Geir agreed and stepped out into the darkness.

Flakes swirled furiously in the pools of light cast by the street lamps as he strode through the ankle-deep snow. A scruffy grey 4x4 was parked outside the house. He walked up to the passenger window and tapped on the glass. The window opened a couple of inches and a face half covered with a scarf looked out.

"What brings you here, Inga?" Arnar Geir asked, peering inside so he could see the camera in her lap. "Some scandal in suburbia?"

"What's it to you?" the man behind the wheel asked, leaning over.

"Just concerned," Arnar Geir said blithely. "It's not every day you see Reykjavík's finest newshounds this far from the city centre."

"A tip-off," the girl with the camera said. "We were sent up here. Waiting for a call."

"That was Skúli, was it?"

"Skúli's off sick. This is for something Haukur heard. He sent us up here to wait for confirmation."

Arnar Geir nodded to himself.

"Listen. Let me tell you, there's no story. At least not tonight. You'd best get yourselves off home and call it a day, while the roads are still open."

The man behind the wheel narrowed his eyes, while the girl with the camera looked fearfully at the gathering snow.

"A lawyer telling me there's no story tells me there has to be a story," the man said. "We'll wait for Haukur to let us know. But thanks for your concern."

The window hissed shut.

Arnar Geir set off along the street, scrolling through the numbers on his phone as he walked until he found the one he was looking for. In the lee of the wind outside Katla's house he pressed the call button and there was an instant reply.

"Hey, Haukur," he said breezily. "How goes it?"

"Not bad. What can I do for you? Something you want to whisper to me?"

The journalist's voice crackled in his ear, drowning out the moaning wind.

"Not exactly. Listen, I just ran into a couple of your guys parked up at the back end of Asparsel, freezing themselves to death."

"Ah," Haukur said, and paused. "Not far from where your sister-in-law lives, you mean?"

"That's it. Can you do me a favour and call them off?"

"Any particular reason?" There was a harsh new note of suspicion in Haukur's voice. "Do I owe you any favours?"

"Maybe not," Arnar Geir said. "But I'm sure it could be arranged."

Ingvar slid his key card across the desk and the receptionist looked up enquiringly.

"A change of plans, I'm afraid," he said. "Something's come up and I need to get home right away."

"I'm sorry to hear that, Mr Tallaksen," the girl said smoothly, tapping at a keyboard. "I'm afraid it's after seven, so I'll have to charge you for tonight as well."

He slid a credit card across the desk.

"Of course. It's not a problem."

"Not bad news, I hope?" she said, slotting his card into a reader and handing it back for him to punch in his PIN.

245

"Not good. A serious illness in the family, so I need to be there as soon as I can."

"You're flying tonight?" she asked in surprise.

"Early tomorrow. The first flight I could get."

The girl looked dubious and her keyboard clattered again.

"You might find there are delays. There's been a severe weather warning and a lot of this evening's flights have been cancelled," she said, squinting at her screen.

Ingvar shrugged and sighed.

"You're going to the airport now?"

"That's the idea. I've booked a room at the airport hotel, so I can just walk over there in the morning and find out how things are looking."

"That's a smart move," the girl said. "There's a weather warning for the road out to the airport too, so it might be closed soon."

"I'll have to chance it in that case," Ingvar said, shouldering his bag and folding up the collar of his coat. "It's a cold night for travelling."

"It is," the girl agreed. "This is unusual. I hope it won't be like this next time you come to Iceland."

Ingvar grinned.

"I'll come in summer next time."

The *Spotlight* intro rolled and Gunna put her phone down.

"Steini!" she called out. "It's starting!"

As the studio and three figures appeared, Gunna immediately recognised Laufey's silhouette against the backdrop.

"Activism for a worthwhile cause, or economic vandalism for its own sake?" the sharp-suited, neatly goateed presenter suggested, looking into the camera as he squared sheets of paper in his hands. "Our guests today are from opposite ends of the spectrum. We have Moderate Alliance chairman Vilberg Sveinsson, described as Iceland's foremost climate change denier, and environmental activist Laufey Oddbjörg Ragnarsdóttir, who made a strong impression speaking after yesterday's protest outside the Chinese Embassy here in Reykjavík. First I'd like to —"

"If you don't mind," Vilberg broke in, his chin already jutting angrily forward. "I resent being described as a climate change denier. My opinion is that climate change may well be taking place, although to my mind that hasn't been proved conclusively. My position is that changes in the climate are not necessarily due to human activity, nor for that matter are they anything to be unduly concerned about. If you must, you can call me a sceptic, not a denier."

He sat back in his chair, shoulders back and arms folded in challenge as he glared at Laufey.

"I was going to say," the presenter went on smoothly, as if the interruption had been a mere technical glitch, "Laufey, you and your associates were very vocal yesterday outside the Chinese Embassy and you made some startling statements. Would you like to clarify these? You mentioned that time is running out, for instance."

Laufey nodded sagely and Gunna felt a surge of pride.

"For some of us, it's already too late," she said, speaking in measured tones. "There are island nations in the Pacific and Indian Oceans that are in the process of disappearing already, and those islands' inhabitants are set to become the first climate refugees." She glanced at the other guest. "With respect to Vilberg's opinions," she continued in a tone that implied no respect whatever, "time has already run out. We are already seeing concrete effects of climate change taking place, which makes it very difficult to deny that this is happening. I can also cite changes in weather patterns, the reduction in polar ice coverage —"

"When I was a boy, winter started in September and stayed with us until Easter, and we had six months of knee-deep snow," Vilberg snorted. "So I'd be inclined not to complain about winters that are a little warmer than they used to be."

"Certainly, and I think this demonstrates my point," Laufey shot back at him. "You're from a fishing region, Vilberg; I'm sure you'll appreciate that the changes are already having far-reaching effects on your constituents. There was no capelin fishery last year, and this year's looks unlikely too. This doesn't appear to be because of a shortage of capelin, but their migration patterns are shifting away from our waters. Are you telling me that this isn't a concern?"

"Of course it's a concern," he said, sitting back and hoisting his folded arms even higher. "But this is the natural way of things. One species moves on, another takes its place. In a few years we'll be fishing sardines and anchovies off Selvogur."

"Laufey, is that the case? Is the environmental movement as a whole guilty of scaremongering?" the presenter broke in with a glance at Vilberg.

"I don't see exactly what Vilberg and I are arguing about. He seems to accept that climate change is in fact taking place and that it will have some extensive consequences: species shift, rising sea levels, desertification and more. As far as I can see, we agree on everything but the cause of the change."

Vilberg opened his mouth and his face turned a shade redder before the presenter again cut in.

"So the key issue is how to respond, rather than arguing about the origins of climate change?" he suggested, looking over at Vilberg, but Laufey beat him to it and Gunna found herself hunched on the edge of her seat, reminding herself to breathe.

"The reality is that the reasons for climate change are highly significant," Laufey said. "They tell us where we've been going wrong and what needs to change."

"Such as what?" the presenter asked.

"To start with, a realistic carbon tax without easy opt-outs. An end to coal-fired power stations around the world — it's completely scandalous that these are still being built in some places. Realistic subsidies for green energy; that's solar, wind and tide."

"We have to adapt," Vilberg said, visibly agitated as his arms unfolded and he slapped the desk in front of him. "There are colossal advantages to be had from a climate that's a couple of degrees warmer. It's something to be welcomed."

"Welcomed?" Laufey retorted. "Tell that to the island people already losing their homes, and the millions who will be displaced when half of South East Asia is under water. The migrations we have seen as a result of conflict in the Middle East are going to be small potatoes in comparison. Do you have suggestions as to where these people can all go or what they are going to live on?"

"Of course there are challenges, but these can all be met," Vilberg replied.

"What you mean is that these people are collateral damage?"

"I'm sorry, young lady, but you and your sort are deluded if you continue to think that this is a disaster in the making. Stop trying to save the planet, will you? Embrace what can't be changed and take advantage of it."

"I assure you," Laufey said, glaring at him for a second as Gunna held her breath, "saving the planet is pretty much at the bottom of our list of priorities."

"There, you see," Vilberg shot back with a smug look on his face. "Opportunism, self-publicity. That's what this is all about."

"Laufey, is that correct?" the presenter said, a quizzical look on his face. "Isn't the health of the planet the key issue at stake?"

Gunna watched as Laufey fixed the presenter with the steely look she knew so well.

"No. The planet's health isn't the issue here," she said, and paused just long enough for effect. "Earth will be absolutely fine. We haven't done any damage nature can't fix, if you look at things in a geological time frame. But humans are a remarkably delicate species that requires some very particular conditions in order to survive. We don't have to change a lot before this planet becomes uninhabitable, and when we're gone, after a few millennia and an ice age or two, it'll be as if we were never here. The planet will be fine. It's humans who need saving."

She delivered her words with an understated emphasis that left the presenter at a moment's loss, before he turned back to his other guest.

"Vilberg, we're almost out of time. Your final word?"

"Pure, unadulterated speculation," Vilberg said. "I —"

"Based on the best available science," Laufey broke in.

"And that's all we have time for," the presenter said, quickly silencing them both. "I'd like to thank my guests Vilberg Sveinsson and Laufey Oddbjörg Ragnarsdóttir, and over to my colleague Erlendur."

He looked to one side as an almost identical young man appeared on the screen, and Steini quickly turned down the volume.

"Wow. Powerful stuff," he said in admiration.

"So are you going to go out and buy an electric car now?" Gunna asked.

"I'll tell you what, I'm not far off being convinced."

Arnar Geir had never much liked his sister-in-law, but he had always admired her and saw precisely what had attracted his brother.

He sat on a stool with one ankle resting on the other knee, his back against the wall, and carried on admiring her. Katla had looked after herself, he reflected. She had been stunning back when she had married Ingvar. Now, closer to fifty than forty, she was no less fascinating, but the innocent exuberance of her younger self had been replaced by a confidence she had made herself develop, and which could be abrasive when she failed to keep herself in check — especially if there was a drink in her hand.

"You knew, didn't you?" she rasped, glaring at him.

Arnar Geir nodded.

"Sure I knew, but not right away," he lied. "It was only a couple of years ago that he got in touch, just after our mother died. Up until then, I didn't know anything."

Katla slopped wine into a tumbler and gulped.

"So where does he live now?"

"I don't ask. Didn't you suspect he was alive? Didn't you hear anything from him?"

"Not a word," Katla said, running her hands through her mane of blonde hair so that it fell around her face. She looked up at Arnar Geir with narrowed eyes. "But I knew, yeah."

"How?"

"He cleaned out our savings account a few days after the tsunami."

"And you never said anything?"

She shook her head.

"It wasn't until at least a month later that I remembered to check it. A pile of money was taken out just before New Year. The only other person with access was Ingvar. So I took out the rest and closed the account." She reached for the wine bottle again.

"So you knew all along?"

"Let's say I had a strong suspicion, and kept it to myself. Anyway, why are you here? Why has the hotshot lawyer-politician come to see me now? It's not as if you didn't know where to find us."

"I always had the impression that you didn't want anything to do with Ingvar's family any more, especially after your new guy came along," Arnar Geir said. "Although I gather he wasn't exactly new, was he?"

"Yeah," Katla sighed. "It's awkward, I suppose." She poured more wine, and gestured with the bottle to Arnar Geir, who shook his head. "Come on. Why are you here?"

"I was wondering how come a couple of hacks were hanging around outside. A sniff of something that might make news?"

Katla sat up and her face twisted into a frown.

"Who I talk to is my business."

"Sure it is. But there are people it's not a great idea to share secrets with," Arnar Geir said. "In any case, I thought you'd prefer to be left alone, so I told them there was no story to be had and sent them on their way."

"Fuck you, Addi," Katla spat, banging her glass down on the table. "Who do you think you are, shoving your nose into my business?"

Arnar Geir leaned forward and concentrated on holding her eyes.

"I'm your brother-in-law, and I have both your and my brother's interests at heart," he said in a voice that managed to combine velvet with underlying steel. "I'm concerned that if you're going to go to your friends in the media, who are nobody's friends but their own, you need to tread extremely carefully."

"You mind your own business and I'll mind mine."

Katla poured half a glass and knocked it back quickly.

"As I say, I've nothing but your best interests at heart," Arnar Geir continued. "So I'd hate to see you turned out of this house after all these years."

"What the hell are you talking about?" Katla demanded once she had stifled the bout of coughing that shook her for half a minute.

"Look," he said, slowly getting to his feet, "Ingvar disappeared all those years ago and you were left pretty comfortable. Just suppose that someone finds out he's not at the bottom of the Indian Ocean after all, but living a quiet, comfortable life somewhere. Do you really think the insurance company that stumped up to pay off the house is just going to shrug it off?"

He paused and watched Katla's eyes widen.

"I . . . I . . ." she stammered. "But it was years ago. Surely they wouldn't after all this time?"

"Believe me, they would. I've acted for insurance companies in the past and I can assure you that these people are not running charities. If they think they've been swindled, they'll want their money back." Arnar Geir paused a moment to let his words sink in. "They'll make sure they get their money back, every single penny of it, plus interest. They'll take everything you have, and turning you out into the street won't lose them a moment's sleep. So maybe you'd better think long and hard before you open your mouth, especially if it turns out that you suspected your husband wasn't dead all along," he said, his voice soft but clear. "I'll see myself out."

Gunna poured the last of the wine.

"Guys who can cook are great, aren't they?" Ursula said, glancing at where Steini lay stretched out on the sofa, a book splayed across his chest where it had dropped as he fell asleep.

"Shh. He might hear you," Gunna said. "It's been a long day for both of us."

"Cheers," Ursula said, lifting her glass. "Your daughter is fantastic, and it's really kind of you both to let me use her room, otherwise I'd have had to get a taxi at four in the morning to catch my flight."

"And you might not have made it anyway. The weather's been appalling these last few days and there's a good chance the road out of the city will be closed to traffic tonight." Gunna paused and they could hear the moaning of the wind outside. Snow had piled against the back door and window, and Steini had spent most of the day at the controls of a digger, clearing Hvalvík's streets. "Laufey's staying in Reykjavík tonight, so it's no problem for you to use her room."

"You have just the one?"

"I have a son as well. He lives not far from here with his girlfriend. He's a seaman, and considering the weather, I have to confess I was massively relieved when I knew that his ship is docking tonight. That'll be his last trip for a while, as there's an addition to the family on its way in a few weeks."

As Steini slumbered, Gunna dimmed the living room lights, leaving just the dining table in a pool of light.

"You said on the day I arrived that you're from the west of Iceland as well and that you remember my mother," Ursula said, swirling the wine in her glass. "What do you remember about her? Did you meet her, have anything to do with her?"

"No, not really. In these small places everyone knows who everyone else is, even though you might spend a lifetime in the same village and never actually speak. I remember her working in the Co-op in Vestureyri, and that must have been not all that long before she left. She didn't look happy, as far as I recall."

"There must have been gossip about that, surely?"

"Naturally," Gunna said, with a trace of bitterness. "There's always small-town gossip flying around and it doesn't have to be based on any kind of reality. I had the same when my son was on the way, and he's only a few years younger than you. To be honest with you, I had to get out. That's one of the reasons I made the move down here. So I sympathise with Birna completely. But I was a little too young to be all that interested in whatever scandal people had dreamed up about her at the time." She sipped her wine thoughtfully. "What triggered the gossip was that she refused to name your father. The local scandalmongers wanted sordid detail, so you can imagine how much speculation went on."

"Villi," Ursula said. "That's all I know. One time when she had put away half a bottle of wine, I pestered her about all this, asking why she had left Ósvík and gone to live in Sweden instead, and she said something about someone called Villi. *It's all because of that arsehole Villi*, she said, and she seemed to think it was funny. So I'm guessing that might have been his name. That's all."

"I've no idea who that might be," Gunna said. "You haven't tried to find out?"

Ursula finished the last drops of wine in her glass.

"Not yet. Maybe I will one day. When it feels right."

CHAPTER
SIX

Strong northerly wind, possibly gusting gale force. Some cloud cover. Isolated snowfalls during the day, possible widespread snow overnight. Widespread sub-zero temperatures, dropping to — 5°C overnight.

The road was surprisingly clear by the time Gunna reached the city, an hour earlier than usual. She had dropped Ursula off at the airport, where the sight of the milling crowd inside the terminal made her heart sink.

"It'll be fine," Ursula said, looking glum. "If there's a delay, I'll just have to sit it out."

"Call me if you're stuck," Gunna had made her promise. "Let's hope you get home. But I'll be in touch when I have something to tell you."

The storm had dropped from its furious overnight howl to a stiff wind from the north, but the snow had stopped falling and the main roads through the city had already been cleared and gritted as she drove through what had come to feel like permanent roadworks to the old harbour.

She slapped Matti's shoulder in the harbourside café that had become increasingly gentrified but which at this time of the morning was still a magnet for dockers and taxi drivers.

"G'day, cousin Matti. How's life?"

He looked up from the sandwich he had been making progress on as he leafed through a two-day-old newspaper.

"Cousin Gunna. Not bad. And you? Keeping the streets safe from rogues and villains?" He handed her his mug. "If you're getting yourself a coffee, you can get me a refill at the same time."

Gunna placed two mugs on the table and slipped off her coat to hang it on the back of her chair.

"What can I do for you?" Matti asked with mock suspicion.

"Just thought I'd see how my favourite cousin is," Gunna said from behind her mug.

"Get away with you."

"There is one thing," she said.

"I knew it. It could hardly be a social call. What are you after?"

"Gossip," Gunna said. "Small-town scandal, the kind that our beloved mothers are so fond of."

Matti shuddered.

"You'd find yourself in court if you repeated some of the stuff they used to come out with — and probably still do for all I know."

Gunna tapped the table with a forefinger.

"You're a few years older than me. You remember Birna Bergthórsdóttir? Bergthór Bjartmarsson's daughter?"

"From Ósvík? Hair red like a fire engine?"

"That's her."

"What happened to her?"

"She died. A few years ago."

"Something you're snooping into, cousin Gunna?"

"Let's say I'm taking an interest. I'm looking for a Villi from Ósvík, someone she might have had something to do with."

Matti sat back and chewed the final remnant of his sandwich.

"Only one man that can be," he said with satisfaction.

"Go on. Spill the beans."

"You young people . . ." he gloated. "Villi can't be anyone other than the highly respected former mayor of Ósvík, surely. Birna worked for him for a while, and then left town suddenly. You could always give your mother a call and ask her."

It was Gunna's turn to shudder.

The twelfth hotel had been the one, to Helgi's relief. The man could just as easily have rented an apartment for his stay in Iceland, but somehow he had been sure that Ingvar Sturlaugsson would want to be somewhere central, as well as in a place where he wouldn't have to fix his own breakfast.

Even better, it was within walking distance of the Hverfisgata police headquarters. Helgi trudged through the snow that had piled up overnight. The wind had dropped towards dawn and the snow had stopped falling, so the ploughs had been out since long before daybreak to clear the main roads through the city.

He shoved open the door, hearing it grind in the gravel that had collected on the floor instead of swishing across smooth tiles, and a young man in a suit looked up and gave him a welcoming smile.

"Morning," Helgi said, stamping snow from his shoes. "Pétur?"

"That's me. You're the policeman?"

"Helgi Svavarsson." He unbuttoned his coat and took out the printout he had been carrying around. "This guy. Erik Petter Tallaksen. He's staying here?"

Pétur shook his head sadly.

"I'm sorry, but he checked out last night."

"Shit," Helgi grunted to himself, in disappointment but not surprise. "When?" He looked up at the electronic eye that scanned the lobby. "CCTV?" he said hopefully.

He watched the jerky replay of Erik Petter Tallaksen sliding a credit card across the desk to the receptionist, and noted the time stamp on the recording.

"There's no sound on this, is there? Just images?"

"That's right."

Helgi pointed at the screen.

"The girl behind the desk. Is she at work?"

"That's Sunneva. Her shift ended at midnight. She's not on again until this afternoon."

"Where does she live?"

"I've really no idea," Pétur said stiffly.

"All right. I need to speak to her. It's urgent."

"Is this person dangerous?" Pétur asked, eyes widening.

"Not exactly dangerous, no. But it's urgent that we track him down."

Pétur took out a smartphone and tapped at the screen until it hummed to itself a few times and a sleepy voice answered.

"Hæ, Sunneva. It's Pétur here. I'm sorry to wake you up, but this is important. There's someone here who needs to talk to you."

"Good morning, Sunneva," Helgi said, taking the phone. "My name's Helgi Svavarsson and I'm a detective with the city police. I'm looking for Erik Petter Tallaksen, who was a guest at the hotel until last night. I understand he checked out. Is that right?"

"Yeah. About seven, I think it was."

"Seven twenty-five, according to the CCTV. I can see from the recording that you had a conversation with him."

"Has he done something? He seemed like a decent guy. Very polite."

"Did he say where he was going?"

"He said he was going home, but I didn't ask where he lives," Sunneva said with a yawn. "He was going out to the airport and had a flight this morning. Or that's what he said. So unless his flight was delayed, you might have already missed him."

"Just like the old days, Gunnhildur. A little fresh outside this morning," a jovial Ívar Laxdal said, stripping off his leather gloves and unbuttoning his coat. He hung up the black beret that had come with him to the police force all those years ago from his time in the Coast Guard.

"You mean closed roads, delayed flights, no post or newspapers for a week and empty shelves in the shops?"

"It wasn't that bad, surely?"

"Maybe not for city types, but for those of us who lived in rural backwaters, that's exactly what it used to be like."

"I know, Gunnhildur," he said gently. "I have been outside 101 once or twice."

"About Áskell Hafberg, and more to the point about Birna Bergthórsdóttir . . ." Gunna began.

"Yes. Ursula got to the airport, did she? Remarkable young woman, very knowledgeable."

"I dropped her off there, and that's more or less what she said about you as well."

"She did?"

Ívar Laxdal looked visibly pleased and Gunna wondered if she had ever seen him so clearly taken by surprise.

"She did, yes," she assured him. "I think you'd be welcome in Gothenburg."

"What do you have to tell me? Something stinks, otherwise you wouldn't be here."

Gunna took a deep breath and wondered where to start.

"I suspect that Ursula is the result of an affair between Birna and the Moderate Alliance guy, Vilberg Sveinsson. One of Vilberg's main political allies is Arnar Geir Sturlaugsson, who was present at the house at Hafravatn when Birna died. This is according to Arnar

Geir's ex-wife, who appears to be either frightened or withholding more information, or both."

Ívar Laxdal's eyebrows lifted.

"And? Vilberg's star is rising. A dangerous man."

"Arnar Geir's frightened. Helgi has him cornered over this business with his brother, the one who disappeared all those years ago."

"And what do you want me to do?"

"Nothing," Gunna said. "Let's see what Arnar Geir has to say when he appears. It's possible that he may have been responsible for Birna's death, or . . ." She fell silent for a moment.

"Or what?" Ívar Laxdal prompted.

"It could have been done deliberately to kill a scandal that could hit Vilberg and both of their political ambitions. On the other hand, I came across some video footage shot that night, and I'm fairly sure I know who drowned Birna. But there's some work to do to actually build a case that'll be strong enough for a prosecution."

"And Örlygur? Where does he fit into this?"

"This is where it really stinks. He ticked the boxes as quickly as he could, and put his feet up. I can't tell if this was because he's naturally lazy, or if there might be some other reason. If there's a link between Örlygur and the people behind the Moderate Alliance, then there'll be heaps of awkward questions to answer."

Gunna looked up and watched in bemusement as Helgi hurried in and sat at his computer, muttering to himself.

"Everything all right?" Eiríkur asked politely.

Phone at his ear, Helgi nodded quickly.

"Yeah, fine," he mumbled, listening to the dial tone. "Andri?" he snapped as the call was answered. "Listen, I want you to check some passenger lists for me. Can you do that? Tallaksen. Yeah, the guy I was asking about before. Call me back when you know, will you? Yeah, it's urgent. Thanks," he said, banging down the receiver.

"Helgi, what's the fuss?" Gunna asked.

"Ingvar Sturlaugsson. He's only been staying at Hotel Atlantic, right under our noses."

"But he's not there any longer?"

"Nope. Checked out and vanished last night." Helgi snatched at the phone as it rang. "Yes? That's right," he said, the pitch of his voice rising as he spoke, words tumbling out. "Look, grab him, pull him to one side. I don't care what you tell him. Don't let him get on the flight. I'll be there, don't you worry." He paused and listened. "Yes. Absolutely. Thanks, Andri. See you soon."

He put the phone down and sank back in his chair with a sigh of relief.

"And?" Gunna asked.

"He's on a flight to Copenhagen. Or so he thinks."

"So I imagine you're off to the airport?"

"Absolutely, not going to miss this one," Helgi said. "By the way, that break-in should be sorted out. With any luck, all the stolen property will be returned tonight, and we can drop that case."

"A word in someone's ear?"

"It's amazing how that can work sometimes," he said.

The place was spartan, very different from the plush hotel room he had left behind. It was also quiet, deserted all night apart from the occupant of Room 6.

Ingvar tapped his phone to check the time as he returned from the shower along the hall, and saw that by now there should be some staff in the place, though nobody had yet shown up.

He pored over his iPad at the minimalist desk in his room, an idea starting to form in his mind as he went through a very long list of contacts. His burner phone ringing startled him. He grunted into it as he answered.

"Yeah?"

"Hæ, Dad. Tekla."

"Hi. Sorry, didn't mean to be abrupt with you. Didn't recognise the number."

"That's all right. Listen, what's going on? Uncle Addi was here last night. He stopped Mum from telling some journalist that you're alive and in Iceland, but it was close."

Ingvar's heart sank and he wanted to groan.

"What did she say?"

"I don't know, and there's no point asking her. I think she spoke to someone she knows at *Fréttablaðið* but didn't tell them the whole story, just that she had something to say."

"Right. And then Arnar Geir turned up?"

"Yeah, and told her to keep her mouth shut if she wants to stay out of trouble."

"You mean he threatened her?"

"Not exactly," Tekla said. "I didn't hear the whole thing, but he said that if anyone finds out that you're not dead after all, the insurance company that paid for the house is going to want its money back."

"I get it," Ingvar said, and wanted to laugh. "Appealing to her wallet is always the best argument with your mother."

"Really?" Tekla asked, her voice frosty. "Hey, you weren't here and didn't see all the shit she's gone through. It hasn't exactly been a bed of roses."

"You think I don't know? You imagine I haven't regretted the past and haven't thought about you all every single day?"

He heard Tekla sigh.

"Whatever. Look, Dad, this is stuff I'd really like to talk over with you when we have a chance. But right now we just need you out of the way again. Otherwise we're all going to be out on the street. That's me, Mum, Einar, Inga Lára and María Vala. Sturlaugur will be the only one of us with a secure roof over his head if someone finds you."

Gunna inspected the page and wondered where the photograph of Ragnar Sæmundsson had come from, while Laufey fumed quietly.

"It's absolutely intolerable," she muttered. "What does my dad have to do with any of this?"

A full inside page of the free-sheet paper was filled with an unflattering image of Laufey taken during the protest outside the Chinese Embassy, her mouth open in mid-speech. The headline read: *Eco-Firebrand's Father was Coast Guard Hero*.

Gunna guessed that the picture of Ragnar Sæmundsson had been lifted and enlarged from a group photograph. He was in uniform, his cap tilted as far back on his head as was acceptable, on his face the familiar cheeky smile that made her heart beat a little faster even now, almost twenty years after his death.

"'Environmental activist Laufey Ragnarsdóttir had a tough upbringing, raised in a single-parent family after her father, Ragnar Sæmundsson, was lost at sea when she was only a year old. One of the crew of Coast Guard ship *Ægir*, he died in a diving accident while working to clear the propeller of a merchant ship drifting towards the fearsome rocks of Garðsskagi in heavy weather. His loss has never been satisfactorily explained'," she read out. "Nothing new there that couldn't have been found on the internet, is there?" She sighed, spreading the paper out on the café table in front of her and sipping her coffee as she skimmed through the article. "Pleased to see they left my name out of it."

"They wouldn't dare put you in there," Laufey said.

"It wouldn't worry me a lot. I've been through all this before, after your father died. Although I was a bit numb back then and didn't really take it all in until afterwards."

"But what am I going to do about this?" Laufey asked.

"Do about it? There's not much you can do," Gunna said, closing the newspaper, folding it in half and passing it to her daughter. "I suppose you can try and manage how the press treat you. But this one's aimed at crusties who are adamant that a woman's place is shuttling between the washing machine and the stove, so they're giving their readers what they want to hear."

"Like Vilberg Sveinsson, you mean?"

"Exactly. Tell people what they want to hear and then blame someone else when you fail to deliver," Gunna said. "So what's he like? I've heard him on the radio and he sounds like a complete bigot. But he's been successful in local politics in the past, so I'm wondering if it's an act."

Laufey took a small sip of coffee and a large bite of Danish pastry as she nodded.

"He's no fool," she said. "We were in the green room before the interview and he was charming, intelligent, knowledgeable. He was even polite. But as soon as the cameras were on us he turned into a mad dog, coming out with all that crap he must know is bullshit."

"I thought as much."

Laufey opened the paper again. "Look, they even said that I'm a student politics radical and that I'm associated with a group of extremists," she said, and groaned.

"Don't worry too much about what the papers say about you. This'll be lining someone's cat litter tray before too long. But if you want to manage your image, you need to talk to the media, not wait for them to come to you or just let them make it up."

Laufey drained her fruit juice, yawned and stretched. "How, though?"

"Come on, it's not that hard." Gunna checked her phone, found a number and jotted it down on a corner of the newspaper's front page. "We have to do this sort of thing as well, although it's normally Ívar Laxdal who does the press stuff. This guy," she said, tapping the number with the end of her biro, "Skúli Snædal, works for *Reykjavík Voice*. Have a chat with him and tell him I sent you. He'll give you good advice."

"I'll do it when I get back," Laufey said.

"Going somewhere?"

"I've been asked to take part in a workshop with the Pirate Party that they're holding in Akureyri. There have even been hints of standing as a candidate at the next election." She dropped her voice and glanced from side to side. "Then the week after next, we're going to Amsterdam for the environmental conference, me and Finnur and a couple of others. There's a ferry from Seyðisfjörður to Denmark, and then we can get trains to Amsterdam. Looking forward to it."

"So you're going to be travelling with Finnur? I like him. He's a decent lad."

"Did you see this?" Laufey said with a frown, scanning the newspaper on the table between them. "In here they described him as my partner. Finnur. Good grief."

Gunna leaned forward to peer at the page.

"And isn't he?" she asked. "I mean, aren't you . . . ?"

"Mum." Laufey gave her a withering look. "I'm certain Finnur is gay. He's not interested."

"You're sure about that?" Gunna murmured, recalling the look of longing on Finnur's face as the group had finished making their banner in Steini's workshop. "I'm sure you could find out if you put your mind to it."

Helgi returned disconsolately to the control room and its row of screens. He had spent the last hour fruitlessly scouring the departure lounge and then studying the faces of passengers for the Copenhagen flight as they lined up for boarding.

"We could have stayed in here, you know," Andri told him gently, patting the top of a monitor. "We could have watched the whole thing without having to stand up."

"Hell and damnation," Helgi muttered to himself. "Damn. What went wrong? Why didn't he show?"

"What's he done, this guy? Anything serious?"

"Well, you could say that," Helgi said. "Let's say it's complicated. Now I'm wondering what he's playing at."

"How do you mean?"

"He booked a flight and checked in online a few minutes later, but didn't show up. So I'm wondering if there's some last-minute reason he didn't show, or did he book a flight and not catch it simply to lay a false trail?"

He shook his head in frustration.

"Ring him up and ask him," Andri suggested.

Helgi glared.

"What?"

"The airline will have a contact number. You have to provide a phone number when you book a ticket. So ring him up. Or just get comms to track the phone.

That way you'll know where he is and you can go and ask him yourself."

This was more like what he was used to, Ingvar decided as he drove through the industrial estate that had spread around the harbour. This was the side of his country that he knew best, away from the brasseries and tourist shops of the city centre that he had been surrounded by for the past few days.

Here he could smell the sea and hear the crash of forklifts and the idling of engines as he strode across the bare quayside, already scraped clear, its night-time covering of snow bulldozed into the black water of the dock.

He stopped to cast a critical eye over the squat bulk of the unlovely red-and-white trawler that lay at the quayside, and the steel wire being steadily spooled through a block hanging at its quarter.

"Hey," he said gruffly, choosing the youngest of the group of men in heavy padded overalls, smoking as they watched the wire inch its way on board from a machine on the far side of the quay.

"Yeah?"

"Is Bogi on board? Bogi Isaksen?"

"On the bridge. But hold on." The man muttered a few words into a handheld radio and listened to the reply. "He says who are you?"

"Tell him Ingo."

The man nodded and murmured again into his handset, then jerked a thumb at the gangway that lay at an alarmingly steep angle.

272

Ingvar took it three battered aluminium steps at a time, headed for the nearest door and followed the steps up to the wheelhouse.

"You look healthy for someone who's dead," the pot-bellied man leaning on a console by the aft window said, turning his head as Ingvar appeared.

"And you look good for someone who's been in the wheelhouse chair for the last twenty years."

"Good to see you," Bogi said, extending a hand and gripping Ingvar's in a grip that made him wince. "Is this a social call?"

"Not exactly."

"That's a shame. If it was, I'd offer you a drink. Except this is a dry ship, and I've been dry myself for a few years now. But there's coffee over there by the chart table."

Ingvar poured thick black coffee into a paper cup and sipped, looking around him.

"The ship's looking good."

"It is. Getting old, but steers good and tows well."

"Sailing tonight?"

"When the warps and the new trawl doors are on board. The cook's gone for stores. We're sailing when he's back."

"Greenland?"

"Yep. And landing in Fuglafjörður in four weeks."

"Good trip so far?"

"Not bad," Bogi said, fingers deep in his heavy beard as he thought, looking at Ingvar with curiosity. "I can't deny it's a pleasure to see you, Ingo, and I'd heard a

273

whisper you were still in one piece. But what can I do for you?"

"I need a way out of the country that doesn't mean going through an airport."

Bogi's eyes narrowed.

"Did you hurt someone, Ingo?" he asked in a soft voice. "I'm not asking your reasons. But did you do someone harm?"

Ingvar hesitated.

"My former wife and I hadn't been on good terms for a long time. Once the shock had passed, I reckon she was happy to see the back of me. Apart from that, no."

"You don't sound convinced."

"I made mistakes. And now I've made another one by coming back. I thought I might be able to help my son, but that was a mistake as well. I can't. Not yet, at least," Ingvar said. "So do you have room for a passenger?"

"It'll be a month."

"I can live with that."

"Or . . ." Bogi leaned forward to look down at the deck below. "You remember Níels? Níels Jøkladal?"

"Your cousin?"

He nodded.

"He's bringing the *Thule Star* in here this week to put their gear ashore on the way to refit in Hirtshals. I can ask him. He might have a spare bunk, and you'd be in Denmark in a few days."

It felt strange being the only one staying in this deserted guest house. He hunched over the white desk

274

built into the white wall, plugged in his iPad and waited for a reply.

Lizzie's face dissolved into pixels and reappeared, the image jerky as the picture failed to keep pace.

"Hi, when are you coming home?"

She looked tired, cheeks pale, hair pulled back from her face and drawn into an untidy plait. Ingvar felt a pang of concern.

"Soon, sweetheart."

"Are you all right?"

She got the question in first.

"I was going to ask you that," he said. "How are you feeling?"

"Sick," she said. "I haven't thrown up yet, but I want to."

"I'm sorry, I should be there with you."

"You should," Lizzie said, and coughed. "When are you coming back?"

"In the next few days, I hope. It shouldn't be long."

"Why can't you just get a flight today? You could be here tonight."

Ingvar paused with his mouth half open.

"It's complicated, sweetheart," he said eventually. "Some trouble to deal with."

He watched her frown.

"Trouble? What sort of trouble?"

It needed an answer that would take half the day, or none at all, he decided.

"It's all right. Some work stuff I need to sort out. But —"

"But what?" Lizzie snapped.

"Hey, back off, will you?" Ingvar protested. "Look, this is serious and I need to keep out of sight. You understand, darling? Otherwise I might not be coming home for a very long time."

"What have you done?" This time there was a new depth of concern in her voice. "Is this something illegal?"

"It's old stuff, but I need to deal with it. Once that's done, I'll be back and I won't be going anywhere."

"Are you sure, Erik? Do you mean that?"

"Sure. I won't need to go anywhere much. I'll just be getting the ferry over to Berbes and back, and the office is as far as I'm planning to travel. But listen." His voice dropped. "There's something I need you to do for me."

"Tell me. What?"

"If anyone comes looking for me, the police or anyone like that, I want you to tell them I'm in Africa. Tell them I've gone down to Dakhla to get one of the boats fixed up, and I'll be back in a week, ten days or so."

"Erik, what are you doing?" He watched Lizzie's eyes widen and then narrow in suspicion. "Why do you want me to lie for you?"

It had been easy enough to fix the phone's location, and what was interesting was that it wasn't moving.

In the evening gloom, Helgi threaded his way between the banks of snow on either side of the pavement.

"Still not moving?" he asked.

"No. Same position. And no calls," the voice coming through his communicator confirmed.

Helgi looked around at the battleship-grey concrete walls of the old-fashioned houses, and at the cars parked either side of the road.

"Hold on. I'm going to call it and see what happens," he said, tapping the number into his phone and holding it to his other ear.

"It's ringing," the voice from the communications section said.

"And nobody's answering," Helgi growled back.

It was the faint chirrup of a phone from a car parked a few metres away that alerted him. He strode over to the grey 4x4 and peered through the passenger window, shading his eyes with his free hand. The phone continued to trill, and he jammed his mobile between shoulder and ear as he played the light of a small torch through the window. An old-style phone with buttons flashed and buzzed in the footwell, and he felt a surge of triumph.

"Found it," he muttered into his communicator as he walked around to the front of the car. "Check BI-853 and give me the owner's details, will you?" he said.

There was a sticker in the rear window of the 4x4, and as he brushed snow from the glass, he made out the name and number of the car hire company before it was relayed by the control room to his earpiece. He called the number and waited for a reply.

"Hello? Hi, my name's Helgi Svavarsson and I'm a detective with the city police force. I'm looking for information on a grey Hyundai Santa Fe that's on your books," he said, reading out the registration again. "I need to know when was it rented and who by."

"Er, one moment, please," the voice on the line said, and he heard fragments of a whispered conversation.

"Hello?" A new voice spoke. "This is Magnús Pálsson and I'm the manager. You're from the police, you say?"

"That's right. Helgi Svavarsson, serious crime division. This Santa Fe, I need to know how long it's been rented and in whose name."

"I can't just give that information over the phone," Magnús Pálsson protested. "How do I know you're a police officer and not someone running some kind of scam?"

"You can either take my word for it right now — and I'd appreciate it if you did, as this is urgent," Helgi said, telling himself not to snap back in irritation. "Or else you can call four-forty-four-one-thousand and ask to be put through to Helgi Svavarsson. Or if you prefer, you can just call the emergency line, because it'll go through to the same place anyway. Up to you."

He could hear the man muttering and a mouse clicking, while cars rattled along the street in the afternoon gloom, their lights forming a kaleidoscope of converging beams as they passed by.

"OK," he heard Magnús Pálsson say at last. "It was rented on the eighteenth and it's due back a week today. The guy's name is Tallaksen. He's Danish."

"Thanks. That tells me what I needed to know," Helgi said. "You can see my number, can't you?"

"I can."

"Right, I need you to text me a contact number so I can call you out of hours, just in case we need to impound this vehicle. And tomorrow I'll be along to your office to pick up copies of the rental paperwork."

"Has this guy done a bunk?" Magnús asked in alarm.

"I've no idea," Helgi replied. "But for the moment your car is safe and well. I'll let you know."

After his conversation with Bogi in *Northern Pride*'s wheelhouse, Ingvar had abandoned caution and gone to Múlakaffi, leaving it until after the lunchtime rush of tradesmen with thirty minutes to wolf a plateful of food had subsided, where he had treated himself to old-fashioned fried fish and potatoes of the kind he hadn't tasted for years.

Lizzie's call had left him angry and restless, although his frustration was directed more at himself than at her waspishness. The girl was pregnant, he reminded himself with a sigh. It wasn't something he would have wanted, and he wondered how accidental it had been. All the same, it meant that now was the time to take stock and get a grip on things, to extricate himself as best he could from this mess he had managed to get himself into.

He shivered as he reminded himself that he had caused someone's death, although he told himself that it had been unintentional, on top of which Aron Stefánsson had been the one who had put his son behind bars. The bastard deserved it, he decided. The boy was no loss, although he felt a burning guilt at the anguish he must have caused Gréta.

He tapped his iPad into life and opened the ship-tracker app, nodding to himself as he saw that Bogi had sailed. The snub-nosed *Northern Pride* had left Reykjavík's Sund freight dock behind as it punched its way through the weather towards East Greenland. *Thule Star's* icon showed on the screen, which gave him a warm feeling. He could keep track of it, and with any luck he would be leaving Iceland behind him before long.

He felt a lurch in his belly as the thought came to him that this might be the last time he would come here, the last time he would see his own country. His one brief encounter with his granddaughter could turn out to be the only time they would meet.

Spending too much time alone, he told himself. It was time to get out, and to fill the empty hours with a long walk. He hoped there would be a chance to speak to Tekla before he left. If so, he would have to see her tonight. He reached for his jacket and went through the pockets, looking for the anonymous cheap phone with a local number. He found only the smartphone he had brought with him, and cursed himself for leaving the other phone in the car.

Outside on the street, he shivered. The pavement was crusted with snow that was hardening in the evening frost, turning the flagstones underfoot into sheets of ice. This was a busy part of town, and there had been no choice but to park in the next street. He stepped carefully, turned the corner and was about to click the fob of the car key in his pocket when instinct stopped him.

280

He could see the 4x4 slotted neatly into a bay by the kerb. Someone was standing by it, shining a torch through a window, scanning the interior.

Ingvar crossed the street, taking his time, keeping as far as he could out of the glare of the street lamps as he acted as if he were simply walking past. He pulled on his woollen hat and tugged it low over his eyes, and when he felt it was safe, he turned and watched to see who was showing such an interest in the car.

As the man straightened his back and looked around, Ingvar felt there was something familiar about him. Helgi from Efstibær, he realised. This was Helgi who had been at school with his older brother's sons all those years ago, the same Helgi who had spent years as one of the Blönduós coppers with the uncanny knack of appearing at the side of the road with a speed camera where they were least expected.

Now Helgi Svavarsson from Efstibær was taking photographs of the car before walking along the street with his phone to his ear.

Helgi dropped into his chair. After only a few days back at work, he already felt as tired as he had been before he had gone on holiday.

"The car's parked on Baronsstígur. The phone's inside."

"You're not impounding it?" Gunna asked.

Helgi ran a hand over the top of his head before rubbing his eyes with his knuckles.

"No. If he's still around, then he'll be back for the car, and comms are tracking the phone. As soon as it goes from one mast to another, or there's a call made, they'll let us know. Then, with any luck, Ingvar will be all ours."

"What next, young man?"

Helgi groaned.

"I want to go home and put my feet up, sip a cold beer and be waited on hand and foot until I fall asleep in front of the TV."

"Like you usually do?" Gunna said. "Anyway, it looks like we don't need to panic about that house fire out near Hveragerði, Erling Larsen's place. The conclusion is there's no indication the fire was deliberate. Aron's remains were found in the kitchen doorway and the post-mortem identified all sorts of gunk in the guy's bloodstream. The thinking is that he was out of his head when he deep-fried a snack, and probably fell asleep without turning off the hotplate. The position of the body would indicate that he could have woken up and been aware of the fire, but by then he would have been overcome. At any rate, the expectation is that smoke inhalation was the primary cause of death."

"A stupid boy playing with fire, then?" Helgi said.

"We'll see. Sævaldur's team have been interrogating Erling Larsen. It seems Aron was supposed to be there overnight to keep an eye on the place, and he was pretty blasted when Erling left for the night. The two Polish guys who were putting up a fence are being interviewed as well, and they're terrified they've been caught up in something out of a gangster movie. They weren't impressed that Aron was left behind in that condition, but they back up what Erling's saying."

"Aron's mother has been informed?"

"Yep, that's all been done. Eiríkur has been interviewing the dead man's mother. So he's had a great day of it."

"There's still something spooky about all this," Helgi said. "Those boys. One in prison and one dead. It just stinks."

"Not least because the one in prison is your friend Ingvar's son. How do you square that with this man being in Iceland right now after all these years?"

"I've no idea," Helgi said. "If I could get hold of the bastard, I'd ask him."

Gunna glanced at her phone to check the time.

"My shift's almost over, and I need to pick Laufey up in an hour. What are you up to next?"

"There are two people out there who might know what Ingvar's doing here," Helgi said, standing up. "That's assuming he really is here and it's not all in my imagination. His ex-wife, and his brother. Of the two, I reckon the brother is the more likely one, but he's a tough nut to crack. So I'm going home, but I'll have another go at Arnar Geir on the way."

"Sounds good. Want me to come with you?" Gunna said. "I can be the good cop."

He hadn't expected to see Helgi Svavarsson's face right there in the street. Fortunately he had been able to watch him at work, and realised that somehow Helgi had tracked down the phone that he had left in the car. He wondered how they had found the number, and decided that the police must be able to locate a phone with remarkable ease.

He shivered as it dawned on him how fortunate he had been that it had dropped out of his pocket, otherwise he might have had Helgi banging on the door of the deserted hostel instead of being able to give him the slip in the street.

But now he might have to kiss goodbye to the car, and the phone, although neither was a concern. What worried him more was that Helgi had been able to track down Erik Petter Tallaksen, and that could lead him right to his door. Once he was back home, he would have to pull strings, treat the right people to expensive meals and maybe the professional night-time services he sometimes relied on when a visiting businessman or an official needed an extra-special sweetener to conclude a deal.

He grimaced at the thought of the late night that would entail, and returning home to Lizzie smelling of smoke and whisky. In the past it wouldn't have bothered him even slightly and he would have relished mixing business with suitably debauched pleasure. But now . . . Now things were different, he decided.

All the same, he would have to make sure that a report eventually reached the Icelandic police declaring that Erik Petter Tallaksen had been interviewed, and that while the unfortunate gentleman had been on business in Africa on the dates on question, it appeared that his personal details had been purloined and used by an unknown person. A few favours in the right places would make him the innocent victim of identity theft, he decided.

284

He toyed with the idea of tossing the 4x4's keys into the road to be flattened into the snow, but decided to hold on to them for the moment. In the morning he could just take a taxi, and until then, walking would do him no harm.

He pulled out his Spanish phone and punched in a text message as he walked.

Arnar Geir made no effort to conceal his exasperation at yet another visit from the police, any more than Helgi tried to hide his impatience. Gunna said nothing and watched Helgi, and hoped that he would not be tempted into an angry outburst that the lawyer on the other side of the desk could use to spin the situation around. In all the years they had worked together, she had never seen him so frustrated.

Arnar Geir glanced at her, then looked at Helgi.

"Brought some moral support, have you?"

"This is Gunnhildur. She's my boss," Helgi said, fidgeting with the phone in his hands. "You spoke to your brother yesterday, so I imagine you have an idea where he is."

Arnar Geir looked blank.

"Excuse me?"

"There's a mobile phone number associated with the gentleman who arrived from Portugal via Amsterdam. I have a list of calls made to and from that number."

Arnar Geir's composure began to waver. A mobile phone on the desk in front of him started to flash and buzz, and Helgi held up his own phone.

285

"See?" he said. "I'm calling a number from that call list right now, one that connected to Ingvar's phone seven times in the last few days. Your phone, Addi."

"I have nothing to say other than that it must be some kind of mistake. I get crank calls all the time," Arnar Geir said.

"Where is he, Addi?"

"I'm not Addi to you," Arnar Geir shot back. "I don't know what you're talking about. As I said, I haven't seen my brother since 2004."

"Then you must have a plausible explanation for those half-dozen conversations over the last few days."

Arnar Geir took off his glasses, folded them shut and tucked them into the pocket of his jacket. He picked up some papers from his desk, tapped them square and then opened a diary, leafing through the pages.

"If you don't mind," he said, "I have a meeting to attend in a few minutes, here in this building. Tomorrow morning, eleven o'clock, I'll be at the central police station with my lawyer to make a statement."

Helgi glanced at Gunna and raised an eyebrow. Gunna shrugged in reply.

"Later," she said. "Make it twelve. You're not the only one who leads a busy life."

Arnar Geir opened his mouth and lifted a finger, then nodded, lips pursed.

"Twelve. On the dot."

"If this is the way you want to do things, Addi," Helgi said, frowning across the desk.

"You made it official by bringing your boss with you," Arnar Geir said. "We're both lads from the north; we could sort this out amicably between ourselves without jumping through hoops. But if that's the way you want it . . ."

Helgi stood up, shoving his chair back behind him.

"See you at twelve," he said. "Shall we, Gunna?"

"I've just been admiring the pictures," Gunna said. "That's Vilberg, isn't it?"

"Surely you know?" Arnar Geir snapped. "He's a prominent figure and we've worked closely together."

"Thought so. I'm from that part of the country myself and remember seeing him around before he moved south and went into politics."

"You're from Ósvík?"

Arnar Geir's hostile tone softened and he turned his back on Helgi to speak to Gunna.

"The next town along, Vestureyri," Gunna said. "But I left a long time ago. My brothers used to talk about Vilberg sometimes, but our paths never crossed."

"He's a remarkable man," Arnar Geir said, almost reverently.

"That's interesting," Gunna said, picking up a metal ornament from between the framed pictures on the sideboard and looking at it closely. "It's made out of some old tools?"

Gunna put it back down. The metalwork gleamed, the curve of the handle of a pair of pliers forming the back of a tiny dragon, the arms of a set of calipers making up its legs, and the body and head fashioned from twisted bolts and washers.

"Scrapyard art, it's called," Arnar Geir said carelessly. "An old guy I used to work for gave it to me back when I was still doing legal stuff, years ago."

"Right," Gunna said brightly. "I was wondering if you'd bought it somewhere, and I was going to ask where."

"No," Arnar Geir said. "The guy only made a few of these, and he's dead now."

"So this one's a collector's piece?" she said. "Shame." She turned to Helgi. "Shall we leave this gentleman to it?"

"This is it. Let me know how you get on, won't you? Keep in touch," Ingvar said. He wanted to hug her, but something held him back. Instead he reached out and touched her cheek gently with the back of one curled finger.

"Sure, Dad."

Dad. The word still made him shiver.

"You're the only one who knows where to reach me," he said. "So keep it to yourself."

Tekla leaned forward and kissed his cheek.

"I hope I see you again sometime," she said. "We have a lot of catching up to do."

He saw her eyes widen, and she stiffened as a man appeared from the darkness, snatching at Ingvar's arm and moving to pin it behind his back. He was a fraction of a second too late, and Ingvar twisted around to face him, fists already balled. He heard Tekla yelp, and glanced to one side, where another figure in a black jacket had an arm around her neck.

He tried to think quickly, but knew he had to concentrate first on the man facing him. A long wooden club appeared from behind his back and swished through the air, missing Ingvar by inches as he backed away. The man swung the club a second time, and Ingvar wondered why he noticed it was a ship's ice club. He realised that one more step would put his back against a wall, with nowhere to go, and he told himself to think rationally, to wait for the club to swing one more time.

The man lunged forward as he swung again, and this time the club caught Ingvar's shoulder a glancing blow on its downward sweep towards the ground, just as Ingvar launched himself at his opponent, wrapping both arms around his forearms and the club, his momentum propelling them both into the dirty snow at the side of the street.

He heard the man roar with furious frustration, their faces inches apart.

For the moment, Ingvar knew that his weight gave him the upper hand, pinning the man to the floor, but he had to find a way to end this quickly. He squeezed his assailant's arms as hard as he could, hoping to damage an elbow joint or at least to inflict a little distraction pain, and pulled his head back. As the man in his grasp glared at him through narrowed eyes, Ingvar smashed his forehead as hard as he could into his opponent's face, feeling his nose crack as he did so. He relaxed his grip and rolled away, leaving the man to put his hands to his shattered nose, and glanced around, scrambling to his feet to rush to Tekla's side.

He was just in time to see the man who had held her in the crook of his elbow perform a graceless pirouette and sprawl into the snow as Tekla swung him over one hip in a throw she had practised so often as to make it instinctive.

"We need to get out of here," Ingvar gasped. "Who the fuck are these bastards?"

"I don't know, but they don't like one of us."

He could already feel a dull pain spreading across his upper arm, and wriggled his shoulder.

"Hurt?"

"Don't know."

"Fingers moving?"

He flexed his hand.

"It all works," he said, and looked around. "Are you all right?"

One of the two men sat in the snow with his hands to his crushed nose, while the other was getting to his feet, casting around for the wooden club his friend had dropped.

"Of course I am," Tekla snapped back. "But we won't be if we hang around here. Go, Dad. Get out of here."

CHAPTER
SEVEN

Stiff north-easterly wind veering easterly by mid afternoon. Snow showers and possible sleet. Temperatures around 0°C.

Einar Ingvarsson sat slumped over the kitchen table and Katla held his hand, sitting bolt upright with her eyes smouldering. She watched as Helgi sat down and gave him an amiable smile.

"You must be Einar," Helgi said.

"Yeah."

The boy nodded. His hair was a shaggy mat of jet black and he wore a black hoodie, both of which contrasted with the ashen shade of his face. A livid bruise had formed under one eye.

"Are you going to tell me what happened?" Helgi gently suggested. "I don't suppose you walked into a lamp post?"

"I should be at school," he said petulantly, glaring at his mother.

"I've already called the school and told them you're sick. You're not going anywhere until you tell this man what happened to you, and who did this."

Einar looked from his mother to Helgi and back again.

"A couple of guys," he grunted.

"You've seen them before?"

He shook his head.

"All right. Where and when did this happen?"

"Last night. We were using the music room at school in the evening and they were waiting when I came out."

"This is the further education college on Ármúli, right? I've already spoken to your teachers and they said that you've had a few problems. Anything to do with these two men who were waiting for you?"

Einar shrugged and said nothing.

"What did they want?" Helgi asked gently. "I mean, why did they single you out? Have you seen these men before?"

"A couple of days ago," the boy mumbled. "There were three of them that time." Einar looked imploringly at his mother, his mouth half open. "They wanted to know about the old man," he said quickly. "I said he's working in the east, and why were they asking me? Then they said not Valgeir, they meant my real dad. So I said he was dead and they just laughed."

"And then what?"

"And one of them did this." Einar felt the tender side of his face and flinched at the touch of his own fingers. "They said it was so I wouldn't forget."

"Did they say any more? What were you supposed to not forget?"

"To let them know if my real dad turned up and they gave me a number to call. They said, nice house you live in, and tell your sister we'll be back. And they said, don't talk to the filth and we'll know if you do."

Helgi looked at Katla, whose face had turned red with fury.

"Where's your daughter?"

"She's at college, of course. What are you going to do about this?"

Einar pushed his chair back, zipping up his hoodie as he stood up.

"Where do you think you're going?" Katla demanded.

"I feel like shit. I'm going to lie down."

He padded from the room, and a door banged in the distance.

"Where's your husband? Valgeir, I mean?"

"Like Einar said, he's working in the east. He should have been back last night but the roads have been blocked."

"And Ingvar?" Helgi said, his eyes on hers. "I know he's not dead. So where is he?"

"I don't know what you're talking about. Ingvar died in the tsunami all those years ago."

"Come on, Katla. What the hell is going on here? Don't think this is going to go away. I've seen Ingvar with my own eyes, so it's going to take more than that to convince me. Though right now I'm more concerned about your children and whatever threats they're facing. Someone wants to get hold of Ingvar, and doing it through you or the children is the obvious route."

"I don't know! My husband's dead and my son's in prison, and now this . . . I don't know which way to turn and your crowd are no help. What kind of protection are we entitled to?"

★ ★ ★

293

The door to Lind Ákadóttir's apartment was open an inch, and Gunna stopped to listen to the muffled sound of confrontation inside before cautiously easing it open and stepping over the threshold. The sound was clearer now, although still distant: sharp cries of distress.

She glanced into the bedrooms as she crept towards the living room, which appeared to be deserted until she felt the cool draught from an open door and saw two figures on the balcony: a man's bulky figure forcing a woman's head far out over the iron railing, a hand clamped over the back of her neck. Gunna could make out indistinct angry voices and watched in horror as the man reached down with his free hand to catch hold of the woman's ankle, lifting her leg high in the air as her face was pushed further out into space.

She hauled the sliding door open and in one quick movement took hold of the man's arm. He dropped the woman's leg and Gunna spun him around into a heap on the floor, grasping his wrist and elbow in a lock that made him roar with surprised anger.

"What the fuck . . .?" Arnar Geir barked as he looked up and saw Gunna glaring down at him. "Could I ask what you're doing here?" he said once he had managed to catch his breath.

"Looking for this lady here," Gunna said, glancing over to where Lind had collapsed against the balcony railing, her hands at her throat as she struggled for breath. "And I'm wondering if this was really what it looked like, and how it would have ended if I hadn't turned up."

Lind nodded, coughed and nodded again.

"Are you going to let me stand up so I can offer an explanation?" Arnar Geir asked.

"No. You can try and explain from where you are," Gunna said.

"My wife had a coughing fit and I was assisting her."

"Ex-wife, you mean? And you were assisting her by holding her neck against a metal bar?"

"Officer, it's easy to misconstrue circumstances," Arnar Geir said as smoothly as he could with one cheek pressed against the floor.

"And sometimes first impressions are the right ones," Gunna said. "Put your hands behind your back."

"What are you doing?"

"What I'm supposed to do under the circumstances. Now do it."

Arnar Geir shifted as Gunna eased the tension on his arm. She placed one knee in the small of his back and snapped handcuffs on his wrists.

"Fucking handcuffs? What for?"

"You can sit up now," she said, clicking her communicator. "Control, ninety-five fifty."

"Ninety-five fifty, what can we do for you?" asked a businesslike voice in her earpiece.

"What are you doing now?" Arnar Geir demanded as Gunna crouched next to Lind, speaking into her communicator as she did so.

"Just ordering you a taxi," Gunna told him. "You have an appointment with Helgi at Hverfisgata anyway, so you're going to be early."

Lind was hunched over with her head between her knees. Gunna felt for her wrist and found her pulse racing. She put a hand into the curtain of hair shrouding Lind's face and lifted her chin with one finger, exposing a couple of livid red marks on one side of her neck.

"I think we'll get you to hospital and have that checked out," she said, and clicked her communicator again.

"You'll be collected after school and driven home," Helgi told Tekla as the principal gazed impassively at them from behind half-moon glasses. "We are taking this extremely seriously, and any information you can give us could be vital. This appears to concern the safety of the whole family."

Tekla looked down at her hands.

"Is it about Sturlaugur?"

"We can't be sure," Helgi said. "But it seems to concern your supposedly late father, Ingvar."

"What?" Tekla demanded. "Dad died years ago. How can this be anything to do with him?"

"You tell me, Tekla. You tell me. I have very good reason to believe that Ingvar is alive and in Iceland right now. So if there's anything you have to tell me, then let's hear it. I'd love to know what could have brought him back after all these years."

"I don't know anything," she said, but Helgi noticed that she dropped her eyes to the floor as she spoke.

"Sure about that? No strange calls? No social media messages? Nothing like that? No new friends on Facebook?"

"No. Nothing at all."

"All right," he said. "Don't leave the building here. Don't go outside. Clear?"

"Yeah."

"There'll be a police officer here to collect you this afternoon. And please take this seriously."

"Fine, understood," she said petulantly, standing up and swinging her bag over her shoulder.

"She's hiding something," Helgi said as the door shut behind her.

"You can tell?" the principal asked.

"I can feel it, and she's not a good liar." He fumbled for his phone as it buzzed in his pocket. "Helgi," he barked into it.

"Hæ, it's Anna Björg. The car you wanted impounded isn't there any more."

"Shit," Helgi grunted, and saw a look of sadness cross the principal's face. "Stay right there. I'll be with you in ten minutes."

"What was all that about?" Gunna asked.

Lind Ákadóttir sat stiff and shocked, looking at the pattern that reassuringly repeated itself on the heart-rate monitor she was hooked up to.

"I don't want to talk about it," she said. "And I don't want to bring any charges."

"You were close to being pitched into the street. It's a long drop," Gunna said. "This is serious enough as it is, so you don't have to bring charges. Assault, even attempted murder. Apart from that, you need to get an injunction to keep Arnar Geir away from you."

"I know a good lawyer," Lind said bitterly. "I used to be married to him."

"Another few seconds and you'd have been all over the pavement."

Lind shook her head and pursed her lips.

"He would never have done that. Arnar Geir has a temper that flares up occasionally, but he'd never go that far. And how do I explain to our son that I've taken out an injunction against his father?"

She looked up at Gunna with wide, questioning eyes.

"That's a bridge you'll have to cross when you come to it. What was the problem? Why was he upset enough with you to want to throw you off a balcony? That's not what most of us would regard as normal behaviour. Come on, this wasn't just a minor disagreement."

"I don't want to talk about it," Lind repeated, pulling tighter the grey blanket wrapped around her shoulders.

"This is about Hafravatn," Gunna said, and watched Lind's eyes begin to bulge. "Let's have the truth, shall we? I have evidence that Arnar Geir was present the night Birna died, even though you carefully kept quiet about that. So if you're determined to continue to cover for him, then my inclination would be to assume that you either have an involvement in Birna's death, or you're deliberately obstructing an investigation. That's a crime in itself."

"No, I wouldn't . . ." Lind said as the spikes on the monitor quickened and a red light flashed. "I mean, Arnar Geir would never . . ."

"You're sure about that?" Gunna said. "You'd have been on the pavement three floors down if I hadn't turned up and if Arnar Geir hadn't been in too much of a hurry to shut the door properly. You wouldn't have been in a comfortable room being checked out. You'd have been downstairs in the mortuary. You were lucky."

Lind blanched at the thought.

"Don't think I'm not grateful."

"Why didn't you mention that Arnar Geir had been there that night at Hafravatn? And how come you went home with Simoni?"

"I did not!" Lind yelped.

"That's not what he said. He said you shared a taxi back to town after the altercation between his assistant and your toyboy."

"Of course we didn't," Lind snapped, her face hard with indignation. "I would never, ever allow myself to be alone with that dreadful man."

"So why cover up for Arnar Geir?" Gunna said. "Did your husband murder Birna to keep her from making accusations against his friend Vilberg Sveinsson?"

Lind's mouth fell open as she gaped at Gunna.

"You . . ." she said with an effort. "You can't be serious."

"That's my suspicion. So how about you come clean?"

Lind groaned. "What have you heard?"

"You were at Áskell's house. Róbert said you were hysterical because you found your date on top of his assistant, and he offered to take you back to town. Now let's hear what really happened."

"I heard them arguing," Lind said with a sigh. "I told you this before, you know. All I saw was Tolli punching Róbert. Not hard, but enough to get the message across. I made him come back to the party."

"Go on," Gunna said as Lind paused.

"Róbert got quite drunk, and he and Arnar Geir were arguing about something, then he had an argument with Mímir as well."

"And where was Birna at this time?"

"At the barbecue, with Jónatan. But Birna was everywhere. She had so much energy."

"And you definitely didn't leave with Róbert?"

"Certainly not. I was still there in the morning when the man from next door raised the alarm."

"So why was Arnar Geir about to push you off a balcony just now? What do you have on him that's so sensitive?"

The space was empty, and Anna Björg stood guard over it, waving away motorists seeking parking slots as they approached.

Helgi parked in a spot reserved for residents of a nearby apartment block, and hurried through the snow to where the 4x4 had been the night before.

"Was this someone important?" Anna Björg asked, waving another car away.

"Ingvar from Vesturhæli," Helgi said as he surveyed the empty space. "Any idea how long it's been gone?"

"Ingvar Sturlaugsson?" Anna Björg asked, eyes widening. "It's really him?"

"Yep. He's right here and there's a proper storm brewing around him. This afternoon I need you to go and collect his daughter and take her home. She's studying at MH. Between now and then I need to figure out what we can do for protection, if anything."

300

"That's Tekla, right?"

"That's her. And she knows something she's keeping to herself."

He scouted around the edges of the parking space, kicking through the remaining loose snow. Flakes of white had again begun to drift gently downwards.

"Can you put out an alert for the number? If anyone sees the car, we need it stopped and the driver hauled in," he said as he crouched down to check under the next car in the street. He lay down and used the torch in his phone, reaching as far as he could to retrieve the remnants of Ingvar's phone from beneath it.

He got to his feet and fitted together the battery and body, and pressed the red button to bring it to life, but the phone remained obstinately dead.

"What's that?" Anna Björg asked.

"His phone, the one we managed to track. It had been left in the car, which is how we found the vehicle. I had a call from comms to say it had been switched off at eight forty this morning, so we can assume that's when he took the car. He must have figured that the phone was being tracked, or just guessed. Whatever, Ingvar's no fool, and I reckon he didn't want to take any risks."

"All right, anything more you need here?"

"No. That's it. We'll just have to hope the car turns up before too long, and hopefully Ingvar with it."

"You carefully didn't mention that Arnar Geir is your ex-husband," Gunna said.

"I must have forgotten. I've been trying for years to forget about that man," Lind said with a laugh that failed to sound careless.

"We have a good idea of who was there, who was present at the time of Birna's death. We've spoken to almost everyone —"

"Tolli as well?" Lind broke in. "You've seen him?"

"Of course I have."

"How is he?"

"I wasn't asking after his health and happiness," Gunna said. "Let's say he answered all my questions, which is how I came to hear that Arnar Geir was present as well. What took him out there among all the arty types?"

"Arnar Geir has the unlikeliest friends in strange places," Lind said. "He's a lawyer and now he's in politics, and that's because he has filth on everyone around him, all the secrets nobody wants out in the open. He was also Áskell's lawyer, represented him once when someone accused him of plagiarism, which was just ridiculous. But it still had to go to court and a settlement had to be reached. Every now and then Arnar Geir would go out there and they'd spend an afternoon in Áskell's workshop with a bottle of brandy."

"So why didn't you tell me when I asked you who was there?"

"I forgot," Lind said, swinging her legs off the bed.

"Come on, you can do better than that. You're not the type who forgets."

Lind stared at Gunna as if being challenged was the worst affront possible. She scowled and her face hardened into a tight frown as she got unsteadily to her feet.

"All right. He lies and cheats, but he does it with charm, and it seems like I'm the only one who can see through him," she said, and sighed. "But he still owns half of this place. We have a son, although he's grown up now. I should have told you Arnar Geir had been there. I don't know why I didn't."

"He threatened you?"

"Of course not," Lind said with a flash of unconvincing anger. "Generally we get on fine, like normal adults do."

"And that's why you took a toyboy to a party where you knew you'd see him?"

Arnar Geir's face was a picture of injured pride as he sat in the interview room, his lawyer at his side. Helgi sat with his back to the window, the wind outside hammering at the glass with all its strength as Gunna took a seat beside him.

"I understand you have a statement to make," Helgi said. "So let's hear it."

Arnar Geir sat impassively and gestured to his lawyer.

"All yours," he said.

"My name's Snorri Gunnlaugsson and I am representing Arnar Geir Sturlaugsson in this matter."

"We know that," Helgi said.

Snorri cleared his throat and squared some sheets of paper in his hands before reading in a voice that rose in pitch as he spoke.

"'My client has no knowledge of the whereabouts of his brother Ingvar Sturlaugsson, who is presumed to have lost his life in the twenty-sixth of December 2004 disaster in Thailand. His last communication with his brother took place before Ingvar and his family flew to Thailand, departing from Iceland on the fifteenth of December 2004. Ingvar Sturlaugsson was subsequently declared deceased, even though no body or remains were located. My client has nothing on which to base an assumption that this might not be the case.'"

He paused and cleared his throat again.

"'Approximately one week ago, he was contacted by someone claiming to be Ingvar Sturlaugsson. Over the course of a number of mobile telephone conversations, my client became convinced that this was a fraudulent claim and that the person calling was not in fact Ingvar Sturlaugsson. His firm opinion is that the person making the calls, from an Icelandic phone number, is in fact seeking to extort money from Arnar Geir and possibly from other family members.'" Snorri spoke with a flourish, as if he were delivering a verdict. "'In conclusion, my client would appreciate it if the police could make urgent efforts to locate the person making these fraudulent calls, which have caused significant distress, and place appropriate charges against this person.'"

"That's interesting," Helgi said, speaking to Arnar Geir. "All right, what made you think this person was a fraud?"

"My client states that the person calling him addressed him as Arnar," the lawyer replied for him.

304

"Within the family and among friends, he has invariably been addressed as Addi, never as Arnar."

"Did you think to record any of these calls?"

"Unfortunately, my client did not."

"And there have been no more calls?"

"The last call was the day before yesterday," Snorri said. "Is that all, officer? I think we have been through the key points and see no reason to continue."

"I'm not so sure," Helgi said, laying out fresh printouts of all the pictures he had collected. "This is Erik Petter Tallaksen, the gentleman who flew to Iceland from Portugal a few days ago." He placed his finger on a photo of Ingvar that he had retrieved from the driving licence archive. "This is Ingvar a few years before his disappearance. And this is Tallaksen as he used to be, his passport photo from around thirty years ago. There are two different people here, and only one of them is Erik Petter Tallaksen." He held up a photo of a sharp-faced man with brown hair that lapped at his collar.

"My client recognises the photograph of his brother, naturally. The other two are strangers. Whether or not they are the same person is immaterial."

"I'd prefer it if you didn't try to patronise me, young man," Helgi said with sudden sharpness. "In my opinion, this is the same person, fifteen years apart." He lined up Ingvar's picture with the airport CCTV image. "The computer agrees. I've put the images through a couple of facial recognition systems, and they all say the same thing. Same man, no question."

Snorri sat back for a second and muttered something to Arnar Geir, who nodded.

"In that case," he said, "if you are certain of this person's identity, my client would be delighted if you could locate his long-lost brother. So, are we finished?" he asked brightly.

"You might be," Gunna said, speaking for the first time. "But Arnar Geir and I have some other business to deal with"

There was one more class before her lessons would be finished for the day, but she would have to skip psychology. This was more urgent. The string of text messages that had appeared on her phone during the German class had left her numb and angry at her own helplessness.

There was no question that the sender knew where to find all of them and that one of them would be made to suffer if she failed to do what she had been told. For a moment she wondered whether to disobey the final instruction and let the police see the messages, but something inside told her she would have to deal with this herself.

She would have to explain that Ingvar had left the country and that she had no idea where he had gone. She had to hope that once her father had disappeared, yet again, the family would be left to go back to its normal mundane existence. She was surprised to find that her inner fury was directed not at Ingvar, or even at the heavy-handed criminals who were determined to get hold of him, but instead at her brother. Sturlaugur was the one who had drifted into drugs and crime and had screwed things up for them as well as for himself.

Now he was safe and comfortable in a centrally heated cell with three square meals a day and all the time in the world to devote himself to getting a qualification that would give him a helping hand later in life, while Einar struggled with his own difficulties in relating to the world around him, and Tekla was on her feet from morning to night juggling college and a couple of dead-end jobs in her spare time.

She slung her bag over her shoulder, wrapped her scarf around her neck, snug under her chin, and thought through the instructions again. No police. Not a word to anyone. The anger that was growing inside her spurred her on and she strode through the gathering darkness, kicking snow aside in impotent fury until the lights of a car parked on the opposite side of the street flashed twice.

"We meet again," the man said warily as she approached, and she recognised him as the leather-jacketed thug she had swung over her hip into an undignified heap.

"I can't say I'm pleased to see you," she spat back. "What is all this about? Why are you harassing us? Why can't you leave us in peace?"

"My boss wants to speak to your old man. He's upset, and that's not good," the man said, a humourless smile showing a missing tooth. "When Erling doesn't get his own way, people get hurt."

"Innocent people, you mean. Like us."

"Yeah. Now get in the car."

When Tekla was settled in the passenger seat, the man sat behind the wheel.

"Listen, you're going to call your old man."

"Why should I?"

The man's eyes hardened.

"Otherwise it's going to be painful for someone. Your old lady's still tasty, even if she's an old bird. The boys would love to play games with her. And your brothers are just waiting to fall down some stairs. That could even be fatal. So maybe you'd better remember that phone number."

Gunna tapped the screen of her iPad and propped it up on a table in the clinic's waiting room.

"Watch carefully," she said. "Tolli's videos. You probably know all these people, so I need you to identify as many as you can for me."

Lind looked miserable and coughed as she hunched in front of the screen, a pair of John Lennon-style round glasses giving her an owlish look.

The first sequence was in bright daylight, with cheerful people talking and laughing as they sat in a wide semicircle around the barbecue.

"That's the neighbour."

"Jónatan," Gunna supplied.

"And those two are Mímir and Magnea, still sober at that point."

"And this one?" Gunna said, pointing at a tall man with sand-coloured hair.

"Another neighbour. I don't think he stayed long. He's the one who found Birna in the morning."

"Óttar."

"Yes," Lind said, and lapsed into silence as the sequence played out. They watched a noticeably pregnant Ursula make an appearance, taking a seat while her husband fetched food for her from the barbecue and Birna fussed over her.

"That's me there, and there's that old weirdo Gussi," Lind said as an elderly man with a flamboyant cravat appeared and made a short speech, ending it with an elaborate bow. "He's in a home now, the poor old thing."

A second, shorter clip had clearly been recorded later in the evening, with long shadows cast by the trees as Áskell and Birna sat on a bench side by side, answering questions from someone out of shot.

"That's Róbert," Lind said. "That's definitely his voice."

"This was before the incident behind the workshop?"

"Oh yes," Lind said, her voice turning sharp as she pointed to a willowy woman with silver hair who laughed musically at everything Áskell said. "And that's Eyrún, the one who waltzed off with Tolli."

"Róbert's assistant."

"If that's what you want to call her," Lind sniffed.

"And that's Arnar Geir."

"I recognise him all right."

A third video was more grainy and less steady, shot after darkness had fallen, with Jónatan feeding pieces of wood to a flickering fire that provided most of the light.

"This is after Tolli smacked Róbert?" Gunna prompted as she paused the recording. "Names?"

"That's Mímir being his usual grand self, and Magnea next to him," Lind said as the lens swung to take in the group. "There's Birna, of course, and Róbert." His face turned to the camera for a second and twisted into a furious scowl.

"That's Róbert? He looks different."

"It's the hair," Lind said. "A couple of years ago he gave up pretending to not be losing his hair and had it cropped short, but there he's still trying to make out he can carry off a ponytail."

"And this was taken some time after dark, so obviously he didn't flounce out as soon as he'd had that fight with Tolli."

"It doesn't look like it. I really don't remember. It was a dreadful night and I've been trying ever since not to think about it."

"One more," Gunna said, clicking on the final video file. The screen was black to begin with, accompanied by the sound of feet crunching on gravel and throaty laughter. The interior lights of a car came to life and the headlights bathed trees and rocks in a harsh white glare as the car began to move. "This must be Eyrún driving?" Gunna asked, and Lind nodded slowly.

"I suppose so."

The car bumped along the track that Gunna remembered from walking up to Áskell's workshop, with an alarming crunch as the exhaust grounded, prompting a flood of laughter from the driver. At the end of the track it halted before turning onto the unmade road around the lake, and its lights flashed over two figures in the moonlight by the jetty jutting out into the lake.

"And you know as well as I do who those two people are, don't you?" Gunna asked, pausing the recording just as the car's driver whooped in delight. She scrolled back to show the two figures standing by the jetty, illuminated by the car's harsh headlights, one of them staring at the camera with a face twisted in furious surprise, the other looking the same way, clearly amused.

"Róbert," Lind whispered. "That's Róbert, and that's Birna. That's where her body was found in the morning."

It seemed like an age as she sat next to the man in black. She coughed as he lit a cigarette and he looked scornfully sideways at her but wound down the window and blew the smoke into the cold air outside.

As he sent the butt spinning into the gloom, her phone rang.

"Tekla? What's the matter? You said it was urgent."

"Dad . . ." she said, trying not to allow her voice to quaver. "You have to help us out."

The man in the driver's seat held out a hand and she passed the phone to him. He peered at the screen and tapped once to put it on speaker.

"Listen, my boss and I want to have a proper word with you."

"And who are you?" Ingvar's voice rasped through the loudspeaker.

311

"You don't need to know that. All you need to know is that we know where your old lady and your kids are. So if you don't show your ugly face, you know who's going to pay the bill."

"When?"

"Now. You're going to drive out to Garðabær and park up —"

"No," Ingvar said. "If all you want to do is talk, then it has to be somewhere public. Outside the university, the gravel parking lot on Sæmundargata."

The man was silent for a moment.

"All right. We can do that. Be there in an hour, not a second less."

"What are you driving?"

"Grey BMW. I'll be waiting for you, and I'll be slicing a chunk off your little girl for every five minutes you're late."

Helgi grumbled to himself as he kicked off his soaked shoes under his desk.

"Gunna, we need to talk."

"Don't tell me, you're tired of this materialistic lifestyle and you want to renounce all earthly wealth so you can go and live as a monk in chastity and poverty?"

"Don't tempt me," Helgi growled. "That sounds just perfect right now."

"Go on, young man," Gunna said, dropping into Eiríkur's chair next to him. "Tell me all."

"It's this crazy family from Vesturhæli."

"Vesturhæli? Where's that?"

"Sorry, I mean Ingvar Sturlaugsson's family. Their old man owned a farm called Vesturhæli, one of the Skagi farms that's miles from anywhere."

"Arnar Geir's been released," Gunna said. "His ex is reluctant to press charges, and as he's already reminded me, any lawyer is going to rip the case the shreds unless Lind changes her mind. Even then it's doubtful."

"We have a problem with the rest of Ingvar's family. The younger son has been intimidated and beaten up by a couple of heavies wanting to know where Ingvar is. So he's upset someone, we just don't know who that someone is. The daughter isn't saying anything, although my gut feeling is that she's holding back all sorts. Ingvar's crazy wife is also playing it close to her chest and is demanding protection for the children."

"We don't have any manpower for that, unless I can persuade the Laxdal to sign off a whole stack of overtime."

"Yeah, I know. Anna Björg is going to collect Tekla from school and take her home. The younger boy, Einar, should also be at home. We have a patrol checking their street every hour or so. But it's after dark that I'm more concerned about. If anything's going to happen, it'll be then."

"What can you do?"

"That's about it. Ingvar has either figured out that his phone was being tracked, or else he's simply being cautious. The car he was using has gone, and that's a fuck-up on my part. I was banking on being able to track the phone when it moved, but the car's disappeared and the phone had been dumped in the street." Helgi pulled an evidence bag containing the remains of Ingvar's phone from his coat pocket.

"So what are the options?" Gunna said.

"Not a lot. There's an alert out for the Santa Fe he was driving, and until that shows up, I'm back to square one." Helgi shook off his coat and hung it on the back of his chair. "I'm convinced that Arnar Geir has seen his brother, no question, but he's going to stonewall until the bitter end. I'm wondering which of the children he might have been in touch with, or even Katla, though she bears him no goodwill as far as I can see. If he turned up, she'd gladly put his balls in a blender."

"And we're not the only ones who want to get hold of him. Your best option right now is to get Einar in here and go through as many faces as you can find, and I'll continue to make Arnar Geir's life a misery."

Tekla sat in silence next to the man in black as he lit another cigarette. This time he wound down the window without having to be asked. The car park opposite the imposing university building was practically empty, scattered with mounds of piled-up snow that continued to freeze into rock-hard hillocks in the sub-zero chill.

The man tapped the clock on the dashboard.

"He'd better be here soon."

"What is all this about?" Tekla demanded. "Why are you doing this to us?"

"It's not about you, darling. It's about your old man and what my boss reckons he's done."

314

"And what's that?"

"You don't know?" he asked, turning to her, his eyes half closed. "You don't know what kind of a guy your old man is?"

Tekla stopped listening as she saw a compact 4x4 drive into the car park and head slowly around the edge.

"That's him?" the man asked as the Santa Fe approached and parked parallel to the BMW, leaving a windswept no-man's-land of a couple of spaces between them.

He felt in a pocket and extracted a carpet knife, holding it in his hand where Tekla could see it.

"These things are nasty," he said, sliding the blade forward. "Don't make me use it. Understand?"

Tekla nodded, and shuddered. In the other car, Ingvar glared from the driver's seat.

"Now, we're going over there," the man said. "We're just going to sit quietly and talk. Don't do anything fast, don't do anything stupid. Just get out, and we'll go and talk to your old man."

Tekla felt numb as she stepped across the space between the cars, opened one of the rear doors and got in. The man settled in the seat next to her. It was dark in the car and she could make out his face only as a shadow. The car park's few lights cast little brightness, and fat flakes of damp snow drifted down in the orbs of light around them. Occasionally a flash from the lights of a passing car lit up the man's narrow face, tight with tension.

"You're Stulli's old man, right?" he said.

"Yeah. What do you want with me?"

"You've been asking questions and that's upset a few people. Erling wants to know why."

"And who's Erling?" Ingvar asked, twisting around in his seat.

The man grinned.

"If you get on the wrong side of him, Erling is everyone's worst nightmare, and he'll be here any minute. He wants to talk to you in person. There's been some damage to his property. One of his friends was hurt and he seems to think you might know something about it, since you've been asking the wrong people questions."

"I've been asking a few people about my boy. That's all. Nothing to do with you or your pal."

"That's what you think." The man dipped into his pocket and brought out the carpet knife, balancing it in his hand, and Tekla shrank away, tucking her hands inside her coat. "Erling's house. It burned down a couple of nights ago. You were there."

"I don't know what you're talking about," Ingvar said.

"Wrong answer." He slid the blade out and jerked his head towards Tekla. "Cute girl, isn't she? A shame to spoil that pretty face."

Ingvar breathed deeply and forced himself to be as calm as he could.

"Listen, I've been here for three days. I haven't been back in this country for years. I've no idea what you're talking about."

The man clicked the blade in and out of the knife a couple of times, and hissed with nervous frustration.

"I'm not playing games. You were there."

"You want me to tell you a lie? I'm telling you the truth, man," Ingvar protested. "You think I'd take a chance with my daughter's life? Maybe you would with your kid's life."

"Don't fuck with us, pal. Last warning before there's some damage. That's why we're in your car. This could get really messy."

"Is that your boss?" Tekla asked suddenly, sitting up and peering between the seats as lights briefly illuminated the car's interior.

His attention distracted, the man glanced up, and Tekla took her chance, stabbing downwards with the biro she had plucked from an inside pocket of her coat, holding it in both hands and driving it with all her strength into the muscle of the man's thigh.

His screech of pain took her by surprise. He jerked and his arms flailed, the knife slicing a gash in the upholstery. Ingvar shot out a hand to catch hold of his wrist, wrenching the man's arm forward and bending the elbow joint against the side of the passenger seat, squeezing the wrist as hard as he could as he tried to force him to drop the knife.

As the man fought and yelled, Tekla pulled her scarf from under her coat and stretched to wrap it around his neck, twisting it into knots around her hands as she tightened it. His yells dissolved into grunts. The knife clattered from his hand and he slumped back.

Ingvar relaxed his grip.

"I don't believe it . . ." he muttered to himself. Opening the door and tumbling out of the car, he hauled Tekla out of the back seat and reached inside to feel for a pulse in the man's neck.

Einar sat sulkily in front of the computer with Helgi as he put together as detailed a description as he could of the two men who had intimidated him. The boy answered questions with as few words as possible. Helgi suspected that he was already frightened of repercussions, and was furious with his mother for having taken the matter to the police. He admitted that they had accosted him on a dark street, taking care to keep their faces obscured, claiming that he could recall few details, other than that the pair had been very similar in build, with the same close-cropped hair and beards.

"What sort of age are we looking at here?" Helgi asked. "Could you guess?"

"Thirty, forty?" Einar hazarded. "I don't know. Just old."

"Older than me?"

"Nah. You're well old. They were younger."

"I'm forty-seven, so we're no nearer, are we?"

"You oldies all look the same," Einar complained.

Helgi assembled an image on the screen and pointed.

"Is that close?"

"I don't know."

"Look at the eyes. Do they look right?"

"One of them looked different."

"All right, different. But how?"

"I don't know. Not like that."

"Were the eyes further apart, or should the brow be heavier?"

318

"I don't know. It was dark. I couldn't see them very well. One of them had a plaster on his nose."

"Like a sticking plaster?"

"Yeah. I could see it because it was white."

Helgi sighed. An hour's effort had given him nothing more than a vague description that could apply to half of Reykjavík's adult male population. He had already been to the location to check out the possibility of the pair having been caught on CCTV, but had drawn a blank there as well. The two men had known what they were doing, choosing a spot far from any cameras and with any street lights so distant as to provide no help.

"How about their voices? Anything different or odd about the way they spoke to you?"

Einar sat in thought for a while and Helgi wondered if he would come up with anything.

"One of them talked a bit like you."

"How do you mean?"

"You know, sort of slow. And he sounded like he had a cold, like his nose was full of snot."

"Did he use any strange words, anything like that?" Helgi asked. "Or did he have an accent?"

"No. They both talked like you. Slow and old-fashioned."

Helgi sighed, stood up and took his mug to the coffee corner. He put his head round the door and whistled until Einar looked up.

"You want a coffee?" He saw the boy wrinkle his nose. "Juice? Milk?"

"Any chocolate milk?"

"No," Helgi said, scanning the contents of the fridge.

"Juice then."

"Juice then, thank you, Helgi, you mean," Helgi muttered under his breath as he went back to his desk, coffee in one hand and a carton of juice in the other.

"Where were we?" he began, just as his phone buzzed and he saw Anna Björg's name appear on the screen.

"Talk to me, Arnar Geir."

He sat with his arms folded, facing her. The hours he had spent in a cell had not been kind to him. The suave manner had fallen away and his voice had taken on a raw quality. He had been released after having been presented with an injunction preventing him from going near his former wife's home, and was now back in his office.

"About what?"

"Ingvar. It's him, isn't it?"

Arnar Geir shrugged. "You tell me."

"I am telling you. There's no doubt in Helgi's mind."

"I have nothing to say."

"But that's not my main concern," Gunna said. "The night Birna Bergthórsdóttir lost her life in Hafravatn, you were there."

"Says who?"

"There's evidence. Birna didn't simply drown in the lake. She wasn't drunk, and she wasn't suicidal. She was drowned, and someone made it happen."

He slumped in his chair behind the desk that seemed even more crowded than before, piled high with stacks of documents.

"To answer your questions before you ask them, my brother Ingvar still hasn't returned from the dead as far as I know. I haven't been anywhere near my former wife, and I don't have anything more to say on the matter."

"That night six years ago, you were at Áskell's place at Hafravatn," Gunna said. Arnar Geir glared as she made herself comfortable in the deep leather chair that faced his desk. "So maybe you can enlighten me on a few things I've been trying to piece together."

"Do I have to? We could have gone through all this shit earlier at the police station."

"True, but I felt a need to do it away from curious eyes, and without any records. An informal conversation."

"I'm busy right now. I have to be out of here today."

"Holiday or something?"

"I'm stepping down," he said in a grim tone. "Maybe temporarily, maybe not."

"No more politics?"

"Don't know yet. It depends."

"On whether or not Lind decides to press charges?"

Arnar Geir sighed.

"Yeah. Pretty much. If this goes to court, I'm out of politics."

"Hafravatn," Gunna reminded him, leaning forward and tapping the desk with one forefinger. "It seems that Birna's death wasn't an accident. It was treated as one, but I don't believe it was. People don't drown in water that's less than knee deep. Now, for a while I had you pegged as having been responsible."

"What?" Arnar Geir's jaw dropped and the colour drained from his face. "You're not serious, surely?"

"Don't worry, I've changed my thinking on that now that I know more. What I really want to know is why you went to such lengths to make sure it was all dealt with as quickly and quietly as possible. Who has your balls in a vice?"

"I . . ." he spluttered. "I don't see where you're going with this."

"It was investigated by my former colleague Örlygur Sveinsson. Now, I was able to go through some internal records from that weekend six years ago, and you know what? Örlygur was on leave. He was off duty. But all the same, he turned up and went through the motions, ticked the boxes, made sure everything was dealt with as discreetly as possible."

"You're making assumptions."

"Not at all. Nobody called the emergency line, which is what any normal person would do. Instead, someone called Örlygur, and rather than handing the case to an officer on duty, which he should have done, he dealt with it in person. So who called him?" Gunna said. "If it was you, you might as well say so and save me the bother of requesting the phone records."

Arnar Geir groaned.

"OK, I called him. It seemed to be the easiest way. Personal connections, you know. Cuts through the bureaucracy."

Gunna half closed one eye as she glared across the glacier of paperwork that filled Arnar Geir's desk.

"As a lawyer, you are undoubtedly aware of the importance of making sure things are done by the book. So I'm still wondering what prompted you to do that. If there has ever been a police officer inclined to take every possible shortcut, it's Örlygur. You couldn't have found anyone with less professional motivation." She caught Arnar Geir's eye and held it. "Of course, he also just happened to be your pal Vilberg's half-brother. So you did Vilberg a real favour there."

Arnar Geir's face froze and his lips parted for a moment, as if he was about to say something. Then they shut tight and he looked at Gunna over the stacked documents on the desk in front of him.

"All right. Off the record," he said at last. "Completely off the record. Áskell invited me to the party because we had known each other a long time. It wasn't exactly a friendly gathering. Áskell had an argument with Róbert. Then there was that stupid fracas over a girl between Róbert and the toyboy Lind had dragged along in some pitiful attempt to embarrass me. Anyway, everyone had way too much to drink, and I slept on the couch."

He sat back and gazed into the space over Gunna's head.

"And?" she prompted.

"The neighbour — not the barbecue guy, but the other one — banged on the door early in the morning."

"Óttar."

"That's him. He woke us up. I went down to the shore with him, saw what there was to see and said I'd deal with it."

"So you called Örlygur?"

"Not exactly. I called Vilberg and told him what had happened, because I knew his brother was a senior detective."

"You knew there was some history there?"

"Oh yes," Arnar Geir said quietly.

"And you told Vilberg who the victim was?"

"He was overjoyed. But you can ask him about that."

"Is he dead?"

Tekla stood stock still, willing herself not to collapse, not to allow the shock to stop her from thinking.

"If he isn't, he soon will be," Ingvar said, opening the back of the 4x4 and pulling out a plastic can of diesel.

"What are you doing? We should call the police."

"No. Not going to happen," Ingvar said shortly, taking the rental paperwork out of the glove compartment and ripping it up into a pile under the car door. He poured diesel over the man's legs and the seats, laying a trail of fuel that dripped out of the door onto the paper on the ground. Then he went around the other side and rummaged in the dead man's pocket, extracting a lighter and a pack of cigarettes.

"Stand back," he ordered, suddenly starkly illuminated by the headlights of a car as it swept into the car park and bumped to a halt. "Well back. This is going to go up like a firework."

He glanced from side to side and clicked the lighter a couple of times to light the cigarette between his lips, coughing as he puffed until the tip glowed fiercely. He held it for a moment in front of his face, then threw it onto the pile of paper, which instantly caught light. Then he snatched at Tekla's arm and dragged her into a run.

She heard the rush and roar of the car catching light and felt the raw burst of heat as they hurried into the darkness, neither of them daring to look back. It was only as they waited for a break in the traffic that hurtled along Hringbraut, already slowing as people craned their necks to see the blaze in the university car park, that she looked over her shoulder, just as the first siren could be heard.

Ingvar strode across the main road, dodging cars and hauling Tekla along with him. Once they were on the far side, he stopped to look behind him. Blue lights were already flashing as a police car turned into the university car park, heading off a dark car that looked to be on its way out, and the sound of distant sirens could now be heard from both directions.

"What do we do now?"

"We walk into town like law-abiding citizens. You can catch a bus home as usual," Ingvar said, taking her arm and steering her down a quiet street of imposing white-fronted houses. "Don't hurry. We're just taking a stroll."

"What about you?"

"It'll be like I was never here."

"Again?"

"What else? The last thing you need is me hanging around," he said.

Tekla squeezed his arm, a kaleidoscope of the moments in the car running through her mind: the click of the man's knife, his teeth bared in anger, the high-pitched screech of pain as she stabbed the pen into his leg, the sounds he had made as she choked the life out of him.

The reek of burning followed them as they left Hringbraut behind, walking along the bank of Reykjavík's lake towards City Hall and the town centre. Ingvar hoped that Arnar Geir wouldn't be looking out of his office window.

It was a short walk from City Hall to the Parliament building, and Gunna strolled through the modest crowd of people who appeared to be emerging from hibernation after a day and a night of snow and wind had kept much of Reykjavík's population off the streets. Beyond the Parliament building was the old house with burgundy walls where the Moderate Alliance had its offices.

The man looked older in real life and up close than he had appeared on the screen. There were lines around his eyes that gave him the appearance of being tired, but there was no doubting the intensity of Vilberg Sveinsson's eyes as he looked Gunna up and down.

"I have ten minutes," he said in a curt voice. "What's so urgent that the police can haul me out of a meeting?"

"My name's —" Gunna began.

"I know your name," he snapped back. "I know all about you already. Could you please make this quick?"

"You knew Birna Bergthórsdóttir some years ago?"

"You're not serious," he said in a low voice laden with concern, his attention now fully on Gunna. "That was so long ago it's practically in the Stone Age."

"But you were close, weren't you? I've looked up your family history and that tells me that Birna's daughter was born about six months after your eldest son. So you were a prominent person in local politics at the time, having an affair with a young woman?"

Vilberg gulped and stared.

"Come with me," he said, and hurried to an alcove, where he glanced around. "What's all this about? Birna died years ago."

"Exactly," Gunna said, interested to see that she now had his undivided attention. "New information has come to light and there's reason to believe her death wasn't an accident."

"And why have you come to me?"

"I'm interested in any connection Birna may have had with you."

"Connection?" Vilberg snarled. "It was years ago. How can her death have had anything to do with me?"

"Birna never identified her daughter's father, and I'm inclined to believe that could be you. I could ask for a DNA sample so it can be confirmed."

"And I could decline to supply one," Vilberg snapped back. "In any case, nothing to do with me."

"That would look good, wouldn't it?" Gunna said softly. "The leader of a movement that's all about standing up for old-fashioned values declines a paternity test. That would really go down well with your supporters."

"Ridiculous. Nobody would be bothered."

"You think so? Especially if it turned out that she had been quietly got rid of to keep the truth from coming out. I know politicians don't make a habit of resigning, but it looks poor for a party leader, even a small party like yours."

Vilberg's eyes narrowed.

"Small for the moment," he said. "Are you threatening me?"

"I wouldn't dream of it. Just asking for your input," Gunna said. "Are you telling me that you didn't have a fling with Birna? By the way, your colleague Arnar Geir Sturlaugsson is in all kinds of shit at the moment, and there's no telling what he'll let fall when he starts to get desperate."

"She's definitely not there?" Helgi barked.

"No, I've had the staff search the whole place. No sign of her. She's not in the building anywhere."

"Shit," Helgi groaned. "Not going our way today, is it? Can you go to her home and stay there? Her mother will need to know that the girl's gone walkabout, and I'll bring the boy so we have at least two of them under one roof."

"Hold on a moment," Anna Björg said, and Helgi heard a muffled conversation in the background. He fought back impatience, pulling on his coat as he listened and motioning for Einar to do the same. "Still there? One of the kids just said he saw Tekla walk out around an hour ago. So she's gone."

"That wretched girl," Helgi muttered to himself. "She must have what she thinks is a good reason for going off on her own. Can you get over to her home right away and get the girl's phone number from her mother. We should be able to track it, so that'll give us an idea of where she is even if we don't know what she's up to."

"Right, on my way," Anna Björg said, and Helgi felt a warm glow of affection that he immediately stifled, reminding himself to keep his mind on the job in hand.

"I'll see you there when I've brought Gunna up to date, and I'll bring the lad with me."

"Villi?"

The door swung open and a young face adorned with an old man's beard appeared around the frame and looked Gunna up and down in surprise, taking in the uniform trousers with their chequered bands.

"Parked somewhere you shouldn't have, Villi?" he asked, and Vilberg frowned at him. "Are you coming? They'll be waiting for us."

"I have a meeting in Parliament in a few minutes. The nation's needs take priority, I'm afraid," Vilberg said, making an effort to be courteous.

"That's all right," Gunna told him, gently blocking his path. "This won't take more than a couple of minutes and I can walk with you. Your colleague Arnar Geir was adamant that there are a few questions only you could answer."

Vilberg looked flustered for a moment, shrugging on a thick overcoat as he thought.

Outside the building, the bearded man waited, along with a young woman with sharp eyes who scanned Gunna critically.

"Sonja, would you stand in for me while I deal with this?" Vilberg said to the woman. "I'll be a few minutes, but this is something urgent that I need to nip in the bud."

"If you say so."

"What now?" Vilberg said as the pair strode towards the Parliament building.

"Birna."

"Again?"

"Yes, again," Gunna said, pointing to a bench. "Sit down for a minute."

Vilberg hugged his briefcase as he perched on the bench, and Gunna sat next to him.

"There was nothing accidental about Birna's death. My concern is that it might have a connection to your relationship with her."

"There was no relationship," Vilberg spat angrily. "How many times do I have to tell you?"

"Then why were you overjoyed when you knew she was dead? Why did you jump at the chance to bring in the laziest policeman in the world to investigate her death?"

Vilberg looked shocked and at a loss for words.

"What has Arnar Geir said?"

"Don't worry about what Arnar Geir said. I want your side of it. You had an affair with Birna when she was working for you."

"I most certainly did not," he retorted. "Don't listen to smalltown gossip."

"What, then? Why did she leave so suddenly? Why did she go abroad?"

Vilberg sighed and hugged his briefcase tighter.

"I did something I shouldn't have. Birna knew and she wanted money."

Gunna stared.

"Birna blackmailed you?"

Vilberg nodded mournfully.

"Come on. Let's hear it."

"Back when I was the chief executive at the local authority in Ósvík, I overlooked a few irregularities," he said, and shivered as Gunna looked at him questioningly. "There were people on the payroll who shouldn't have been. Two of my cousins, and my brother Örlygur."

"Even though he was a policeman in Reykjavík?"

"Yes." Vilberg gulped. "Birna was the receptionist there. Somehow she got into the payroll and found out. One day she asked me for a private meeting. She said she had evidence," he added in a small voice. "Hardly anyone knows about this. She wanted enough money to leave the country. It's as simple as that."

"And did she have evidence? Documents?"

"She had paperwork and she had copied computer files. I couldn't deny it. She threatened to go public with it unless I contributed a one-time-only payment to her travel fund."

"So you did?"

"I had to sell shares in one of the banks to pay her off," he said with a bitter laugh. "Just think, shares in a bank that went bankrupt a few years later."

"And this evidence Birna had? Where is it now?"

Vilberg shrugged.

"I've no idea, and that's what worries me. When she died, I was delighted as it meant she couldn't come looking for me ever again. But it also meant that all that stuff could be anywhere, and if it ever surfaces, I'm in the shit."

331

"So that's why you paid that little thug Ellert Ásgrímsson to go up there and search the place?"

Helgi was flustered and angry, while Einar sat in brooding silence as they drove to his house and pulled up outside behind the patrol car Anna Björg had taken.

The door swung open as they walked up the path and Katla stood there with arms folded, glaring at Helgi.

"So you've let him out?"

"Of course. He hasn't done anything. All he's been doing is trying to identify the arseholes who gave him a black eye."

"That's just as well, then," Katla muttered as she stalked away.

Anna Björg appeared in the doorway as Einar kicked off his boots.

"No sign of Tekla?" Helgi asked.

"Nothing. She's not picking up the phone. It goes straight to voicemail so I reckon it's switched off. I'm waiting for comms to get back to me with a trace."

Helgi leaned against the wall and ran a hand over his face.

"Come into the kitchen," Anna Björg said gently. Her hand on his arm sent a jolt through him. "Katla's going crazy in there not knowing where the girl is."

Einar had already disappeared into his room, while Katla leaned against the kitchen worktop, shoulders slumped, staring out through the window into the darkness outside.

"You haven't heard anything?" she said, her voice bleak.

"Not a thing," Helgi said.

"I've lost one child already. I can't lose another one."

"Sturlaugur won't be inside for ever."

"You don't understand, Helgi. Sturlaugur is gone. I visit him in prison every couple of weeks, and he looks like my boy, but he's not the person I brought up. For all I know, he might have killed someone. He's turned into a man I don't recognise, and if it wasn't for María Vala, I'm not sure I'd want to know him."

"I can't imagine what you've been through," Helgi mumbled to himself, his thoughts elsewhere.

"So I can't face the prospect of losing Tekla as well."

"Helgi?" Anna Björg stood in the kitchen doorway. "I have to go. There's an emergency, car on fire outside the university. Hringbraut's blocked and everything's at a standstill."

Helgi sighed.

"No problem," he said. "I'll stand guard here. Let's hope the girl shows up before too long."

They parted among the hurrying people on Austurvöllur Square in the centre of the city.

"This is goodbye again?" Tekla asked. She had stopped shivering, but a new terror was beginning to take hold. Images of her brother's life behind bars were already flashing through her mind.

"Again," Ingvar said. "Unless you want to come with me?"

"Come with you? When? Where to?"

"Now. Spain. Right now."

She shook her head in regret.

"I can't," she said. "Mum has already lost you, then she lost Sturlaugur when he went to prison. She can't lose me as well. It would finish her off completely. I couldn't do it to her."

"You know how to reach me. Whenever you're ready. But don't give that email address to anyone else, all right?" He put out a hand and placed it on her shoulder. "You're tough, much tougher than I was at your age," he said quietly.

"It hasn't been easy since you vanished. And don't think I'll forgive you for that. At least not right away."

"I wouldn't ask you to."

"But we have a lot to talk over one day, when we get a chance."

"Before too long. But not here. I won't come to Iceland again."

Tekla reached up and wrapped her arms around his neck, taking him by surprise.

"Look after yourself, old man," she whispered into his ear. "I want to see you again."

Katla fried eggs and dropped them onto slices of brown bread.

"I can't cook anything more complicated than that," she apologised, handing Helgi his egg sandwich on a plate. "I'm just a bag of nerves right now."

She hesitated, reached out and twitched back the curtain in the kitchen window to reveal a bottle of wine.

334

"Want some?"

He shook his head. A glass of wine would be perfect, taking him back to the carefree couple of weeks in the villa in Portugal that already seemed so far in the past.

"No thanks. I'm on duty," he said sorrowfully. "And I have to drive."

"More for me," Katla said, slopping wine into a tumbler.

Helgi poured himself coffee from the flask on the table and wished it would kill the aroma of wine that mingled with the smell of eggs.

"Nothing from Tekla, I suppose?" he said through a mouthful of sandwich.

"Nothing. Her phone must be out of battery. She'll be home soon. I'm sure of it."

Katla sounded more hopeful than confident.

"This is unlike her, isn't it? Normally she's pretty responsible."

"Always has been. Ever since she was tiny. She's always been the sensible one. I don't know where she gets that from. Not from me, and definitely not from her father."

"Speaking of which, he's alive, isn't he?" Helgi said, seizing on the opportunity.

"How would I know?" Katla snapped. "When he was here, I was always the last one to know what the hell was going on. That hasn't changed just because he disappeared."

"I saw him, Katla," Helgi said gently. "I saw him with my own eyes. I know damn well he's alive."

"What? When?"

"A week ago, when I was flying home from a holiday in Portugal. I saw him at the airport. I knew it was someone I recognised, but it wasn't until afterwards that I realised who it was."

Katla shook her head.

"You must be mistaken," she said without conviction, and pushed away her half-eaten sandwich.

"You don't want that?" Helgi asked, eyeing it.

"No appetite," she said. "Have it if you want."

An icy draught suddenly snaked around his ankles and a door banged somewhere at the back of the house. Katla leaped to her feet and was about to hurry from the room, but met Tekla in the doorway. Helgi saw the tousled fair hair and the serious look on the girl's face, and breathed a sigh of relief.

Katla threw her arms around her daughter and squeezed her tight with a moment's delight, until frustrated anger took over.

"Where the fuck have you been?" she yelled. "Have you any idea how worried we've been, you little bitch?"

"Go home, Helgi," Gunna told him sternly. "You've had enough."

Helgi rattled his car keys in his coat pocket.

"Where is everyone?"

"Eiríkur's down at Hringbraut and so is practically everyone else who's on duty, including the Laxdal."

"Because a car caught fire?"

"Because someone set fire to a car, and there was someone in it."

"Shit, I see what you mean. Any ideas yet?"

Gunna grimaced.

"It's a mess. Unidentified male corpse on the back seat, car completely burned out. There's a chance it could be identified from the number on the engine block, but it's going to have to cool down first. Someone really wanted this thing to go up in smoke. But there's one positive about it."

"Which is?"

"There was a patrol car on the spot almost immediately and they found Erling Larsen and one of his people leaving the scene. So you can imagine how happy Sævaldur is, like Christmas all over again. He's putting Erling through the grinder, whether he had anything to do with this or not. At any rate, he's going to have to come up with convincing answers to some tough questions, including why there was a firearm in his car."

"Sometimes there can be a silver lining," Helgi said.

"On top of that, it opens up a whole new can of worms concerning the fire at Erling's house, and whether or not that was accidental. So I guess that's what we'll be assigned to first thing tomorrow. How's your bunch of crazy people?"

"All right. Anna Björg was called away because of the car fire, so I was left with them and the girl turned up. There's something weird going on there. She said she'd left school early, went to find her mother in the Kringlan shopping centre, but the shop was closed so she spent an hour or two in the library before going home. It sort of fits, but I'm not convinced."

"She's lying?"

"Or not telling the whole story. That girl's smart," Helgi muttered to himself. "Smart like her dad, wherever he's got to."

"You didn't get to the bottom of who intimidated the boy?"

Helgi shook his head.

"No. I've left them with instructions not to answer the door unless they're certain who it is, and asked for a patrol to check the street during the night. Apart from that, I've hit a wall. Ingvar's trail has gone completely cold since he dumped the phone."

"Like I told you, go home," Gunna said. "Your shift was over hours ago."

Flakes of snow whirled in the fluorescent glow of the deck lights as the mutter of the engine far below increased to a growl, a burst of black exhaust whirled away into the night and the side thruster roared into life, gradually pushing *Thule Star*'s bow into the wind and away from the quayside.

Ingvar shivered in borrowed overalls, jacket and boots, his fingers numb in spite of heavy gloves, as he looked down over the gunwale at the dark dock below. The bright yellow helmet handed to him before going on deck felt odd; too tight for comfort. A figure on the quayside, swaddled in a padded snowsuit against the cold of the winter night, unhooked the bow rope from a bollard as the roar of the thruster died away and *Thule Star* slipped astern under its own momentum.

Ingvar felt the sweat break out on his back as he hauled at the mooring rope, straining to cope with its weight to begin with, then hand-over-handing it faster and faster until the long spliced eye dropped onto the deck at his feet. He was feeling his age, he decided. It had been years since he had done this kind of thing on a cold night. He stowed the rope carefully, looping it around the bitts and lashing it securely in place before heading for the door that would take him to the ship's warm insides.

There had been nobody on the quay to see him off; only the ship's agent, who had been there to let go the rope, and he had been back inside his van and on his way home before *Thule Star* was even underway.

"All right?" Ingvar asked as he opened the wheelhouse door and stepped inside.

"All good," Níels said, looking at him quizzically. "An extra hand is useful when there are so few of us on board."

Ingvar watched as Níels brought the ship around slowly with a quick burst of power from the thruster that subsided as he increased the main engine's revolutions. *Thule Star* surged ahead. The line of lights on the shore took on a new brightness as Níels turned off the lights in the wheelhouse and stood at the control position, eyes on the radar screen in front of him as gentle touches on the tiller brought the unwieldy ship into the main channel.

Picking up speed, the city's lights were gradually left behind as *Thule Star* slid into the channel leading to the open sea.

339

"Want me to take a watch?" Ingvar asked.

"You can go below and get yourself some dinner," Niels said. "I'll take her past Reykjanes."

CHAPTER
EIGHT

Moderate southerly wind. Occasional sunshine.
Fair. Temperatures 5_8C.

Spring was on its way, with winter fighting a losing
battle to keep the countryside firmly in its grip, Gunna
decided as she got out of Ívar Laxdal's black Volvo
outside the tiny white-walled church.

There were a dozen mourners already waiting.
Ursula hugged Gunna, shook Ívar Laxdal's hand and
kissed his cheek. Her husband, almost as tall as she
was, shepherded three young children ahead of him in
an effort to keep them if not quiet, at least not arguing
with each other.

"Áskell didn't have much time for God and wouldn't
have wanted to be buried in a churchyard," Ursula said
with a wan smile. "But my mother did, and he would
have wanted to be next to her. So here we are, burying
a godless heathen in holy ground."

"How long are you staying?" Ívar Laxdal asked.

"For a week. There's all sorts of legal stuff to be
done. We need to arrange to clear the house," Ursula
said. There were black lines under her eyes. "We're still
deciding whether to sell the place or keep it. Lasse
thinks we should sell. I'm wondering whether to hold
on to it."

341

"If there's anything I can do to help . . ." Ívar Laxdal said.

"Thank you." Ursula turned to Gunna. "Is your daughter here? It was good of her to let me use her room when I was here last."

"No, she's at an environmental conference in Amsterdam at the moment."

"Give her my regards, please," Ursula said, looking over Gunna's shoulder as more cars arrived in the little church's car park. "Excuse me. I must speak to everyone, and I don't know who most of these people are . . ."

There was no funeral service, no prayers. Gunna felt that the blonde woman in vestments looked far too young to be a priest as she read a short eulogy for Áskell at the graveside and the mourners bowed their heads. Then a bell tolled from the church as Ursula, Lasse and four of the others present took hold of the bands while the deacon removed the boards supporting the pale wooden coffin.

It was lowered jerkily into the ground and the priest scattered a handful of earth that echoed on the coffin's lid along with the words of the funeral service. Ursula followed, and Gunna joined the back of the line.

"You've a nerve being here," she muttered to Róbert Simoni in front of her.

"What do you mean?" he hissed back, looking over his shoulder.

"You know exactly what I mean." She took a step forward and hurried him ahead of her.

Róbert elected to use the little tin-plate shovel to scatter his offering of earth from the pile at the graveside, while Gunna buried her hand in the cold soil and let it fall from between her fingers onto the box deep in the earth. Ívar Laxdal stood for a moment at the graveside.

"I have no idea what you're talking about," Róbert sniffed.

Gunna turned to face him, blocking his path. She nodded towards the car park, where a patrol car had pulled up. Anna Björg, smart in uniform, and Helgi in his shabby overcoat came towards them.

"These two colleagues of mine have come to collect you, Róbert."

"What the hell are you talking about?"

"So we can do this discreetly or we can do it the uncomfortable way," she continued. "My colleague Helgi will go with you in your car to the police station on Hverfisgata and you can wait for me there."

"I . . . I have appointments this afternoon," he protested.

"Then you had better cancel them, as I expect you to answer a lot of questions."

"About what?"

"I'm sure you can guess," Gunna said softly. "Helgi, would you accompany this gentleman to Hverfisgata? I'll go with Ívar and we'll be right behind you."

Gunna watched Róbert's shoulders slump as if a burden had been laid on them as Helgi ushered him towards his own car, taking the keys from his fingers.

"Ready, Gunnhildur?" Ívar Laxdal asked.

She glanced around, saw the figure she was searching for heading for the car park and set off after him.

"I'll be right with you. Two minutes," she called over her shoulder.

Arnar Geir was grinding the butt of a cigarette into the mud as she approached. He looked older, and there were streaks of grey in his hair that looked fresh.

"Morning," Gunna said.

"Oh, it's you."

"Nobody's ever pleased to see the police. Don't worry, I'm used to it."

"Sorry. Good morning, I mean. Funerals always make me miserable. I hate these things, especially when it's someone I actually liked a lot."

"I thought I'd let you know as you're here that the assault case isn't being followed up," she said grimly. "Unfortunately, you were right. There's no real prospect of a conviction, so it's been moth-balled. Unless it happens again."

"Which it won't," Arnar Geir said.

"I see your pal Vilberg is retiring."

"That's right," Arnar Geir said with a humourless grin. "Time for a change of scenery. Time to take out the trash."

"Between you and me, did he jump or was he pushed?"

"Let's say he was encouraged to jump."

"Because someone might have come across a treasure trove of embarrassing documents?"

The smile vanished from Arnar Geir's face as if a switch had been flipped.

"I have no idea what you mean," he said frostily, and got into his car, slamming the door behind him.

Gunna walked back to where Ívar Laxdal waited beside his sinister Volvo.

"Satisfied customers, Gunnhildur?" he asked softly as she sat in the passenger seat.

"Some customers are never satisfied," she said, looking out at the glow of the midday sun on the roof of the tiny church. Róbert's Mercedes was bumping out of the car park with Helgi at the wheel, tailed by Anna Björg in the patrol car. The mourners had begun to make their way back to town and the two gravediggers were already shovelling soil. "I hate it when we get tangled up in politics. I'd much rather deal with old-fashioned criminals any day."

ACKNOWLEDGEMENTS

After *Cold Breath*, I made a promise to myself that I wouldn't write any more novels, but somehow that promise didn't last long.

As this story made its gradual way from my imagination and onto the page, I'm deeply grateful to my posse of experts, Bylgja, Kalli, Lúlli and Gummi, for their patience in coming up with answers to even the most ludicrous questions, for some fine meals, and for providing much food for thought. Thanks to Ewa, Dr Noir, Lilja, the elves and Col Scott for their encouragement, support and generally being the coolest, kindest bunch of criminally inclined types. Guðrún deserves grateful appreciation for putting up with it all, and for not taking any more notice than usual when I swore not to write another novel.

Other titles published by Ulverscroft:

COLD BREATH

Quentin Bates

Gunnhildur has been taken off police duties to act as bodyguard to a high-profile stranger. Hidden away in a secure house outside Reykjavík, the pair are thrown together — but they soon find they are neither as safe nor as carefully hidden as Gunna had thought. As conflicting glimpses of the stranger's past start to emerge, the press sniff him out — and they're not the only ones interested in finding him. As they move from safehouse to safehouse, Gunna struggles to come to terms with protecting the life of a man who may have the lives of many on his conscience. And as the friction grows between them, Gunna realizes they are increasingly out of their depth as the trail leads from the house outside Reykjavík to Brussels, Russia and the Middle East.

THIN ICE

Quentin Bates

When two small-time crooks rob Reykjavík's premier drug dealer, their plans start to unravel after their getaway driver fails to show. Tensions mount between the pair and the two women they grabbed as hostages, when they find themselves holed up in an isolated hotel that has been mothballed for the season. Back in the capital, police officers Gunnhildur, Eiríkur and Helgi find themselves at a dead end investigating what appears to be the unrelated disappearance of a mother, her daughter and their car, and the death of a thief. But Gunna and her team soon realise that all these unrelated incidents are, in fact, linked — while at the same time, two increasingly desperate lowlifes have no choice but to make some big decisions on how to get rid of their accidental hostages . . .